INTRODUCTION

Santa's Prayer by Diane Ashley
God has a plan for all His children, and Nick Jackson believes that His plan is for Nick to bring Delia Wilkins, his ex-girlfriend and current boss, to a relationship with Jesus. He discovers the perfect gift for her—a new Santa Claus figurine for her much-loved collection. What better way to witness to Delia than to present her with the exquisite bisque figurine of Santa kneeling at the Christ Child's manger! But will she be willing to hear Christ's message? Or will it only be foolishness to her ears?

The Cookie Jar by Janet Lee Barton
When Cindy Morrow loses her mother in an automobile accident, she decides to keep her mother's dream alive by opening a shop called Carly's Cookie Jar. Trying to get her cookie business on firm financial footing keeps her busy—almost too busy to admit to the attraction she feels for a widower from her church. Will she recognize the plans the Lord has for her when she's presented with a cookie jar full of love?

Stuck on You by Rhonda Gibson
Sheila Fisher loves to collect Foster's Woodland Creatures ornaments, which inspire her to plot children's stories. This Christmas she decides to meet the creator and request permission to write and sell her stories based on Morgan Foster's ornaments. Will Sheila find herself writing stories about her collection and falling in love at the same time? Or will Morgan take away her dreams once and for all?

Snowbound for Christmas by Gail Sattler
Rochelle McWilliams collects snowflakes. Kade Guildford hates snow—real and plastic. When Rochelle starts decorating, snowflakes appear everywhere, first invading his office building and, worse, his place of worship. As the snow thickens into a layer of ice around Kade's cold heart, can Rochelle be the one to make it melt?

A
CONNECTICUT
CHRISTMAS

Four Modern Romances Develop at a Christmas Collectibles Shop

DIANE ASHLEY · JANET LEE BARTON

RHONDA GIBSON · GAIL SATTLER

BARBOUR
PUBLISHING

Our mission is to publish and distribute inspirational products offering exceptional value and biblical encouragement to the masses.

 Member of the
Evangelical Christian
Publishers Association

Printed in the United States of America

Santa's Prayer

by Diane Ashley

Dedication

To Gene, my husband, my better half.
Thanks for your steadfast encouragement
and for reading my stories even when they
don't have aliens, monsters, or secret agents.
I love you.

Thanks to my publisher, Rebecca Germany,
for taking a chance on me
and to Debbie Cole, my editor,
for your kind words about my publication.
And a special thanks to the Bards of Faith
for the polish they add to every manuscript.
Who's next?

Chapter 1

I'm dreaming of a white Christmas. . . ." Bing Crosby's mellow crooning floated through the mall and made Delia think of the classic movie she and her family watched every year. What more fitting way to spend a cold Sunday in Connecticut? Dad always fixed a big bowl of popcorn, and Mom heated up hot chocolate for all of them to drink. She sighed. It would be a relief when her parents got back from their cruise. Not having her family around had made Thanksgiving Day a total drag.

"Earth to Delia." Frances's voice brought her back to the present.

"I'm sorry. I was just thinking—"

"Don't tell me. You were thinking of Nicholas B. Jackson again. Come on, honey. I know his Southern drawl stole your heart, but you're the one who told me it's over. You've got to move on."

Delia forced a smile as they threaded their way through the crowds of people at Village Mall. She did not need to be reminded of her romantic problems. Especially on the biggest shopping day of the year. As general manager of the mall, she had plenty of crises to distract her. "Actually you've jumped to the wrong conclusion. I was thinking about Mom and Dad."

"Sure you were." Frances winked and patted her arm. "I understand. Everyone misses their loved ones during the holiday season. Parents, siblings, friends, and. . .um. . .other friends. That's why I insisted you join me for lunch."

Delia gritted her teeth and reminded herself that she and Frances had been best friends since the second grade. Frances had been a newcomer, arriving in Snowbound Village in the middle of the school year. She had been tiny even then, and some of the other kids had teased her relentlessly about her red hair, comparing her to the freckle-faced icon of a national hamburger chain. Delia had sided with Frances, and together they had vanquished the bullies. That day had cemented their friendship, and the two girls had been practically inseparable ever since.

"Speaking of 'other friends,' I imagine you've talked to my brother since I have. When's he supposed to get back here?" Delia's smile broadened at the blush on Frances's face. It was a source of great satisfaction to her that Frances and Carl had lately begun to act like a pair of lovebirds. For years she had hoped they would quit competing against each other and admit they made the perfect couple. She resolutely pushed away the painful fact that she had also recently thought she and Nick made a perfect couple.

Frances fanned her red cheeks. "You need to speak to

someone about the temperature in the mall. It's gotten awfully hot in here."

"Maybe it's the crowd." Delia looked at her friend, and they both laughed.

"As a matter of fact, your brother did have a few minutes free between shifts last night. I'm so worried about him, Delia. That hospital is working him way too hard."

"That's what they're supposed to do to residents. I think it's a rite of passage." She shrugged. "I guess it's supposed to make him a better doctor."

"I don't see how it can. Poor Carl has only had two hours of sleep over the last three days. And he's expected to continue working like he's well rested." Frances tsked her sympathy. "He needs someone to take care of him so he can make it through the next two years."

"I just hope he makes it home for Christmas this year. Between his work schedule, my sister's ski trip, and my parents' decision to cruise Greece, I found little to be thankful for this year."

"I could shoot you for not calling me, Delia. You know my family would have been happy to have you come over for Thanksgiving dinner when things fell through between you and Nick. You could have helped Mom and me clean up while the guys shouted at their favorite football quarterbacks."

Delia had not been in the mood to talk to anyone yesterday. She had cried about a dozen buckets of tears. She still couldn't believe Nick had dumped her. Never mind that she'd told him to choose—she had never doubted he would choose her. Two years of dating—six months exclusively. Everyone knew they were destined for a wedding. In fact Nick had hinted he might give her a "sparkly" reason to be thankful this year. But then everything had changed, and she had spent her Thanksgiving holiday all alone with her face buried in her pillow. She could never have let Frances's family see her red and swollen face. Nor could she have endured their boisterous attempts to cheer her up. "I needed to spend some time cleaning my apartment anyway."

Frances sniffed. "I only wish I could keep my place as spotless as yours. No dust particles would dare alight on your furniture."

"I got out the Santa collection, too. In fact I was hoping we could go by that new Christmas shop, Deck the Hall, during our lunch break. I'd love to find a new figurine to add for this year." Delia stopped walking, because she realized Frances had dropped back and was staring at something that had caught her interest.

"Don't look now, but I think your erstwhile boyfriend is coming out of the camping store."

Delia gasped as she caught sight of Nick's wide shoulders and square chin. It was not fair for him to look so good when she felt so awful. He was talking animatedly to one of his new friends, and he looked like a million bucks, from his crisp button-down to his shiny loafers.

She turned and looked in the plate glass window of the home-decor shop. She should have put on some mascara this morning. It was the curse of being born blond—invisible eyelashes and infantile jokes. Delia noticed her bangs were mussed, but at least her new flip was holding its shape. Her green suit, the one she had donned this morning in an attempt to embrace the upcoming Christmas shopping season, looked more like a Girl Scout uniform to her eyes now. Sensible shoes were a must for a job like hers that required numerous trips from one end of the mall to the other several times a day, but they did nothing for her legs. It was too late to worry about that now. Fate seemed to be conspiring against her. During the last few days, she had imagined seeing Nick and being in total control of the situation. In her daydreams, she had wounded him with a cutting remark and coolly walked away, leaving him with an aching sense of what might have been. Instead she had to run into him now. She was not prepared.

Could she slip away? Her gray eyes widened as the fight-or-flight impulse flooded her body with adrenalin. Feeling a little like a hunted animal, she looked around for somewhere to hide, hoping he would not notice them. She could have died when Frances called out his name and waved.

"You've got to face your demons," her friend whispered as she grabbed Delia's hand and dragged her forward. In a louder voice, she addressed the guys. "What are you doing here? A little Christmas shopping?" She paused, put her finger on her chin, and winked at Delia. "It's not Christmas Eve already, is it?"

Delia closed her eyes, but she could still hear Nick's laugh. It sounded stilted to her ears. She opened her eyes and looked directly into his deep blue gaze—those beautiful blue eyes surrounded by thick dark eyelashes. His eyes were what had drawn Delia to Nick in the first place, and they were still as magnetic as ever.

"It's good to see you, Delia." His voice washed over her like warm Southern air. "How are you?" The drawl she had always loved was as deep and thick as ever. It raised tiny hairs along her forearms and the back of her neck. Although he had lived in Connecticut for the past two years, his voice still held the Mississippi accent that pulled on her heartstrings.

Frances, the rat who claimed to be her friend, was chatting with Nick's companion, leaving her and her former boyfriend on their own. What could she do? She wanted to run and hide— escape from the pain in her chest and the pain she could see reflected on his face. "Fine." It was the only word she could choke out.

"Me, too."

He looked toward his left in response to a question from his friend, and she followed his gaze. Not a hundred feet away was the entrance to the Christmas collectibles shop. Salvation was at hand!

"Excuse me. I think I see someone. . . ." Delia moved away and practically ran to the door of the new shop.

❧

Nick watched Delia for a minute through the plate glass window. He was such a sap. How could he ever hope to witness to nonbelievers when he could not even summon up a convincing hello for his girlfriend—ex-girlfriend, that is. Pain struck him again. How had it all gone so wrong? Just a few short weeks ago, he and Delia had been the perfect couple. Now they could not even maintain social pleasantries. He had to be crazy to think about trying to work with her.

"Come on, man." Tom's deep voice interrupted his thoughts. "Didn't you say you had to be somewhere by 2:30?"

Nick sighed deeply. "Yes, but—"

Tom, the broad-shouldered ex-football player who had become one of his closest friends since he had joined New Life Church, looked sympathetic. "Was that her?"

"Yes." Nick bit off the word and squared his shoulders. Pity was something he could not abide. "Let's get over to the mall offices. I really need that job."

"Explain this to me again. You and. . ." His voice trailed off.

"Delia."

"Right. You and Delia broke up because you're saved and she's not. And you apparently still have feelings for her. That's fine. I understand your heart may take longer to convince than your head. But you know you made the right decision to break things off, right?"

Nick hesitated. Was it the right decision? Or should he have stayed in the relationship and witnessed to her? Had he given up on Delia too soon? But she had been the one to insist he choose between her and his newfound relationship with Christ. "Yes."

"Okay. You had me worried there for a moment." Tom punched his shoulder. "I know it's hard for new Christians to separate themselves from their old lives. Sometimes it's hard for old Christians, too."

Nick looked at Tom's earnest face. "You mean it won't ever get any easier?" Would he always struggle to make the right decisions? Since he had begun his walk with Christ, everything was simpler but more complicated. He shook his head in disgust. How could things be both simpler *and* more complicated? Nick felt the urge to return home and study his Bible. There was so much he did not understand.

"Oops. I was trying to reassure you, not make things worse."

"I doubt things could get much worse. I'm broke, broken-hearted, and worried about every decision I have to make."

Tom's forehead drew together in a frown. "I'm certainly no expert, but I know things could get a lot worse. You have a loving family—"

Nick snorted. "About a million miles away from here."

"And friends. And a roof over your head."

"If I don't find a job, I won't have a roof for long. And my friends may feel differently if I have to come begging them for a place to stay."

Tom stopped walking and pointed a finger at him. "You're welcome at my place anytime."

"Thanks, man. But if I get this job, I should be able to make it."

"It might be better for you not to get it since it would mean working directly for your former girlfriend."

"I understand what you're saying, Tom. But I doubt I would be working for her. I'll probably answer to some assistant. Delia is bound to be too busy with managerial stuff to bother with the likes of me. Besides, there aren't many jobs available for full-time students. And I have experience, so I'm sure they'll hire me. Not many people want that job. Too many drawbacks."

"What could be so hard about it? Sitting all day smiling at people and getting your picture taken?"

Nick laughed. "Okay. Why don't you apply, too?" He arrived at the office entrance and pushed the door open wide, beckoning to his friend. "Then you can see what it's really like to be a celebrity."

"No thanks. This is one of the busiest times of the year for home missions. So many people want to give during the holiday season, and it's up to people like us to see that the money and supplies go where they can do the most good."

"Chicken."

Tom waved his hand in dismissal. "Good luck, I guess. I'll see you at Bible study this evening, right?"

"I'll be there." Nick allowed the door to shut behind him, and the noise of busy shoppers dissipated.

Chapter 2

Delia eased her way into the Christmas store and leaned against the doorjamb, one hand pressed to her chest. When would she ever be able to face Nick without losing her cool? Slowly her breathing returned to normal, and Delia noticed the festive ambience of Deck the Hall.

"Can I help you?"

Delia turned to see a teenage girl dressed in a red pinafore and matching Santa hat. Surely this could not be the new owner; she was much too young. But the girl was looking expectantly at her. "I. . .mmm. . .just looking."

"Okay, I'll be right here if you need any help." The girl went back to dusting miniature Victorian houses arranged in a charming village, complete with carolers and tiny horse-drawn carriages.

Delia's attention was drawn to another display, this one filled with cheerful red figures of Santa Claus. Her fingers itched to trace the ruddy cheeks of a large stuffed Santa. She leaned closer to see another figure that barely measured two inches. She smiled her delight. There were so many Santas in the store. She just knew she'd find the perfect one to add to her collection.

The Christmas following Delia's birth, her aunt had given her a Santa carved from a bar of soap. Apparently it had captured her attention even though she had only been nine months old. That was the beginning of the collection. Every year it grew by leaps and bounds as friends and relatives saw the collection and generously gave her all sorts of figurines to add to it. Some of her Santas played songs while others waved or jingled sleigh bells. She even had one that snored and another that blew bubbles. Last year when she packed all of them in protective wrapping, she had counted more than two hundred unique figurines.

A small bell tinkled as the front door swung open, breaking Delia's train of thought.

"There you are. I wondered where you disappeared to." Frances's red hair clashed with many of the displays in the store.

"I told you I wanted to see what they had here." She picked up a Santa and held him up for inspection. "I'm going to have a hard time choosing only one. Don't you love the kitten peeking out of his bag?"

"Whatever." Frances directed a meaningful look her way. "How did your first confrontation go? Did you make him sorry for the breakup?"

"Not so much. I don't know which of us was more embarrassed. I wish you hadn't drawn his attention and then abandoned me. We couldn't find a thing to say to each other."

"If you didn't still care about him, I doubt you'd have gotten so upset at running into him today."

Delia didn't want anyone, even her best friend, to see how miserable she was after breaking up with Nick. "Don't be silly. If you and Carl broke up and I threw you two together, I'm sure you'd find it awkward."

"Nope. Not me. I'd throw myself into his arms and cry like a baby. And I'd wink at you over his shoulder while we patched things up."

Delia shook her head. Frances was like a whirlwind. She rushed through life without worrying about consequences or collateral damage. But that was part of her charm. Delia was the type to consider all angles before acting. She hated being caught off guard. And she had definitely been caught off guard a few minutes ago.

Her face flushed again as she remembered her inability to dredge up any words, not even common phrases, like the weather or the number of people shopping on the Friday after Thanksgiving. His slow drawl had knocked her for a loop, reminding her of soft kisses and whispery promises. Not that Nick had ever gotten out of hand. He had always been the perfect gentleman on their dates, walking her to the front door and seeing that she got safely inside her apartment. Her eyes grew hot with repressed tears. It was so unfair to miss him this much. She clamped down on her emotions, staring at the Santa display and clenching her teeth until she felt like she was once again in control.

"Are you through looking, Dee?" Frances rubbed her flat stomach. "My tummy is trying to eat a hole through my waist."

"Sure." Delia cast one more glance over the display, her eyes lighting on an odd-looking Santa who was perched on one knee and holding his red hat in his hand. She leaned closer to see what he was peering at. It was a manger, exquisitely wrought—so detailed she could see the tiny hand of the baby inside, a hand that seemed to reach upward as if trying to touch Santa's cheek. Her breath caught at the beauty of the delicate figures, but inside a voice chided. Did religious fanatics have to infuse every aspect of the Christmas holiday with theological statements? She went to church every Christmas and had even played Mary in a school drama when she was eight, but she did not see any connection between Santa and the Christ Child. There was a place for religion, but it should be separate from giving and receiving presents. She turned her back on the figurine. "Where do you want to eat?"

"Why don't we go to that coffee shop next door? They have a new cinnamon-flavored bagel that is out of this world. I think I could eat three of them."

Delia laughed. "I'd pay to see that."

"Some friend you are. You just want to see me in pain."

"Misery does love company."

❧

Nick brushed his hair back and smiled at the receptionist. "Busy day?"

The woman looked at him over the top of her bifocals.

"We'd be in trouble if it wasn't." Her voice sounded as dry as the desert. She pulled off her glasses and studied him, a frown drawing her silver eyebrows together.

Nick pasted a smile on his face. He would not let her sour attitude get under his skin. "I guess that's true. Hi, I'm Nick Jackson." He reached in his back pocket and pulled out a newspaper ad. "I have an appointment to interview for the job opening."

He had the satisfaction of seeing her look startled for a moment. She looked from him to the ad and back again before reclaiming her aplomb. "Have a seat."

Nick could feel her gaze on his back as he selected a magazine and made himself comfortable on the long tan sofa. He leafed through the pages without seeing them as he thought back to his encounter with Delia. Was he as crazy as Tom thought? But the mall manager would have no reason to be involved with the temporary help. And he really needed the money. He had blown a lot of money on airline tickets for them to travel to Mississippi during Thanksgiving. When he and Delia broke up, he had not had the heart to make the trip alone. And he wouldn't even think of letting her repay him for her ticket. Instead he'd called the airline to ask for a refund. The lady had been nice, but all she could do was give him a partial credit toward tickets he could use over the next twelve months.

When he called to tell his mom and dad that he and Delia would not be coming home for the holiday, his parents had been concerned but understanding. They even offered to send money to help cover the cost of the airline tickets, but since he knew things were tight at home, too, he had blithely told them he would be all right. It was true. He was young and strong. With God's help, he would get past this rough patch.

"Mr. Jackson." The receptionist's voice stopped his thoughts. Her face had relaxed a bit, so he supposed she had discovered he was a legitimate applicant. "Ms. Applewhite can see you now." She pointed at a door. "Second office on the right."

"Thanks." He smiled at her, hoping to elicit a warm response, but she was a tough cookie. He hoped the rest of the mall staff would be more approachable. Feeling a bit apprehensive, he went searching for Ms. Applewhite. He found the right door and knocked.

"Come in."

Nick whispered a quick prayer before entering. Ms. Applewhite was just hanging up her telephone. She stood as he entered and pushed back her long brown hair before offering her right hand. "I've had nothing but headaches this year trying to line up all the extra people we need through the Christmas holidays. I hope you're going to be the answer to my biggest problem."

Nick smiled in response. "I hope so, too."

"Ooh, I love that accent. Where are you from?"

"Up here you call it Mississippi," he answered, purposely thickening his drawl. "But at home, we say we're from Miss-sippi."

"Delicious. Please have a seat, Mr. Jackson." Unlike the receptionist, Ms. Applewhite had no reservations about being friendly. She winked at him. "I was looking over your application, and I can see you're highly qualified for the job. Even your name is perfect."

Nick smiled. He could not help responding to her bubbly charm. "Thanks. I hear that all the time. So when do I start?"

"Eagerness. . ." Ms. Applewhite nodded. "Another positive trait. But I'd like to go over a few things before I make my final decision. Like your work ethic. I know most people would laugh, but it's very important that we can rely on you, Nick. Of course, no one can help getting sick, but that would be the only legitimate reason for not coming to work. Although this is a temporary job, it's the centerpiece to our seasonal display."

"I understand. And I promise you'll be able to count on me, Ms. Applewhite. Please feel free to check my references. I believe all my previous employers will tell you I'm reliable and hardworking."

She nodded, her large brown eyes seeming to stare directly into his soul. "Your classes won't get in the way of working?"

"No. I finished most of my assignments before Thanksgiving. All I have to do is meet with a couple of professors between now and Christmas, and I'm certain I can work those meetings in when I'm not needed here."

"Perfect." She looked down and wrote something on a sheet of paper before handing it to Nick. "Take this out to Mabel at the front desk. She'll get you everything you need."

"Thanks, Ms. Applewhite."

"Call me Shannon."

Nick smiled. "Shannon. It's been a pleasure to meet you."

"Likewise, Nick. I'll look forward to seeing you a lot more over the next several weeks."

He returned to the dour Mabel, feeling a little guilty for not telling Shannon about his relationship—former relationship—with her boss. But he really needed this job. Nick shrugged. Delia would probably never even know he was one of her employees.

❦

"You did *what*?" Delia's voice squeaked. Betrayal and confusion filled her. "How could you hire *him*?"

"What do you mean? He's cute, experienced, and very likeable. What's wrong?" Shannon paused, and Delia saw her face grow white. "He's not a pedophile or something, is he?"

"Of course not. He's"—she hesitated—"he's just the wrong guy for the job."

"Why?" Shannon frowned, her confusion clear.

"Never mind why. You need to call him right now and tell him there's been a mistake. I refuse to have him hanging around this office, mooning over the past."

"Come on, Delia. You're not making any sense here. You know how hard it is to find a reliable guy for this position. We're lucky to get someone of Nick's caliber to do it. Especially at the salary we're offering. I read about men who do this every year. Once they have a year or two of experience, they get well over ten thousand dollars for the season."

"That's downright ridiculous. I can't believe anyone but the Mall of America would spend that kind of money."

"We've tried other things, but nothing else brings in as many customers."

"Then what about Mr. Dickerson?"

Shannon made an unladylike sound. "He's almost ninety. Don't you remember how he kept dozing off last year? It was a disaster."

Delia closed her eyes and rested her forehead against her fist. Why did everything have to be so complicated? If only she had not agreed to go to lunch with Frances. She could have stopped Nick before he got his foot in the door. By the time she came back, it was all over. When she had told Shannon to hire someone pronto, she'd had no idea what the result would be. And what had possessed Nick to apply for a job at *her* mall? Was he trying to make her life a nightmare? If that was his plan, he had succeeded.

Her memory conjured up the debonair image of Humphrey Bogart. "Of all the shopping malls in all the world. . ." Delia sighed. She supposed it was too late to do anything about it now. She looked up at Shannon. "Okay. He can stay. But I don't want to have to deal with him at all. I don't even want to hear his name spoken in this office."

Shannon lifted her hand in a mock salute. "Yes, ma'am. I promise you won't hear it from me. And I'll take special care of him so you won't be bothered at all."

Delia's heart fell to her toes. And when it returned to her chest, it seemed to have turned green—with envy. What was that all about? She was *over* Nicholas Beauregard Jackson. He had no place in her heart. Shannon was welcome to him. And as soon as Christmas was over, she'd see to it he had no part in her life at all. In fact she was going to take great pleasure in signing his final paycheck.

Chapter 3

Delia's phone played a tinny rendition of "Jingle Bells." With a sigh, she pulled it out of her suit pocket and glared at the display. Mabel! The only reason for her receptionist to call would be to relay a crisis situation that needed Delia's immediate attention. "Delia here. What's the problem?"

"Your new Santa is AWOL."

"I'm on it." Delia closed the cell phone with a *snap*. He wasn't *her* Santa, but it was too late to correct Mabel now. She focused on the problem at hand. How dare he! His first day on the job and Nick was already missing. Her stride lengthened as anger filled her. Hadn't she known something like this would happen? By all rights it should be Shannon who dealt with this problem since she had hired Nick, but Mondays were her day off. So it fell to Delia. The story of her life. Delia would have to deal with it.

Cries and angry voices filled the air as she arrived at the center junction of the mall. Her gaze swept past the crowd.

There was Jean, the elf who kept the line moving and acted as a go-between for the parents and Santa. It was always easier to steer a child toward a particular toy when Santa had insider information.

"What's the problem here?" Delia interrupted a distraught mother who was yelling at Jean over the screams of the child she held in her arms.

The mother turned toward her. "We've been standing in line for nearly two hours. And now this *elf* is trying to tell us Santa has disappeared. I'm tired. Tina is tired. All I know is somebody had better call him and tell him to get his *beard* back up here." She glanced down at little Tina before continuing. "There are other malls with other attractions, if you know what I mean."

Delia looked toward Jean, who explained, "I thought everything was okay, but suddenly Santa said he needed a break. That was forty-five minutes ago."

"I see." Delia turned toward the customers, racking her brain. "I'm sure it's an emergency that's made Santa late." She felt the collective gaze of dozens of children. "Maybe Rudolph caught a cold, and Santa wants to make sure he gets his medicine on time. Everybody knows how important it is for all the reindeer to be healthy, especially at this time of the year."

Silence fell as the crowd absorbed her words. Delia reached in her pocket for her cell phone and quickly scrolled down to Nick's number. It was a good thing she had not yet deleted it. "I'll see if I can find out how soon he'll be back." She punched the CALL button and held the phone to her ear, tapping one foot as she waited to hear what excuse Nick could possibly offer for disappearing on his first day of work. The line buzzed, and suddenly she heard the familiar ring of his phone. She whirled to see where the sound was coming from.

Her face was immediately enveloped in long white fur. Delia sneezed and tried to jump back, but a strong arm circled her waist.

"Ho, ho, ho. Careful there, little lady." The familiar voice made her heartbeat accelerate. She looked up at the laugh lines framing his blue eyes. How many times had she admired his navy blue gaze? Before she could recover her composure, he grinned and turned his attention to the people waiting to see him. "Sorry for the delay, boys and girls. I went to pick up a little something special for Mrs. Claus."

Delia watched as he moved down the line, handing out candy and gum to all the kids from his voluminous pockets. She frowned as he returned to where she stood. "I want to see you in my office before you leave this evening."

"Yes, ma'am." He winked at her. "You be making out your list for old Santa."

Delia could feel her face heating up. She would like to rip into him right now, but she had to remember the children around them. How dare he flirt with her! They were not dating anymore. He had made his choice. She lifted her chin and marched past the line of waiting children. She nodded at the photographer but never slowed down. She couldn't make small talk with anyone. She was too busy rehearsing what she would say to Nick when he came to her office.

❧

Metal gates had been drawn down across the storefronts, and mall security was escorting the last few shoppers out of the building as Nick made his way to Delia's office. He was hot, tired, and sticky. It had been a long day, but sweet. He loved the trust and wonder that shone in the eyes of the children he invited onto his lap. Some were a little overwhelmed by his size and the vivid color of his suit, but most climbed up anyway, pushed by anxious mothers and fathers who wanted photographic mementos of their youngsters.

Nick pulled off his hat and slapped it against his thigh as he walked down the darkened mall. He was anxious to get this meeting over with. What could Delia have to talk to him about? He was pretty sure he'd done a good job today and earned a restful evening at home. After he sponge cleaned the costume that had endured grubby hands all afternoon, he would relax with a tall glass of sweet tea. He licked his lips at the thought of the cool treat.

The lobby was dark, but the door to the suite of offices stood open. The yellow glow of her office light led Nick to Delia's door. Her blond hair gleamed richly as she bent over her appointment book. He stood for a moment drinking in the sight. She was so beautiful. If only. . . He could not let his thoughts stray in that direction, so he knocked on the door to get her attention.

Delia's head jerked up at the noise. A wide smile appeared on her face, and her eyes lit up when she saw him. Nick could feel his own lips turn up in response to her happy expression. An arrow of regret pierced his heart when a curtain seemed to drop over her features. Her eyes dulled, and her pretty mouth straightened. How he wished he could gather her in his arms and kiss her breathless the way he used to. It was hard to believe those days were gone forever, but unless God worked a change in her, the chasm between them would remain.

"Hi, Delia. You needed to see me?"

She nodded and waved him to a chair. "Have a seat, Nick. We have to get a few things straight."

Silence filled the office as Delia hesitated, and Nick assumed she was gathering her thoughts. Delia had never been one to speak hastily. It was probably one of the reasons she had been promoted to manager at such a young age. That and her degree in marketing and her attention to detail and. . . Nick shook his head. No sense listing all her good qualities. From the expression on her face, this was going to be an unpleasant meeting. He used the time to review his first day at work. Had someone complained? He thought things had gone pretty smoothly. He could not recall upsetting any parent too badly or making any children cry.

"I'm not sure if Shannon explained the importance of our Santa display."

Nick sighed. "Of course she did. And I understand. I've been a Santa for several years back home."

"I know things are done a little differently in one's hometown. People you've known all your life tend to overlook certain things." She hesitated again as if searching for the words in a foreign language. "Perhaps there aren't as many children waiting. . . ." Her voice drifted off.

Nick could feel his temper rising. "You think our poor, dumb Southern kids can't afford to have their picture taken with Santa?"

"No, Nick. That's not it at all. I'm trying to imagine some reason your former employer wouldn't mind your disappearing from time to time when you're supposed to be working."

Nick could not believe his ears. "Is that what this is all about? That I was late getting back from my break? The only break I took during an eight-hour shift?"

"Yes, that's exactly what the problem is. Imagine my surprise when I came to check on things and there was a line nearly as long as the mall waiting for you to get back. You're supposed to take several short breaks during the day, not one long one. That is simply unacceptable." Delia's angry gaze met his.

He could almost feel the heat reaching across her desk. A few short weeks ago, his anger would have risen to a level as high or even higher than hers. But not now. Now he was a different man—thanks to Christ's influence in his heart and mind. A praise chorus filled his head, and he could not stop the smile that turned up the corners of his mouth.

"Did you hear what I said, Nick? Your behavior was not acceptable. You made children and parents wait far too long. My merchants may have lost business because of your unexplained disappearance. Unless you can give me a satisfactory explanation, I'm going to have to let you go."

"You might want to hold that thought for a moment, sweetie."

"I'm not your *sweetie* anymore, Nick Jackson, and don't you forget it. I knew this was a bad idea from the beginning." Delia pushed back from her desk and came around the front to face him directly.

Nick stood when she did, as he had been taught. "Calm down, Delia—"

"I tried to tell Shannon, but she was so charmed by you. As I used to be. How you must laugh at all of us, unable to resist your good looks and that sweet Southern accent. You may think you can drift through life on charm alone. Well, it's not going to work on me anymore."

Nick wanted to laugh at the inadvertent compliment in her words. Did she still think he was good-looking and charming? Perhaps there was hope for them after all—if she would only listen to Christ's message. He prayed he would have another chance to share the good news with her, but tonight was not the time.

He put his hand on her arm. "I don't think you've looked at me, Delia. I want you to take a deep breath and look at me real hard." He stepped back a foot to give her some breathing room. He wanted to convince her, not intimidate her.

He saw her gaze rake him from head to toe. Then she looked again, a little more slowly this time. He waited while she took in the rich fur and thick material of his costume. Her expressions were so familiar to him. Anger shifted into perplexity.

"This is not the costume Mabel should have issued to you this morning." She put a tentative hand on the cuff of his sleeve. He could feel her fingers kneading the thick white fur.

"That's right."

"But I don't understand. Mr. Dickerson, last year's Santa, said the old costume was worn out. So after Christmas I went to the novelty store and bought a new one. But it wasn't nearly as soft as this one. Was it too tight for you to use?"

A chuckle bubbled up. "Not quite, Delia. It hung around me like a deflated balloon. I was worried I was going to lose a child in the extra folds. And the fur was a little less, um. . ." He cocked his eyebrow at her.

Delia pulled her hand away as if the fur had suddenly turned red-hot. "Yes, this is certainly a higher quality outfit."

"If you looked at my application, you know I've been doing this for several years. I even went to one of those schools to learn how to be a proper Santa Claus. This costume was part of the tuition."

"But you didn't apply last year when we were dating. I didn't even know you'd ever been a Santa."

He shrugged. "You already had a Santa last year. Besides, it didn't seem appropriate to ask my girlfriend for a job. I didn't want you to be accused of favoritism. But since we broke up, I figured it would be okay to apply this year. I thought you would deep-six my application if you didn't want me to work here."

A blush colored her cheeks. "Shannon handled all the applications. If I had known you were applying, I would have told her about our history."

"And I probably wouldn't have gotten the job." He took a deep breath, warring briefly with his pride. "I could really use the money, Delia."

His words brought an obvious change in the office. Nick could almost see Delia's anger evaporating. He shifted his shoulders. It was hard to let her see his vulnerability.

"I see." Delia shuffled some papers around on her desk before looking at him. "I trust we can leave our personal differences at home and maintain a professional attitude at the mall."

"Exactly my thoughts."

"But you shouldn't expect special treatment. Even if we were still seeing each other, I would treat you the same as any of the other employees here."

Nick dropped his chin in a quick nod. "I'm sorry for coming back late from my lunch break. I thought I could manage it, but I didn't expect the traffic to be so slow. I thought it would take only a few minutes to change into my Santa outfit and get back here. I'll know better than to try to run home again."

Delia studied him for a few moments. Her voice was flat when she answered. "I accept your apology and your promise that it won't happen again."

Now that was interesting. Hadn't she assumed he was in the wrong and jumped down his throat without asking for an explanation? "That's really kind of you, but don't you think maybe you owe me an apology, too?"

Delia's eyes shifted to a point behind his shoulder. Nick wanted to look around to see if anyone had entered the office, but he resisted the impulse.

"I'm sorry for jumping to conclusions." She brought her gaze back to his face and held out her hand. "Can we forget about this misunderstanding and move forward?"

Nick hesitated for a moment before grasping her hand. "Sure, boss." When his fingers closed around hers, he was reminded of their past dates. How often they had walked side by side when leaving the movie theater or a restaurant, their hands forming a link between them. The gesture had always filled him with warmth. Tonight the heat generated between their clasped hands reminded him of that special chemistry.

For a second, he wished they could go back to those days. But then the voice of Christ reminded him of the cost paid for his salvation, and Nick knew he could never go back. Still, it would be so easy to pull her toward him, fold her into his arms, and hug her to seal their agreement. His expression must have betrayed his thoughts. Her eyes grew wide, and she pulled her hand back. Without another word, he grabbed up his red hat and strode out of the quiet office.

Chapter 4

Delia crumpled her empty cup and tossed it into the wastebasket with a yawn. She had tossed and turned all night, unable to banish Nick's smoldering gaze from her dreams. Given her lack of sleep, she'd opted for an extra shot of caffeine in her cappuccino this morning, but her eyelids still felt as heavy as quilts. She shook her head and tried to concentrate on the phone messages Mabel had left on her desk.

The morning passed quietly. Then a knock on her door roused her from the near stupor that had overtaken her. Delia looked up and gasped at the animal that peeked in. It was fuzzy and brown, with large dark eyes and a bright red nose. *"Rudolph!"* She jumped up and ran to the door, pulling it open all the way.

Mabel and Shannon were in the hallway, each holding a three-foot stuffed reindeer. Delia threw her arms around Rudolph, causing its harness's sleigh bells to jingle merrily.

Shannon held up her reindeer. "Say hi to Blitzen."

Delia put her hand on her hip. "How can you tell it's not Comet or Dasher?"

Shannon's mouth opened in mock surprise. "I thought everyone knew the difference between Santa's reindeer."

Delia's eyebrows rose a little. "Rudolph was easy, with the red nose and all, but I didn't know any of the others were so recognizable. Have you been studying reindeer facial features behind my back?"

"Not so much." With a giggle, Shannon turned her reindeer to the side so Delia could see its harness. "His name is printed right here."

The three women laughed as they went back to the main office, strewed with large crates and packing foam. Delia carefully checked all nine reindeer, pleased they looked so sweet and lovable. "We need to get these guys over to the North Pole."

Shannon threw a look at her. "Mabel has to stay here and answer the phones. Don't you think it's going to take awhile with just the two of us?"

"I'll help." In the confusion and laughter, none of the women had heard the door open. Now they turned as one to see who had made the offer. The women seemed caught in a trance, staring at Santa, resplendent from his white mustache to his gleaming black boots. Last night when he'd come by to see Delia, he had worn his own suit, but today it looked more realistic. He even had on a pair of wire-rimmed glasses. He seemed to have stepped magically from the pages of Clement Moore's poem " 'Twas the Night Before Christmas."

The phone rang, sending Mabel back to her desk.

Delia shook her head to clear it. "You're not supposed to be here. You're supposed to be at the North Pole doing what we pay you to do." She winced slightly, wishing her voice had sounded a little less accusatory. Where had her levelheadedness gone? Normally she would not chastise one employee in front of others.

Mabel put her call on hold. Delia was sure she wanted to hear how Santa would respond. Shannon drew away from her and closer to him in a protective gesture. Suddenly Delia felt like the meanest beast in nature. And it didn't help any for Nick to stand quietly in his beautiful red suit with that innocent expression on his face.

"I'm sure he has a valid reason for being here." Shannon's voice was defensive.

Delia nodded her agreement. Why was she so eager to find fault with Nick? "I'm sorry, Nick. Was there something you needed from us?"

"As a matter of fact, yes." He held out a piece of paper that looked a lot like one of the tax forms new employees had to fill out. "I found this with a note on it to sign it and bring it to the office."

"Oh." Delia watched as Nick's eyes swung from her face to Shannon's. Suddenly she felt as if she were in a race. Nick was the judge, she and Shannon the contestants. A flood of emotions filled her chest. She wanted to slap Nick—or maybe Shannon. She wanted to run to her office and slam the door. She wanted to throw herself into Nick's arms and turn her face up for his kisses. But in the end, she did none of those things.

Instead she crossed her arms over her chest and lifted her chin. She would not play his game.

Nick smiled at them, white teeth flashing between his mustache and beard. Delia wanted to stamp her foot when Shannon returned his smile eagerly. She wanted to yell at them to stop it—or at least wait until after hours. Didn't they have a policy about not dating coworkers? If not, she needed to get one added to the employee manual, pronto.

"Since you're here, Nick, you can help." Her harsh tone seemed to break the spell between him and Shannon.

Nick's gaze returned to her. "What do you need me to do?"

Delia motioned to the reindeer that lay scattered around the office. She picked up two of them and tucked them under one arm; then she stuffed a third reindeer under her other arm. "Can you carry three? And you, too, Shannon. I know it's a little awkward, but we can make it in one trip if you guys can manage it."

Nick helped Shannon get her trio together; then he picked up the remaining reindeer. Mabel opened the door for them, and Delia led the way, dodging between benches, stalls, and shoppers. Somehow the other two fell several steps back. She wrestled with Rudolph as he tried to slide out from under her arm. It was a struggle to keep all three of the reindeer balanced—never mind that she had one ear strained to hear what Shannon and Nick were talking about. She wanted to slow down so she could hear what they were saying. Especially when Shannon pealed with laughter. Were they talking about her? Miserably she trudged onward, trying to convince herself it didn't matter what they said to each other. Shannon was a beautiful and charming single girl, and Nick was free to flirt with whomever he chose. But, oh, how she wished she didn't have to witness it.

❧

"Are you about ready to wrap it up for today?" Jean, his elf helper, was beginning to look a little droopy. She sat down on the edge of the podium and rubbed her feet; then she pulled a tissue from the pocket of her belted costume and blew her nose.

Nick helped Brandi, his last tyke, slide from his lap to her mother's waiting arms. "Yes, it's time to get back home to Mrs. Claus." His answer was second nature. It was important to stay in character.

Wide gray eyes stared at him from the frame of the little girl's curly blond hair. "You ride in your sleigh?"

Nick smiled and nodded. He could imagine Delia looking much the same at age three. She still had an air of innocence he found irresistible. When he'd entered the office earlier, he had been charmed by her obvious enthusiasm over the reindeer. How did she manage to balance the demands of her job and still maintain that childlike wonder? And she was not the type to stand back and supervise; Delia always pitched right in.

He remembered her traipsing down the length of the mall earlier this afternoon, those bulky reindeer slipping and sliding away from her as she tried to get them to the center court. He had wanted to help her by carrying an extra reindeer or two, but she'd been so adamant about sharing the load. She had never even considered calling someone from maintenance to help or at least send a cart. Delia was definitely a hands-on manager. He respected that, as he was sure her other employees did. In fact he respected so much about Delia. There was only one problem—she was not a Christian.

For the millionth time, he wondered if he'd made the right choice. What was all that business about being unequally yoked? Why couldn't they continue their relationship? Surely she would accept Christ into her life one day. Couldn't his influence in her daily life bring her to salvation faster?

A bright flash interrupted his reverie, and Nick looked over at the photographer. "What was that all about?"

Devin grinned at him. "Wait until you see that one. Unless I miss my guess, it's a prizewinner. Rodin's Santa Thinker. I'll bring you a copy tomorrow." The photographer packed his cameras into their bags and folded up his tripod. "Good night, Santa."

Nick headed to the exit nearest his car, passed Deck the Hall, stopped, then went in to take a look. Every corner of the shop was filled with objects, their glitter nearly overwhelming him. He blinked a couple of times and sniffed the cinnamon-scented air appreciatively. He heard a Christmas soundtrack playing classical music and recognized it as Tchaikovsky's "The Nutcracker Suite." He'd attended too many of his younger sisters' dance rehearsals to mistake it. The music completed the old-fashioned feeling of the store.

He went straight to the Santa Claus display. They made him think of Delia and her collection. Nick smiled at one that was wearing a straw hat and swimming trunks, apparently enjoying a well-deserved beach vacation after Christmas. There was a beautiful bisque figurine of Santa on his knees beside a manger, praying at the feet of Baby Jesus. The detail was breathtaking, so precise it could have been a miniature sculpture by Michelangelo. How he would love to give it to Delia. It brought the two ideas of Christmas together in one beautiful moment. St. Nicholas, the real Santa Claus, would indeed have worshiped at the feet of the Lord on that wondrous night. Nick turned it over to look for the price tag and whistled. No way could he afford that kind of money this year, no matter that it might be the perfect way to witness to Delia. Or would it? He was so scared of saying the wrong thing to her and pushing her even further away from Christ's love.

He put the figurine down and wandered to a display of a first-century village spread out over the tops of several tables. At one end of the display was the stable housing Mary, Joseph, and Baby Jesus. Barn animals, shepherds, and the three wise men attended them. Farther along the street, the little village was filled with tiny figures who seemed to go about their daily business, unaware of the miraculous birth that had just taken place.

How could the villagers not have known? The innkeeper was busy sweeping the entryway to his inn, a fisherman strode toward the market with his catch, and a woman stood outside a stall, considering baskets of fruits and vegetables. As he looked, Nick began to realize the people in this display had much in common with people today. They were caught up in the daily stress of living, focused on the temporal rather than recognizing the eternal nature of God.

For just an instant, he glimpsed the importance of giving every moment to God. He realized in that moment that it was not up to him to save Delia or judge her. God was in control. He would still like to find a way to purchase the kneeling Santa for her collection, but it was much more important to pray for her.

He left the shop and continued toward the mall exit. Stepping outside, he trudged slowly to his car, welcoming the cold air of the Connecticut evening. His thoughts went back to Delia. Why couldn't he put his feelings for her behind him? Did God want him to witness to her or not? God surely loved Delia even more than he did. Maybe He had led Nick to the Santa figurine for His purpose. The idea made his heart pump faster with hope. Maybe he could borrow the money for the Santa or put it on layaway. He had to buy it for Delia's collection. Nick just knew it was the symbol that would bring them back together.

Last year he'd helped Delia get her collection out of storage for Christmas. Together they had unwrapped the Santas, and he had listened as she told the story of how she'd acquired each one. Some of the stories brought tears to her eyes because they were given by family members who had since died. Then they had laughed over the remote control Santa her brother had rigged to deliver his engagement ring to Frances, his girlfriend.

Nick smiled in the darkness. What a fantastic addition to her collection the kneeling Santa would be! He hoped to one day have the chance to present it to her. He imagined the discussion between them. Gently he would lead her to an understanding of God's mysterious plan to save the world through the birth of an innocent babe. He could almost see the light of recognition in her face. Then they could put their plans back on track for a future together—he hoped.

Chapter 5

T hese bowls are so cute." Frances touched one of the two place settings on Delia's oak dining table. "Oh, and look—even your place mats have Santas on them."

"I know, I know. I tend to go overboard. But those are new, so I couldn't resist using them." Last weekend Delia had spent hours packing up her books, DVDs, and china, replacing them with the jolly figurines that crowded every surface of her home. Each shelf of her glass-fronted china cabinet displayed Santa plates, cups, bowls, and serving trays. A bolt of fluffy cotton covered the surface of her sideboard, and Santas of all sizes gamboled through the snowy-looking scenery. The table's centerpiece was a Santa-shaped cookie jar, surrounded by holly and mistletoe.

"Your apartment looks charming, Delia. I never get tired of looking at your Santa collection."

Delia shook her towel and held it up for her friend to see the smiling image of Santa holding an icy bottle of pop. "I got these last year from my staff."

"Adorable." Frances admired the towel for a moment before sniffing the air appreciatively. "I hope that's our dinner I smell."

"It is. Come on in the kitchen and let me check the bread." Delia grabbed a hot pad that matched her towel and opened the oven door. "Just about perfect. I hope you like this bread. I found the recipe on the Internet last month, and I've been dying to try it."

"You've got to be kidding me. *You* made the bread?"

"I did. And the vegetable soup." Delia pulled the loaf out of the oven, placed it on a cooling tray, and put a holiday scarf in a green basket that sported Santa's face on its side.

"Next thing you'll tell me is that you wove that bread basket or knotted the hearth rug in your living room."

"I'm not that far gone yet." Delia laughed. "I guess I got into homemaker mode when I thought Nick and I would. . ." Her words trailed into silence. Two steps took her to the knife block, and she pulled out a serrated blade as her mind wandered back over the impulse that led her to search out new recipes and begin to experiment in the kitchen—Nick.

She had never been very interested in cooking, much preferring to stop by her parents' home or a restaurant at the mall. Less cooking, less cleanup. But that had changed when things seemed to be getting serious between her and Nick. It was—

Delia nearly jumped out of her skin when Frances's arm circled her waist.

Frances hugged her tightly. "I'm sorry, honey. I don't think I realized until tonight how hard this has been on you."

Delia shrugged, but Frances continued hugging her. "I'm sorry. I should be a better friend. No wonder you were so upset when you ran into him last week."

Delia could feel tightness in her chest, and though tears stung the corners of her eyes, she refused to give in to her misery. She squeezed her friend and backed away. "It's okay. I'm already over him. I have to be. Running into him at the mall was nothing. Wait until I tell you the latest."

Frances's eyes widened. "Tell me."

Delia took a deep breath. How to begin? "Nick is working at the mall."

"Oh no! Which store? Do you see him every day?"

"Not every day, but you still don't understand. He's not working for a store." Delia half concentrated on cutting the bread into even slices and putting them in the basket. "He's working for me."

"What! Have you lost your mind? You're still in love with the man, and you hired him to work for you?"

"Not exactly."

Frances took the knife from her and led Delia to the dining room table. "That's enough bread. Tell me exactly what's going on."

"Shannon hired him to be our Santa Claus."

"When did this happen?"

Delia shrugged. "Last week." She quickly recounted the story of how her assistant had unwittingly hired the worst possible man in town to be the mall Santa.

Frances's frown indicated confusion. "But why would Nick

want to work for you? He had to know it would be uncomfortable for you both. Isn't there some unwritten rule in the dating handbook about working with an ex?"

"If not, there sure should be. But you haven't heard the worst of it yet. I'm afraid I wasn't completely professional with him."

"What happened?" Frances's voice went up an octave. "What did you do, punch him in the nose? Or did you throw your arms around him and tell him you want him to be the newest addition to your collection?"

"No." A slight giggle bubbled up out of her. Trust Frances to make her laugh even while her carefully structured life was falling apart. "I reprimanded him for deserting his station in the middle of the day Monday."

"That doesn't sound like an unreasonable complaint. What happened?"

Delia winced at the memory. "He told me I had jumped to conclusions. And he was right. If it had been anybody other than Nick Jackson, I never would have accused him of misbehavior until I had heard his side of the story. I should have asked him into my office, heard his story, and then decided whether or not to criticize his actions."

"Well, honey, you're not perfect. And there are extenuating circumstances. The two of you have a history, so you're both going to have to maintain a certain distance. Which brings me back to why he applied for a job at the mall—"

"I guess he needs the money. And he is an experienced Santa. He even has his own suit and a pair of the cutest glasses that perch on his nose just like"—she grabbed up a porcelain

Santa that smiled beatifically at his open bag of goodies—"just like him."

Frances raised her eyebrow, but before she could comment, the doorbell rang.

"Now who can that be?" Delia returned Santa to his spot on the sideboard. She left Frances in the dining room and moved quickly to open the front door.

A cold gust swept past her into the warm living room, but her attention centered on the small knot of strangers on her front steps. "May I help you?"

"Miss Wilkins?" A tall, beefy man who looked vaguely familiar held out his right hand. "You may not remember me, but we met at New Life Church a few weeks ago. And I saw you at the mall the Friday after Thanksgiving."

A light bulb went off in Delia's mind. This was Nick's new friend, the one who'd first invited her boyfriend to a men's retreat.

His voice brought her back to the present. "We were wondering if we could take a few minutes of your time."

"I...uh...I don't... This is not a good time."

An unsmiling woman in a white, fur-lined parka held out a pamphlet to her. Delia took it, hoping they would leave if she accepted their literature.

"Are you saved, Miss Wilkins?" The woman's hazel eyes seemed to blaze with a strange light.

"Yes, yes, of course I am. I've been attending church all my life."

"Church attendance is a good habit, but it doesn't guarantee salvation. You need a personal relationship with Jesus if you want to avoid the fires of damnation."

Delia felt trapped, defensive. These people were as bad as Nick. Why did the people from his church think they had the right to judge everyone? She stepped back and began to close the door. "Look. I have company this evening. Maybe we could talk about all this later." She nearly groaned. What had made her say that? She didn't want to encourage them to come back. She could find her own way to church without their help.

"Read the tract, Miss Wilkins." The woman's voice sounded harsh to her ears.

The man frowned at her before turning his attention back to Delia. "We'd be glad to see you back at New Life this weekend. Please excuse us for interrupting your evening."

"That's all right." Delia tossed him a smile. "I'm sure I'll see you around."

She closed the door on the two and dropped the pamphlet on her coffee table on her way to the dining room.

Frances had ladled soup into their bowls and fixed them each a drink. "Who was at the door?"

"No one, really." Delia sat down at the table and frowned. "Just a few people from the church Nick dragged me to. I guess he told them I'm not a Christian." A sense of injustice fueled her indignation. "I've gone to church all my life. What gives them the right to judge me?"

Delia fully expected to hear her friend's enthusiastic agreement. But the only sound was the *pop* and *crackle* from the fireplace in the next room. She looked up and saw an expression of joy on Frances's face. "Oh no. Don't tell me you've become a Holy Roller, too. What does my brother have to say about that?"

"We've been attending New Life for several weeks now. I was going to tell you, but I didn't know how when you told me why you and Nick broke up."

Acid churned in Delia's stomach, and she pushed her bowl away. What was going on with everybody? Was religion contagious? Why hadn't she seen the signs that someone else in her life was defecting? Why did everyone have to change? "I guess this means we can't be friends anymore."

"Don't be silly." Frances reached across the table, her palm up. "We'll always be friends. And Carl will always be your brother."

Somehow Delia doubted her assurances. She remembered Nick starting out the same way, all excited about singing and going to church and reading his Bible. Then he'd decided she needed to jump on the bandwagon, too. Eventually Frances would decide Delia needed saving. As if she wasn't enough of a Christian. It was inevitable. They were all the same.

"If what you say is true, why did Nick dump me when he became a Christian?"

Frances's gaze did not drop. "Didn't you tell me you asked him to choose between his church and you?"

Delia could feel the tears threatening again. "All I did was confront him about the problem. He's the one who was trying to change me. It's true I didn't like all the time he was spending at the church, but his enthusiasm would have faded after a few months. Then we could've gone on like before."

"But that's just it, Delia. Once you invite Christ into your life, you don't want things to go on like before."

"Are you telling me you would have broken up with Carl if he hadn't joined the church when you did? Would you have treated my brother the same way I was treated?" The angry words echoed in the small room. Delia could see the pain on her friend's face, but what about her pain? Didn't that count for something? Had they all lost their minds? Was she the only one who could see the truth?

Chapter 6

Delia shoved at the door to the mall offices. She had to try twice before she mustered enough strength to swing it open. A sigh filled her. Why was she so tired? It had been another busy day, but she should be used to that. This was not her first Christmas as the mall manager, after all. Maybe it was her shoes. She glared at her feet, encased in a beautiful pair of mauve heels that matched her blouse perfectly. They pinched a little, but they couldn't be the real problem. The real problem was more likely the lack of sleep last night.

Frances had left right after their argument. Well, it hadn't really been an argument. Frances had not tried to defend her decision to join New Life. She had merely looked at her with those big green eyes and let Delia rant until she had run out of complaints. Then she had said she'd be praying for Delia, hugged her one more time, gathered her coat and scarf, and walked out into the snowy evening.

Delia had spent the next half hour slamming cabinet doors and scrubbing at her countertops as if rubbing them clean could assuage her guilt. Once her kitchen was gleaming, she had sat down to watch seasonal cartoon movies, but they were either too silly, too sweet, or too Christian.

Finally she had turned off the television and gone to bed to toss and turn and wonder why her life had fallen apart in one short month. Images of Frances's wounded looks melted into Nick's reproachful blue gaze. How had it all gone so wrong?

Delia dragged herself past Mabel's empty desk, looking to see if there were any urgent calls she needed to return before calling it a night. As she wandered down the hall, Shannon's tinkling laughter grabbed her attention. The sound was answered by a low murmur. *Nick!*

Delia could feel her energy returning in a wave of righteous anger. How dare he flirt with her assistant! And as for Shannon, well, she apparently didn't have enough work to keep her busy. It was obviously time to delegate a little more responsibility to her assistant manager.

Professional courtesy and curiosity warred against each other—she ought to go into her own office and close the door loudly enough to warn them she was here—but curiosity won out. She tiptoed her way down the carpeted hall and stood next to Shannon's door, which was slightly ajar. She would only listen for a moment. Then Delia would knock on the door and face them directly.

"I think that's a great idea!"

Shannon's flirty voice made Delia's hands clench. She couldn't hear Nick's voice very plainly. He must be facing away from the door, staring lovingly into Shannon's eyes. The nerve of them, right here at work! She was concentrating so hard on what was going on inside Shannon's office that she didn't hear the noise behind her until someone tapped her shoulder.

Delia let out a shriek that would do a siren proud and jerked around to face the intruder. Eyes as blue as the deep ocean, dark curly hair, a big red coat, and a smile that made her weak in the knees. Oh no! Nick had caught her eavesdropping. But then who—

"What's wrong?" Devin, the Santa photographer, barreled out of Shannon's office, fists up. "Are you okay, Delia?"

Shannon was right behind him, a look of concern replaced by confusion when she recognized her boss and Nick. "What's going on? Is something wrong?"

Delia could have sunk through the carpet. She'd been caught red-handed spying on her employees. What could she say?

"It's my fault." Nick's smile ran a shiver down her back. "Delia obviously didn't realize I was here. I guess I should have—"

"No"—Delia could feel her cheeks heating up, but she wouldn't let Nick take the fall—"I'm the one to blame. I should have gone straight to my office. But I was surprised to hear voices from your office."

"Oh." Shannon's big brown eyes sized up the situation. She raised her eyebrow, but apparently she was going to let the weak explanation pass. "It's good we're all here. Devin and I have been waiting to see you, Nick, to get your permission for an idea Devin has to use in a new holiday promotional spot."

"Promotional spot?" This was the first Delia had heard about it. "What's wrong with the ad campaign we've been using? And why didn't you come to me first?"

Shannon's eyes widened. "Well, you weren't here earlier. So Devin and I decided to get Nick's permission first to use his face. Then we thought we'd show you a polished layout instead of our rough ideas."

Twice in the space of two minutes, Delia had been put in the wrong. What was the matter with her? She was losing it. She swallowed her discomfort with an effort. "I see." She pasted a shaky smile on her face. "I have some things to finish up before I can go home, so you guys go ahead with your plans. I'll be happy to see them whenever you're ready."

"Please don't go." Devin put his hand on her arm. "I've been taking lots of pictures of the mall stores and your new Santa here. I'd love to show them to you, and we can discuss our ideas. I think you'll be pleased with the result."

Delia wondered how she could have ever mistaken the photographer's clipped New England accent for Nick's distinctive drawl. Shannon was urging her to come and see their ideas. Nick just leaned against the wall and watched. She could feel his gaze on her. Was her hair messed up? Probably. It had been a long day. Her hand itched to smooth it back, but she refused to show her insecurity by fussing with her appearance. Let him look. She straightened her back and followed Devin and Shannon.

Delia perched on one of the two faux leather chairs in front of Shannon's desk. Shannon sat in her executive chair with Devin at her elbow as they pored over the pictures scattered across her blotter. That left Nick with two choices—stand or sit in the chair next to Delia's. He sat. Of course. He would never try to make her more comfortable by keeping a physical distance between them. Her conscience assailed her.

What was the matter with her? She seemed to have lost her common sense in the last few days. Nick had always been chivalrous in his treatment of her. Only a few minutes ago, he'd been ready to take the blame when she'd been the one eavesdropping.

"Looks like we may have a romance budding." Nick's low voice interrupted the needling thoughts.

Delia looked at him, but Nick nodded toward Shannon and Devin. She turned her attention their way and caught Devin winking at her assistant. Shannon's cheeks flushed in response, and she fluttered her lashes before looking back at the pictures. Now Delia felt like a complete idiot. Why hadn't she seen it for herself? But she could feel some of the tension leaving her as she witnessed the obvious attraction between them. Her fears about Shannon and Nick had obviously been unfounded.

She sat back in her chair, exchanging a conspiratorial smile with Nick. It felt so natural, so normal. As if their thoughts were on the same wavelength. The intimacy took her breath away.

And then the warm moment was over. Reality slammed into her. They were not dating anymore. Nick had chosen to walk away. She closed her eyes to hide the pain. Why did it have to be this way? Why couldn't things have worked out differently? Why was she still in love with a man who had thrown away their relationship for something he couldn't even see?

Emptiness as deep as a starless night filled her, but Delia

had no idea how to dispel it. Was it grief over the breakup? No, somehow she sensed it was proof of a deeper need.

ॐ

Nick wanted to see the smile return to Delia's face, but she seemed lost in thought. He grimaced. She was lost all right. Lost to the Word. How he prayed she would become more open to the gift of salvation. But every time he tried to break down her wall, she seemed to draw further away.

Unable to come up with a solution, he turned his mind to another matter. Nick could understand why Delia had been a little embarrassed over the scream she'd let loose when he startled her. His ears were still ringing from the sound. She had not been the cool, calm, in-control boss lady. But why had she seemed downright guilty?

Had she been eavesdropping on her employees? He didn't want to believe that because it seemed out of character for Delia. Her approach had always been upfront and straightforward. But she *had* blushed pretty brightly when Devin and Shannon first rushed out into the hall. He frowned at her. What was going on in Delia's head? She'd been acting out of character a lot lately.

Her tight mouth told him how tired she was. Others might be fooled by her crisp suit and polished fingernails, but he could tell when Delia was exhausted. Maybe that was the problem. This was the busiest time of the year for her. He was certain she was putting in extra hours at the mall. He saw her several times during the day, always rushing in one direction or another. She needed to get home and get some sleep. But first he wanted to ask her about an idea he'd had.

"Psst, Delia." Nick kept his voice low, not wanting to disturb Shannon and Devin, who were currently arguing over some dilemma concerning their "brilliant" idea.

When she turned her face toward his, he almost decided to forgo giving her another problem tonight. But then he thought about the kids and his promise. He had no choice.

"What is it, Nick?"

"I need to talk to you in your office for a few minutes."

Her eyes widened slightly. "What's the matter?"

"Nothing much." Nick smiled at her. "It should only take a minute. I need to ask you about making a few adjustments for the rest of this week."

Delia stood up. "Look, you two. You can show me the layout tomorrow. I have a few things I need to wrap up before I go home."

Shannon and Devin hardly paid them any attention, waving at them briefly before returning to their argument. Nick could not stop a smile at the glances the two of them were exchanging. True love. . . It was so sweet during the beginning stages.

He glanced to his right, his eyes tracing the curve of Delia's hair. It had once been that sweet between the two of them. Was that why he ached so badly now? But even though the rift hurt, he knew it was for the best. *Lord, You know my heart. Please give me peace about the situation between us and help me keep Delia at a distance.* He rose and followed her down the hall.

Delia sat behind her desk and nodded at him to take one of

the guest chairs. "What's the problem?"

Nick pulled at the collar of his Santa costume. "I was wondering if we could shut down the Santa visits an hour early for the rest of this week."

"Why do you want to do that?"

"A couple of reasons." Nick realized he was drumming his fingers on the arm of his chair. He consciously relaxed his hand. "I know you've been extremely busy, so you may not have noticed that your elf, Jean, has really been dragging the past few days. I think the long hours are getting to her."

"That doesn't make any sense. Jean's had that job for several years. She knows what it entails."

"And that's exactly why she won't come to you herself. But I'm afraid she's going to collapse if you don't let her get a little more rest by closing down early."

Silence invaded the office space. He could hear the muted voices from Shannon's office and the *creak* of Delia's chair as she leaned back to consider his words.

"I'll think about it. What's the other reason?"

Nick wished he could read her mind. "I have a previous commitment that's very important to me. I'd like to leave an hour early tomorrow so I can take care of it."

Delia's eyebrows came together. "What commitment?"

Had the room grown warmer? If so, it wasn't because of Delia. The expression on her face was as frosty as a snowstorm. He wanted to tell her his plans, but Nick could not stand to see her scornful reaction. They'd been down that road too many times already. "It's a private matter."

Delia's head jerked back as if he'd slapped her.

Nick cringed. He didn't want to hurt her. He opened his mouth to explain, but she raised her hand, palm outward.

"I can take a hint." She looked down and made a notation on her appointment calendar. "I guess I'll have to agree. There's not much of a way to have a Christmas display if neither Santa nor his elf can be present."

"Delia, I'm sorry. It's just that—"

"No, Nick. You're right." She looked away from him, staring at a picture that decorated one wall of her office. "Look—we're both in an uncomfortable situation, but for the sake of Village Mall, let's see if we can manage to get along until the holidays are over."

He nodded and pushed himself out of the chair. "I guess I'll see you around then." He waited for a minute for her answer, but Delia kept her eyes averted. Nick felt awful. He'd made the situation worse than ever, but he had no idea how to mend things tonight.

As he walked to his car, Nick realized God had answered his prayer for distance between him and Delia. He should be more careful about what he asked for.

Chapter 7

Delia's phone rang. She looked at her nails, which sported a fresh, wet coat of Holiday Crimson. No one understood the grueling demands of running a mall. Never mind that it was her day off; she had no choice but to answer her cell. She gingerly pulled open the edges of her purse, holding her breath as she fished out the jangling phone. If she didn't change the tune to another Christmas carol soon, Delia was afraid she would end up with a lifelong aversion to "Jingle Bells."

"Hello?"

"Hi, Delia!" Frances's energetic voice made her wince and move the phone from her ear a fraction. "I know it's your night off, but I've got great plans for the evening. Please tell me you're available."

Delia glanced at the unopened bag of cookies and new novel lying on her coffee table. "I guess you could say that. What's going on?"

"Put on a warm sweater and some old jeans. I'll be there in ten minutes."

A *click* indicated that Frances had hung up. Delia rolled her eyes, wondering what her friend was about to drag her into tonight, but at least the call had not been another crisis at work. With a sigh, she picked up the bag of cookies, uncovering the religious tract Nick's friends had given her last week. Why hadn't she thrown it away? She'd started to when dusting the living room furniture, but something had stopped her. Maybe one of these days, she would have time to look at it—only to reassure herself she had no need to worry about her faith. . .or her soul, of course.

Delia flapped her hands and blew on her fingernails as she went into her bedroom, where she pulled out a cream-colored, cable-knit sweater and a pair of jeans she'd worn while painting her kitchen last spring. Except for a sprinkle of Tantalizing Teal droplets, they looked okay. And they were comfortable. She changed clothes, cringing when she felt her nails drag against the waist of her jeans. Frances really owed her one this time. Maybe she should demand that her friend pay for a manicure to make up for it. Good luck getting Frances to agree to that.

Delia stepped in front of her mirror and attacked her hair, brushing it into some semblance of order. To ensure the style would hold no matter what was on the agenda for the evening, she spritzed the ends with hair gel. As Delia applied a light coat of lip gloss, she remembered a new holiday romance movie was showing at the mall theater. Maybe that's what Frances had in mind for the two of them. That would be good. She always enjoyed a sweet romance story, and she could check in on things at the office while they were at the mall.

Her speculations came to an end at the sound of a horn blowing. Delia grabbed her fur-lined denim jacket and her purse, shaking the latter to be certain her keys were inside. As she opened the door, a cold blast of Connecticut winter made her shiver. It had snowed again last night, and a dozen kids were taking advantage of the fresh powder by sledding down the hillside next to her apartment. Their cheerful shouts lightened her mood even further. It was good to get out.

She slid into Frances's car. "Are we going to the movies?"

"Not exactly." Her friend winked at her. "But I think you'll have a good time anyway. We're volunteering at the soup kitchen."

Delia's buoyant mood melted faster than a snowflake in the tropics. "You want me to *work* on my one night off this week?"

"It's not work. Wait and see for yourself. I went a few times before Thanksgiving, and I've been meaning to get back over there. You'll love it."

Delia crossed her arms over her chest. "Humph."

"Just try it for me, okay?" Frances's tone begged for her acquiescence. "I promise if you don't have a good time I'll never ask you to go again."

Delia let her silence express her disapproval. Her attention centered on the Christmas lights that gave a cheery look to the town's streets as dusk deepened into night. It was the time of year for some of the local young people to make extra money by offering romantic carriage rides through the quaint streets of her hometown, so Delia was not surprised to see a horse-drawn carriage whose passengers leaned close to each other.

Last year she and Nick had taken a similar ride. It had been fun to see the town from a new perspective, especially sharing the experience with the man she loved. . .had loved. Envy and sadness seeped in to fill her chest. Would she never get over Nick? Maybe Frances was right. Maybe she needed to put her own problems aside by focusing on someone else for a change.

They pulled up in front of the shelter, a former storefront that had been recently decorated to look like the entrance to a rustic stable, complete with a large lighted star and an angel who seemed to float above the double doors.

"Doesn't this look nice? Believe it or not, Carl helped mount the star and angel."

Delia was incredulous. "My brother took time from the hospital to come work at the homeless shelter?"

"You'd be surprised at the number of people who volunteer here." Frances pulled open the door, and the two women entered a beehive of activity. Children raced around the large open area, weaving in and out of the long line of people who were waiting for the cafeteria-style serving area to open.

She and Frances were given plastic gloves, aprons, and paper hats before they were assigned to stations in front of the vegetables. They spent the next hour ladling cauliflower, green beans, and creamed potatoes.

Delia smiled and chatted with the people she was serving, slowly losing her reserve. She had to admit, the grateful expressions and words of thanks were rewarding.

"Come on and tell the truth." Her friend tossed a knowing look her way. "You're having a good time."

Delia shook her ladle at Frances. "Don't go getting all smug on me. I—"

"Ho! Ho! Ho!" The words shook the rafters of the remodeled store.

A familiar figure walked through the front door amid squeals from the children. Delia froze in place. Of all the luck. She shot an accusing glare at Frances.

"I didn't know, Delia." The look on her friend's face was a mixture of disbelief and concern. "I never would have suggested we come tonight if I'd known Nick would be here."

Delia wanted to hide behind the counter, but it was too late. Nick's familiar blue gaze met hers, and he seemed to stumble midstride. Her hand went out toward him, and her breath caught; he regained his balance, though, and moved to the Christmas tree in one corner of the room. As she watched him cross the room, realization dawned. *This* was his previous commitment—not a date. Relief washed over her, but she refused to consider why. She was over Nick Jackson—wasn't she?

On the far side of the room, Nick had turned his attention to the children crowded around him. "Are there any good boys or girls here tonight?"

A chorus of yeses answered his question.

"Well, that's fine then. Let's see what I have in my bag." With a flourish, he opened the large bag and reached inside to pull out small books—pink for the girls and navy for the boys.

"What is he handing out?"

"They're Bibles donated by our church."

Delia sniffed. "Don't you think these children need more

than Bibles? Like warm beds and parents with jobs?"

"Oh, Delia, you're so wrong. What better gift to give them than the chance to know Christ?"

The words were spoken gently, but Delia could feel their sting. "But some of those children are too young to even read."

"Then I hope someone will read to them." Frances pulled off her gloves and hat. "If not their parents, then maybe one of the older children. These kids are at such high risk to be drawn into the wrong world. We want them to have a place to turn to, a choice for a better life."

Nick had finished giving out his Bibles. Now the children sat around him and watched as he pulled out a larger Bible from the folds of his coat.

"Do any of you know what day is coming soon?"

"Christmas!" Some of the young voices held a note of wonder, but others sounded resigned and hopeless. It broke Delia's heart to think of these children who had nothing to look forward to on Christmas morning.

"That's right," Nick replied to the children. "And do any of you know why we celebrate Christmas every year?"

"For presents," answered one child.

Nick shook his head. "Presents are nice, but people give them to each other because we are celebrating a special gift that was sent to us a long, long time ago." He opened his Bible, thumbing past several pages until he reached the scripture verse he wanted. "Do any of you know what that gift was?"

An older youngster raised his hand. "Baby Jesus?"

Nick smiled and nodded. "That's right. And it's because of

that one special little baby that we still celebrate today."

Delia could see that Nick had them all enthralled as he read about the birth of Christ. His voice was pitched low, but it carried across the room with ease. He must have learned that technique in Santa school. As he spoke, her mind pictured the rough manger that was the newborn Child's bed. When he read about the shepherds on that long-ago night, she could almost see their fearful, wondering faces.

How would it have felt to see all the angels in the night sky? What if she had witnessed such an exciting event? It had certainly made a difference in the shepherds' lives. According to the Bible, they had not returned to their sheep, hurrying off instead to tell others what they had seen. She wished she had lived back then. It must have been so easy for them. If only God would send her a sign like that. . . .

When Nick finished reading, the silence in the room was eerily complete. Then someone began clapping. Without conscious thought, she joined in the applause. It all seemed like a wonderful dream. But then reality intruded. It was only a dream. Believing in pretty fantasies led to problems, like splitting up with your girlfriend, for example. If she wasn't careful, she would get caught up in all this just as Nick and Frances had.

Delia touched Frances's arm. "Can we leave?"

"Are you all right?"

"I just need to get home." Delia looked down at her cream sweater, which bore evidence of the night's service despite the protection of her apron. Funny that she'd not been aware of her appearance earlier, but now she was. She laid her apron on the counter and looked around for her jacket. A gasp parted her lips as she remembered the cap on her head. A quick grab removed it, but there was no telling what her hair looked like. "Please get me out of here."

❧

Nick's heart banged against his chest with the joy of sharing the true message of Christmas. Sometimes it seemed impossible that he had only recently grasped the importance of Christ's birth. Having grown up in the middle of the Bible Belt, he'd always assumed he was saved. He had been baptized at the same time as his friends and received his first Bible at the age of eleven, but all the supposedly important things of life—dating, football, grades—had seemed to take precedence over faith. Three months ago, however, when he attended a retreat with his friend Tom, Nick realized what a fool he had been, focused on secular issues rather than spiritual truths. That weekend he gave his life over to the Savior, and everything changed.

Nick watched a couple of kids from the mission proudly show their new Bibles to their parents. Maybe this Christmas would be the start of their walks with the Lord. Perhaps their innocent curiosity would also draw the adults closer to God.

A young woman with a gold hoop piercing her left eyebrow held a boy of about three in her lap and was helping him write his name in his new Bible. She looked barely twenty years old. Could she really be the parent of a three-year-old? He wondered if she had run away from home, or maybe she had been dumped by her boyfriend when she got pregnant. Whatever her story, Nick's heart went out to her as she teased her young son. Her love for him was obvious in her smile and the way she protected him within the circle of her arms.

It was funny how God worked things out. The need to share his faith had drawn Nick to the soup kitchen several times since his spiritual awakening, but he had never been able to connect with these people as closely as he had tonight. Luke's account of Jesus' birth had seemed to come alive. As he read the scriptures, Nick had truly felt Joseph's frustration in trying to provide shelter for his pregnant wife, frustration that must have been swallowed up in awe and wonder at the miraculous birth of God in the form of a tiny baby. Had Joseph knelt over the manger? Touched the tiny hand of the newborn babe? Nick's mind flashed to the figurine of the kneeling Santa.

Delia. He'd seen Delia when he came in. Nick's glance searched the workers who were busily cleaning up the serving line, but he didn't spot her. Had he been mistaken? No way. He'd known she was here the moment he walked into the soup kitchen. Like he had a special radar that could detect her even from a distance, even in a crowd of people.

But where was she? Why had she been here? Was she affected by the reading of the Christmas story? Was she softening? Maybe her presence at the downtown mission meant she was changing. Perhaps that hard shell of disbelief was cracking. Sudden hope buoyed him. *Oh, Lord, please let her know You. Even if we are not meant to be together, please draw her to You.*

Nick turned down the offer of a meal, gathered up his

nearly empty bag, and waved good-bye to the children. He still needed to do a lot this evening. Tossing his bag into the front seat of his '98 pickup truck, Nick sat, automatically avoiding the place where a spring poked through the worn upholstery. It might be ugly, but his old truck cranked every time and ran like a dream. He rubbed his hands together and waited for the engine to warm up before negotiating the wintry streets. He pulled off his hat, beard, and mustache. No sense making driving any harder.

Nick's lack of experience on snow had him gripping the steering wheel and moving slowly down the busy streets. When he reached his destination, he breathed a sigh of relief and pulled into an empty spot in front of Tom's apartment. Feeling conspicuous in his red suit, he hurried up the sidewalk and knocked at his friend's door.

"Come on in, Santa." Tom's cheerful face greeted his knock.

Nick followed his friend down the hallway into the living room. Empty pizza boxes and unfolded laundry covered the coffee table. Books and sports magazines obscured the rug, which could probably use a good vacuuming. He caught a distinct odor of stale coffee and old aftershave. "You need a girlfriend to spruce up this place."

"Got one handy in that big bag you carry around?"

Nick laughed at the joke. "I'll have to work on that for you."

"So did you come for those tracts?"

"Yep. I can't believe how quickly they disappear."

"I'm not surprised." Tom pawed through a stack of papers. "They look nice and Christmassy. I like the way they explain the history of St. Nicholas and move to the real reason for the holiday."

Nick's gaze roamed around the room. It put him in mind of the way Delia had responded to his messy apartment when they'd first started dating. She'd immediately begun to organize him, putting his mail into cute baskets, discarding piles of ancient magazines and junk mail, and even getting him a scrapbook for family photographs and newspaper clippings. Since they'd broken up, he'd let things slide. If he wasn't careful, his place would soon revert to its pre-Delia state.

"Here they are." Tom's voice carried a hint of relief. He sidestepped a soda can and a coffee cup, picking up a stack of the tracts and handing them over. "That should be about a hundred. Do you think that will be enough?"

"For a day or two." Nick hesitated. Should he mention the subject that weighed on his mind? He wanted to talk to his friend but wasn't sure exactly what to say. "You'll never guess who was at the soup kitchen tonight."

Tom cocked his eyebrow. "From the expression on your face, I'd have to guess it was your ex-girlfriend, Dahlia."

"Delia."

"Okay, Delia. What was she doing? Donating food?"

"No, she was serving. She was there with her friend Frances. You remember the redhead we met in the mall a few weeks ago?" Nick waited for Tom's nod before continuing. "Something happened tonight. I saw her face when I finished reading the Christmas story to the kids. She was really touched."

"So you think she's ready to listen to the Word? I hope

you're right, Nick. But you need to move slowly. Lots of people, especially females and especially around this time of year, get emotional over stuff. It doesn't mean she's ready."

"But it could be the crack in her armor that leads her to open her heart to God."

Tom shook his head. "I'm not an expert on this. But there's something you don't know."

A cloud of gloom threatened Nick's good mood. He wasn't sure he wanted to hear what Tom had to say. Then he remembered the verse he'd read just that morning in Romans. *"You did not receive a spirit that makes you a slave again to fear."* No matter what Tom had to say, God was in control. Nick drew a deep breath and squared his shoulders.

Tom sighed. "A group of us went to visit Delia last week."

Nick slapped the tracts against his leg to give his roiling emotions an outlet. "Why didn't you tell me? You know I would've wanted to go along. How did it go? What did you say to her?"

"Slow down." Tom leaned against the back of his sofa. "There's not much to tell. She didn't invite us in. Said she had company. She accepted a tract, but I doubt she spent much time reading it. All in all, Delia didn't seem much like she wanted to hear whatever we might have to say."

Nick didn't know how to take Tom's disturbing account. Would Delia never become a Christian? What would it take? He'd been so excited earlier tonight, believing his prayer for the opportunity to witness to Delia had been answered. She'd looked so. . .captivated.

He remembered how her face had glowed, but maybe it had been some Christmas-inspired emotion as Tom suggested. Then he remembered how quickly she'd disappeared, even before the workers cleaned up. Why would she do that if God had been whispering to her heart?

But he refused to give up on Delia. Not only was she missing out on the joy of Christianity, but her eternal soul was at stake.

Chapter 8

Delia knew it was a mistake before the words came out of her mouth, but she couldn't help herself. She had to agree. She could no sooner resist her employees' pleading expressions than she could kick a puppy. "All right."

Shannon clapped her hands. "I knew you were a good sport. The best boss we could have."

"Absolutely the best." Mabel's fluttering eyelashes and falsetto voice made Shannon giggle.

"Enough, enough." Delia took the stack of neatly folded clothing from Shannon's outstretched hands. "You two are pouring it on a little thick."

Mabel's voice fell an octave to her usual no-nonsense tone. "It's obvious the elf costume is best suited to you."

Delia summoned a frown for the benefit of her employees. "Are you saying I need to go on a diet?"

"Not at all. Shannon's about a foot taller than Jean." Mabel glanced down at her ample proportions. "And I'm about three sizes larger."

Shannon held up the boots with pointed red toes and bells attached—and a pair of stockings that had one green leg and one red one.

Delia groaned. "What have I gotten myself into?"

"It'll be fine." Shannon's words were still a little too overeager to Delia's ears.

She took the costume and stomped to her office. How could their veteran elf have gotten sick? Delia thought of all the coughing, sneezing children who had gone through the line since Thanksgiving and shuddered. It was a wonder Santa wasn't sick, too.

Oh no–o–o! Santa! Nick would see her in this outfit. What had she been thinking? Good-bye, navy pumps, creased slacks, and fitted jacket. Instead of a professional manager, she would be a silly elf. How did she get herself into these situations? Was she a lunatic? Or had last night's reading softened her to the point of being unable to say no?

Delia discarded her suit coat and pulled on the forest green tunic as she thought about the tract left by Nick's church friends. Its simple, straightforward words had tugged at something inside her. Delia had grown up knowing about the birth of Christ, but she had never really understood what was so miraculous about it. Babies were born every day, and some of them came to very sad ends. But as she'd read the words in that tract, awareness peeked into her soul like the first pastel rays of sunrise. The look on Frances's face when she'd told her about joining the church, Nick's voice recounting the first Christmas. . . Was it some set of weird circumstances, or was God really trying to get through to her?

Delia's thoughts returned to the present as she wrestled her legs into the multicolored tights and stood, catching a glimpse of her reflection in the mirror that hung above the office sofa. She wrinkled her nose and cinched the wide velveteen belt. The outfit was not too bad. If she stood way back and squinted, it kind of reminded her of her green suit. . .if she ignored the tights, that is. She sighed. And then there were the boots. The bells jangled as she slipped her feet into the kitschy slippers.

With a final sigh for her carefully arranged hair, Delia slipped the garish red-and-green-striped hat on her head. The wide strip of red fur was supposed to fit snugly on her head, allowing her bangs to show. Jean must have a really big head. Delia pushed the hat off her forehead. It slipped back to her eyebrows. She shoved it up. It slipped back down. Up. Down. Up. Down. After several fruitless attempts, Delia wanted to stomp on the thing.

Maybe she could pin it back. But a search in her office yielded exactly zero hairpins. With her hand holding the hat in place, she headed down the hall. "Shannon? Mabel? Somebody help."

"What's the matter?" Shannon poked her head out of her office. "You look. . .elfish."

Delia rolled her eyes. "Just what I wanted to hear. But I guess it's better than being told I look like a complete idiot."

"Seriously, I appreciate your being such a good sport, Delia. I don't know many bosses who would agree to being seen in public looking—"

"You'd better stop right there unless you want to find yourself in this costume."

Shannon's face took on a look of horror. "My lips are sealed. Did you need me for something?"

"Yes, I need hairpins. I looked in my desk, but all I could find were staples and paper clips."

"Sorry. I never use them. Would a rubber band help?"

Delia let go of her hat. It slipped down to cover her eyes.

"Oh, I see. No rubber band will fix that. Maybe Mabel has some."

The two women headed for the front office. Delia kept pushing at the hat, but it was no use. The silly thing insisted on scooting down across her forehead, no matter what. Delia was ready to go back to her office, change clothes, and give this problem to someone else. Why did Santa have to have an elf anyway?

Her boots jingled merrily, and Mabel looked up, her eyes widening and her mouth forming a perfect O.

"What?"

"Nothing." Mabel's voice was suspiciously choked. "I was thinking you make an adorable elf. Santa is going to want to take you back to the North Pole with him."

"You've got to be kidding. The children are more likely to run screaming when they see nothing but a pair of tights, a belt, and a nose."

Mabel pulled open a desk drawer. "Let's see if we can do something about that."

Delia could have hugged the woman when she produced a handful of hairpins. "You're a lifesaver."

Shannon held the hat in place while Mabel anchored the

pins in Delia's hair. The office filled with giggles and an ouch or two as some of the pins went a little deeper than Delia thought necessary.

"Remind me to mention this in your quarterly review," Delia said.

"About how I'm prepared in all situations?" Even a mouthful of hairpins couldn't impede Mabel's saucy reply.

"Something like that." Delia rubbed a sore spot on her scalp and stepped back. "I think that should do it."

"Sounds like someone's anxious to get out there." Shannon's teasing brought a smile to Delia's face. "Maybe she wants to gauge Santa's reaction for herself."

Delia was glad the awkwardness between her and Shannon had eased. She'd apologized several times for eavesdropping on Devin and Shannon. They had graciously forgiven her, even though she could not bring herself to explain exactly who she'd thought was carrying on with Shannon that night. Remembering her unfounded suspicions brought heat to Delia's face.

Oh no! Now her employees would be convinced she was anxious to see Nick. And there wasn't a thing she could do to make the situation better, so she ignored her coworkers' smirks and jingled her way out of the office.

As Delia wandered down the mall to the center court, she noticed the wide eyes and pointing fingers of the children. She nodded, trying to get into character, but she could also see the pitying looks of the parents. They must think she was the most unemployable female in Connecticut. No skills, no experience, no abilities. Why else would she take a job as a Christmas elf?

Delia wanted to stop them and explain why she was dressed like this. She wanted to shout out that they didn't understand. She was a professional. But the evidence was against her. So she smiled at the adults, waved to the children, and hurried to reach her destination.

Delia saw Nick before her jingling boots announced her arrival. Would he make fun of her, too? She thought she'd die of embarrassment if he laughed at her. And how could he resist? She knew how foolish she looked, but she might as well get it over with. She squared her shoulders and marched forward.

Nick nodded at a young girl and deposited her into her mother's waiting arms with a hearty laugh and a wink. Then he reached down in his bag and pulled out a sheet of paper he handed to the mother. Delia was too far away to hear what he said, but she recognized the paper. It was the same tract she had read last night. The tract that had made her want to pray for forgiveness and understanding. She could feel a prick behind her eyes. Was she going to cry? Right here in the middle of the mall?

A *click* and a bright flash startled Delia. She jerked away from the brightness, setting her boots to ringing like a horse-drawn sleigh.

"That's one for the archives." Devin's grin was mischievous.

Delia was horrified. She'd never live it down if Devin passed around a photograph of her dressed up like this. "Please, Devin, have a heart—"

"Ho! Ho! Ho!" Nick's boisterous tones overrode her pitiful plea. "Has anyone seen my elf?"

A host of children answered his question with laughs and pointing fingers.

"Why, *there* she is!" Nick's voice boomed so loudly that Delia wished for a pair of earmuffs. "Come on over here, little helper."

Delia pasted a smile on her face. "Hi, Santa. Sorry I'm late. I was having trouble with my hat."

"Well, I guess that's as good a reason as any. Why don't you start handing out some lollipops to all the good boys and girls in line here?" He beckoned to the next child in line and went to work.

Delia's initial awkwardness over her unprofessional appearance gave way to pleasure as she fell into the role of Santa's elf. She listened to the hopes and dreams of bright-eyed children and chatted with their exhausted parents. She dispensed candy, winks, and hugs. She even got used to having her picture taken nearly as often as Santa.

The only sour note was a group of young men who tried to make her feel uncomfortable with whistles and remarks. Santa, however, came to her rescue. He took the boys aside and spoke to them for a few minutes. She wasn't sure what he said, but the boys drifted off and never reappeared.

When the stores at the mall began closing up, Delia was almost disappointed. She waved good-bye to a sleepy toddler, pushing back the elf hat that had once again crept forward until it grazed her eyebrows.

"Not exactly what you expected, was it?" Nick hefted his bag to one shoulder, carefully picking his way through the Christmas trees and reindeer on display.

"Not at all." She fell in step next to him. "Do you change clothes here or wait until you get home?"

"Usually I wait until I get home, but I have a date with those kids who were giving you a hard time this afternoon. They agreed to meet me at the church gym for a little basketball practice."

So that's what had happened. "How do you do it?" Delia couldn't keep the admiration out of her voice. "You have to be as tired as I am, but now you're going to spend the rest of the evening with some troubled teens."

It might have been a reflection from his costume, but Delia thought she could see a hint of red in Nick's cheeks. "It's nothing. At first I wanted to hit them for bothering you, but that would be the old Nick's response. So I had to take a deep breath and pray for a moment. That's when I got the idea of inviting them to the gym."

Delia put her hand on his arm. "I'm impressed, Nick. And I owe you an apology."

"You don't owe me anything, Delia."

"Please let me finish. I want to get this out before I lose my nerve." She took a deep breath. All around them, the mall was growing quiet, like a weary child at bedtime. Here and there a late shopper hurried out into the cold evening, but for the most part, she and Nick were alone. Even the ever-present Christmas carols had been silenced for the night.

"You were right to break up with me. I was wrong to make you choose between me and your faith. I can see that now. I'm starting to understand that what you have is more than just words."

"Delia." Nick dropped his bag and grabbed her shoulders. "That's the most exciting thing you could have said to me. I've been praying that God would speak to your heart. He is such an amazing God. Isn't it exciting to be one of His children?"

Delia looked up at him for a moment, her gaze caught by his earnest blue eyes. She could nearly drown in their sparkle. She wanted so much to agree with him. But could she? Did she really understand what it meant to be a Christian? Sure, something had touched her heart last night, but how could she know for certain?

She lowered her gaze. A couple of weeks ago, it wouldn't have mattered. She would have said nearly anything to get Nick back. But now it was different. Now she had to be sure that last night had been real. She would not risk hurting Nick. Not again.

"I— You're going a little too fast for me, Nick. I'm not sure exactly what I feel or how to deal with all the questions and problems—"

His hands fell away, leaving her feeling suddenly cold in the quiet hallway. "Delia, one of these days, you're going to have to let God have control of your life. This isn't a game. It's an all-or-nothing kind of thing. When you decide to surrender your life to Him, no problem is too big for Him to handle."

Delia pulled off her bothersome hat and twisted it in her

hands. She didn't know what to say. What did Nick want to hear from her? Wasn't it enough that she was admitting she was wrong? She wished they could skip the awkwardness and go back to the relationship they had before. Then maybe she could figure out exactly what she believed.

She felt something soft at her cheek and realized it was Nick's gloved hand. She looked up into his eyes, eyes so full of love and peace it made her want to cry.

Delia pulled away from his gentle touch. Couldn't he see he was tearing her apart inside? With a choked cry, she turned and ran, the sound of her jingling feet loud in the empty mall.

❧

Nick's warning rang in Delia's ears as she let herself into her office. She had meant to change into her work clothes, but what she was wearing now seemed trivial, an insignificant detail. She sat down at her desk, grabbed her briefcase, and searched inside for the Bible she'd unearthed last night. She knew Nick was right—allowing God complete control was the answer. But how could she do that? What about all the things that consumed her energies, like having to wear elf costumes or succumbing to envy and jealousy? Did God understand about those things? Or was He so far above human problems that the things that were important to her didn't even matter to Him?

A single tear slipped down her cheek. Delia closed her eyes and prayed for an answer to all the questions that seemed to be bombarding her tonight. She remembered the happiness she'd seen in Nick's expression. She wanted to achieve the same joy, but how could she go about it?

Delia flipped through the pages in her Bible, hoping for some sign to help her understand. Time passed in the quiet office as she searched diligently for something, anything to help her.

Impatience built up inside her as she skimmed passage after passage. Then a phrase in Colossians chapter three caught her attention—"know your Creator." She stopped and read the beginning of the chapter more closely. What was this? Chill bumps rose on her forearms. There it was. Her question answered by someone who lived hundreds and hundreds of years ago. This chapter seemed to have been written just for her. "Since you have been raised to new life with Christ, set your sights on the realities of heaven. . . . Think about the things of heaven, not the things of earth."

She laughed out loud, making her footwear ring. *She* was a child of God, destined to shine in Christ's glory. She closed her eyes and talked to Him, words and thoughts tumbling over each other as she tried to make up for all the time she'd spent resisting His Word.

When she opened her eyes, her whole body felt lighter. Wow! She couldn't wait to tell Nick. But how? After the way they'd parted a few hours ago, he would probably think she was only telling him what he wanted to hear if she approached him now. Her gaze scanned the floor-to-ceiling bookshelves that covered one wall, and then she saw it.

God was so amazing! He had shown her the perfect way to tell Nick.

Chapter 9

Nick went to the mall locker room and pulled off the warm Santa costume. A T-shirt and sweat suit would be sufficient for tonight. As he dressed, he thought of the woman he loved. He prayed for God to touch her in a special way.

Nick knew God loved her. God loved her more than he did. As much as it hurt him to see Delia turn away from the truth, it must be so much more painful to Jesus.

His heart squeezed. A prayer filled his mind, seeking forgiveness for all the time he'd spent not believing, for all the missed opportunities. The heartache eased, and peace overwhelmed him, filling Nick with a sense of love and forgiveness that brought him to his knees. His head bowed in submission, and he let go of his desperation. God would take care of Delia. As he drove away from the mall, Nick let God's peace warm his heart.

The boys were waiting for him at the church, and they played hard for an hour. Nick remained patient and encouraged their efforts, letting Christ's love shine through him. He offered to share the message with them. They listened, their eyes challenging at first then becoming uncertain as God's Word spoke to them. He prayed out loud with them, asking for God's love to touch and bless them. When they left, it was with promises to return again on Sunday for Bible study and worship.

It was late when Nick left the church gym. He wished he had someone to talk to. Someone who could help him sort out his mixed feelings about Delia. The last few days had been like a roller coaster to him. Her appearance at the soup kitchen. Then Tom had warned him he was reading too much into her reactions. So he'd played it cool the rest of the week. He'd looked for her to come to church last weekend, but she had not appeared. It had thrown him into a serious tailspin.

And that had been multiplied a thousandfold when he'd gone back to Deck the Hall to look once more at the Santa figurine he wanted to give Delia for a Christmas gift. He'd known from the first time he saw it that the figurine was the perfect tool to witness to her. She loved her Santa collection, and that special figurine was a reminder of the original gift that made Christmas the most holy of days. It also spoke of St. Nicholas's devotion to the Christ and His willingness to sacrifice because of His great love for mankind. The same selfless love Christ taught all believers to have for each other.

But when he'd finally made it to the store last Thursday night, the figurine was gone. He still could not believe it. Of course he saw other renditions of Santa kneeling at the manger, but nothing as exquisitely detailed as the one he had hoped to purchase. He'd left the shop with a heavy heart, unable to take any pleasure in the array of delicate collections.

Weary and downhearted, Nick had dragged himself through the week. And then she had shown up in that absurd elf costume today, all prickly and self-conscious. She'd been stiff at first, but the children had gotten to her.

As the day wore on, he watched her pretensions melt away, leaving the warm and loving woman he'd once been hopeful of spending the rest of his life with. Even if he'd never loved Delia before, he would have fallen in love with her today. She'd been sweet and fun to work with. Having her there had made the hours fly by.

Their talk after closing had given him hope once again. She was opening up to the Lord. He knew it. He could see it in her changing attitude. Why was she still resisting? Nick wanted to beat his hands on the steering wheel with his frustration, but instead he pulled out of the church parking lot and headed home.

He arrived at his apartment and sat in the quiet car for a few minutes. It was nearly Christmas. How could he hold on to his frustration during this miraculous time of the year? He looked up at the night sky, endless and mysterious as the ocean. The moon's glow turned the fresh snow a luminescent blue color. Praise and thanksgiving filled his mind, lifting his spirit out of gloomy thoughts. He stayed in the car until it got so cold he could see his breath. Cold enough for a Southern boy to be seeking his warm bed.

But when he got out of the car, a noise stopped him. It

wasn't a footstep or a voice. It sounded more like. . .like sleigh bells.

Nick's breath caught. Could he be dreaming? But no, there she was—complete with elf boots and bells on. His Delia.

She walked toward him, a gaily wrapped package in her hands. "I know it's not Christmas yet, but I have something I want to give you."

Nick's heart climbed up his throat. A gift? He searched her eyes for the answer he wanted to see. Their gray color was nearly clear in the bright light of the moon. And her expression—it was free of the indecision he had seen at the mall a few hours earlier. This made his heart leave his throat and plunk right down into his chest, where it started beating as wildly as the whole percussion section of an orchestra. He wondered if he was going to pass out at her feet. "What is it?"

Delia's grin warmed him down to his toes. "You'll have to open it to find out, silly."

He took the package and leaned against his car. "Do you want to go inside?"

Delia's head moved from side to side. "Just open it."

Nick pulled the bow off and placed it on the hood of his car. He noticed the shiny label that advertised the collectibles store in the mall. His heart rate kicked up another notch. Could it be?

Trembling fingers peeled away the snow-white paper. Delia held out her hand and took the crumpled paper from him, reaching past him to place it on his car. He wanted to take advantage of her nearness to steal a kiss, but he dared not until he saw what was in the box.

He turned it over in his hands and broke the tape holding the box closed. Carefully he flipped it back over and lifted the lid. A grunt of annoyance showed his impatience as he pushed away several layers of tissue paper. His hands were shaking so hard he nearly dropped the box.

There it sat, the beautiful piece he'd admired for the past month. The piece he'd wanted to buy for Delia to show her the true meaning of Christmas. Delia was the one who had bought the Santa figurine kneeling in front of Christ's manger. Nick could hardly believe it. He wanted to laugh and cry, all at the same time.

"It's perfect, Delia." He looked at her, his vision blurred by tears.

"I'm glad you like it. I thought of you when I saw it. It practically jumped off the shelf at me. And after that night at the soup kitchen, I had to have it. And then I went back to the office after our talk tonight. That's when I realized I wanted to give it to you. To show you I—" Her words broke off. Delia took a deep breath and started again. "I don't know why, exactly. I mean. . .it's not like you have a collection or anything."

He laughed out loud, unable to contain the joy that filled him at the knowledge that Delia had accepted the salvation of Christ. That was even better than her giving him the figurine. It meant no barriers stood between them anymore. God had answered his prayers. "I love you, Delia Wilkins. And I understand exactly why you bought it. It's beautiful and the perfect expression of what Christmas is all about. As a matter of fact, I had hoped to get it for you."

"Oh!" She put her hands in the pockets of her coat and turned slightly away from him. Her boots jingled lightly, reminding him an elf costume could not be considered sufficiently warm dress for the frosty night air.

Soft flakes of snow began to fall as Nick set the figurine on the hood of the car next to the bow and wrapping paper. He pulled Delia into his embrace, thanking God in his heart for the expression on her face. Gone was the old superpractical superachiever. In her place stood a warm, loving woman of God. Delia wrapped her arms around him and laid her cheek against his chest.

Nick closed his eyes. "Thank You, God, for bringing me this Christian woman to love and cherish. At this very special time of the year, may we remember the sacrifice You made in sending Your only Son to save us." He hugged her close, not sure if he would ever be able to let her go.

Delia returned his embrace, and he heard her earnest voice in the quiet night air. "God, I'm not worthy of all the blessings You've sent my way. Thank You so much for opening my soul to You and for sending me this wonderful Christian man, the final addition to my Santa collection."

"Amen." Nick kissed her gently, thankful that God had picked the perfect way to answer his heartfelt prayer.

DIANE ASHLEY

Diane is a "town girl" born and raised in central Mississippi. She and Gene, the romantic, gentle man she married, are active members of Meadowbrook Church of Christ. They are allowed to share their home with their two cats, Shadow and Lightning. Diane has been employed for more than twenty years by the Mississippi House of Representatives, where she currently serves as deputy assistant clerk. When Diane took over the care of her mother after the sudden death of her father, she rediscovered a thirst for writing and was led to a class taught by bestselling author Aaron McCarver. "Santa's Prayer" is her first published novella, and she is elated to work with such talented, award-winning authors in this collection. She and Aaron recently secured a contract for a collaborative novel, the first book of a historical series set in Tennessee. She attributes her talent and success to God's grace, and knows that He will use both according to His plan.

The Cookie Jar

by Janet Lee Barton

Chapter 1

Cindy Morrow unlocked the front gate to her cookie shop and took a moment to enjoy the quietness of the mall in the early morning. The peacefulness would not last long. It was Saturday and the busiest day of the week at the mall. Her hometown of Snowbound Village had expanded well past its quaint name. In the twenty-first century, it could only be called a city. Small compared to many, but certainly it was no village anymore. In fact a few years earlier, a movement was started to change its name to something more fitting with its size. Cindy was thankful the townspeople had voted it down. She loved the quaint downtown area that still kept its feel of times past. She would not want it to change. But she loved the more modern areas, too, like the Village Mall, where her shop was located. But if things went well and she was able to build her clientele, she hoped one day to open a shop in the quainter area of town so she could set her own hours.

She waved to the owner of Deck the Hall, a Christmas collectible store, who was opening her own shop across the way. Even though Thanksgiving was not for several weeks yet, Christmas decorations were already up everywhere. She guessed she should be thinking of decorating her shop. According to her lease, she had to have Christmas decorations up by the time the shop closed the day before Thanksgiving.

Maybe she could make time to run over to the Christmas shop and see if she could find some Christmassy cookie jars she might want to add to her personal collection. They were always handy to use as a display, too. As the piped-in music started to play, signaling the opening of the mall, Cindy smiled and began humming as she went back to work. Soon she'd be hearing Christmas music. She'd opened the shop named for her mother just over a year ago and was hoping this Christmas season would put Carly's Cookie Jar on firm financial footing.

"Here are the Snickerdoodles," her aunt Adeline said as she brought out a tray of freshly baked cookies. They were some of their best sellers.

"Thanks, Aunt Addie." Cindy took the tray and put it inside the display counter alongside the chocolate chip cookies. She turned and gave her aunt a hug. "I don't know what I'd do without you."

"No need to worry about that, Cindy." Aunt Addie patted her shoulder. "There's no place I'd rather be than here helping you bring my sister's dream to life. Besides, I was bored after I retired—I needed something to do."

Cindy just shook her head as her aunt hurried back to the kitchen. Dear Aunt Addie. She might have missed working, but Cindy knew she had been keeping herself busy with volunteer work and various church activities. In fact she had turned down her sister's offer to come in as a partner in the business. That was when Cindy had offered to come in as a co-owner. She was getting tired of her job as office manager in a dentist's office and could think of nothing she wanted more than to see her widowed mother happy.

Cindy knew her aunt had started working at Carly's Cookie Jar for one reason, and that was to help her only niece out after her mother, Aunt Addie's sister, had been killed in a car crash. Not only that, but her aunt had also enlisted her daughter Emily's help. Cindy would be forever grateful to her aunt and her cousin. Without them she was sure her mother's dream would never have become a reality.

"Have you taken a good look at the new manager at Jarvis Jewelers?" her cousin asked, coming out of the kitchen with another tray of cookies. "He is one good-looking man."

Cindy grinned and shook her head. Emily was engaged so Cindy knew she wasn't attracted for herself. No. Em was on a mission to find a man for Cindy. "I'm not interested, Em. You know I don't have time to date right now. Even if I did, I don't think I have the energy for a relationship."

Emily poured them both a cup of freshly brewed coffee and handed one to Cindy. "You need a personal life, Cindy. You practically live here. He really is cute."

Cindy leaned against the counter and took a sip of the warm liquid. "And I'm supposed to do what?"

Her cousin giggled. "Go window-shopping. Christmas is coming up. It's the perfect time of year to start making a list.

You need someone, Cindy."

"If the Lord has someone in mind, He'll see that I meet him. Until then I will be happy baking cookies and seeing this shop succeed. In the meantime, I need to set up the Kids' Corner."

"As crazy as you are about children, one would think you'd be looking for—"

"Emily—" Cindy tried to get her meaning across as a customer entered the store.

"Okay, okay. But you know I'm right," Emily said with a grin. She hurried to help the young woman at the counter.

Cindy sighed and shook her head. Her family was nothing if not persistent, and they were all of one mind. They thought she needed a man in her life. It wasn't that she didn't want someone to love. She just did not have time. She didn't dare take her attention off her goal. If the Lord had other ideas for her, she was counting on Him to let her know. Until then she would keep pouring all her energies into this shop.

She hurried to her favorite spot in the shop. It was the Kids' Corner, where children could decorate their own cookies. She loved to see what color and design combinations they came up with. She made sure she had plenty of aprons on hand and the colored icings she made fresh each morning. Two birthday parties were scheduled for today. She had several tables, but she knew other children would come in and want to decorate on their own. She wondered if Jonathan Griffin would bring in his twins. She hoped so. They made her day. Three more customers came into the shop, and Cindy quickly finished setting up for the first party then hurried to help Emily at the counter. She had a feeling it was going to be a busy day.

❧

Attorney Jonathan Griffin was not sure why he was at the mall on a Saturday afternoon when he had so much to do at home: the wash, not to mention the ironing and the grocery shopping. But he could think of nothing he'd rather do than take his children to Carly's Cookie Jar. It was their favorite place to go nowadays, and he had promised them a treat if they would eat a good lunch first. He wasn't sure how nutritious a meal they'd get at the food court, but he knew they'd eat something. He helped Lydia and Landon out of the car, took their small hands in his, and led them to the mall entrance.

"Daddy, do you think we'll see Miss Morrow?" Lydia asked. "Last time she wasn't there."

"I think she'll be there, sweetheart." Jonathan hoped he was right. His children had formed an attachment to Cindy Morrow. She attended the same church they did, and at first taking them to her shop had been a show of support for a Christian sister. But Jonathan knew, deep down, that he'd begun to look forward to the visits almost as much as his children.

"Look, Daddy! The mall is decorated for Christmas. When are we going to put up our tree?"

A pang of sorrow shot through Jonathan's heart, and he took a deep breath. Christmas was not a holiday he looked forward to anymore. With Leslie gone—

"Daddy?" Landon pulled at his hand.

"Well, it's not even Thanksgiving yet." Both children sighed at the same time, so he told them, "We'll decorate after that."

The twins rewarded him with smiles that made his heart melt. He needed to do certain things for these two, no matter how hard it was. Decorating for Christmas was one of them. He'd gotten out of it last year by taking them to see Leslie's family in Tennessee, but that proved more difficult than he'd anticipated for his late wife's parents and his children. This year they were staying home. Surely it would be easier than last year. *Dear Lord, please let it be.* It had to be.

They reached the food court, and Jonathan was glad he'd decided to come early. It was already getting busy. He put in their order at the chicken place they all liked and let them each carry their own drink to the table. The twins were good children and minded him well. He thought they behaved even better than when his wife was alive, but he put that down to the fact that they didn't want to upset him. They all felt the loss of Leslie. And, as hard as Jonathan tried to give them stability, they knew all too well what it was like to have their lives turned upside down. Oh how he prayed that would never happen to them again.

"Daddy?" Landon called him to the present. His son was dangling a french fry dripping in ketchup a mere inch from his mouth. Somehow he managed to plop it into his mouth just in time.

"Yes, son?" Jonathan tried not to chuckle.

"Do you think Santa would bring us a new mommy for Christmas?"

Jonathan's heart broke at his son's words. Was he having a

hard time remembering what Leslie looked like, too? Whoa. Where did that thought come from? Jonathan looked from Landon to Lydia. The expression in both sets of eyes as they waited for his answer told him what he already knew. They wanted a woman in their lives. They needed a mom—but he couldn't give them false hope. Jonathan cleared his throat and shook his head. "I don't think Santa brings new mommies or daddies, Landon."

"Told you so," Lydia said to her brother. But she looked as disappointed as Landon did.

Jonathan didn't know what to say next.

"Well, if we can't ask Santa, what do we do?" Landon seemed determined.

"We pray about it, like I told you, silly," Lydia said. "God will bring us a mommy."

"Is she right, Dad?" Landon asked.

Jonathan rubbed the bridge of his nose. *Please, Lord, help me find the right words.* He smiled at the five-year-olds. It wasn't as if he'd even been thinking about finding a wife. Well, not seriously anyway. But obviously it was time for him to begin thinking about what was best for his children. "Prayer is always good, and the Lord always listens. He knows what is best for us all, and if it is His will, you'll get a new mommy. But sometimes we have to be patient."

Lydia nodded. "That means we might not get a new mommy for Christmas, huh?"

Jonathan had to laugh. He tweaked his daughter's nose. "That might be a little soon. I haven't even dated anyone yet."

"Yeah, I guess you have to do that."

"It helps."

"Well, you need to start dating, Daddy," Lydia advised him.

"I guess I do. First I have to find someone I like and who you two like, too."

"You do?"

"Well, it would be nice if we all liked her, don't you think?"

The twins nodded at the exact same time.

"Well, we'll just pray that the Lord will help us out. And we'll try to be patient until He thinks the time is right. Okay?"

"Okay," Landon and Lydia said together.

Jonathan breathed a sigh of relief. "Let's go get a cookie."

"Can we decorate them?" Lydia asked.

He was glad the subject of a new mommy was closed for the moment and that Lydia had asked for something he could say yes to. "If it's not too busy, you can."

"Let's go," Landon said, cramming one last fry into his mouth.

Jonathan gathered up their trash and deposited it in the nearest receptacle. He turned to find the twins whispering and nodding at each other. He couldn't help but wonder what they were up to now. He loved how they interacted with each other, but it sure kept him busy. Sometimes he felt as if they were always one step ahead of him. . .if not two or three.

Their angelic smiles didn't fool him. He was more than a little sure they were up to something.

Chapter 2

Cindy turned from cleaning up the Kids' Corner after the party to find her two favorite customers grinning at her. Lydia and Landon Griffin held a special place in her heart. She figured they always would. They attended the same church she did, and she had watched them grow since they were babies. She'd felt a deep connection to them ever since their mother had passed away. Leslie Griffin died in the same five-car accident Cindy's mother was killed in, just over a year ago.

"Hi, Miss Morrow!" Landon said. "We came for cookies, and Daddy said we could ice them if you aren't too busy."

Cindy glanced up at Jonathan Griffin. He was very tall and... very handsome. "That was nice of him," Cindy said. "And you're in luck. A party for eight just left, so give me a minute, and I'll have you set up. Do you know what kind of cookies you want to decorate?"

The children ran over to the display case and peered into it. "Oh, I want the lady pilgrim," Lydia said.

Landon studied the cookies a little longer before saying,

"I'll take the man pilgrim."

"Good choice with Thanksgiving so close—although it's a little hard to remember that with all the Christmas decorations going up everywhere," Jonathan said.

Cindy reached in the cookie case and pulled out the pilgrims. "You are so right. I love Christmas, but it has become so commercial. I'm determined not to put up my decorations until the day before Thanksgiving. I have to have them up by then. And I won't put my Christmas cookies out until the day after."

She led the way to the Kids' Corner and set the trays on the table. Landon and Lydia plopped down in the small chairs and waited for her to bring out the various colored icings. "Here you go. And here are some damp paper towels if it gets messy."

"If?" Jonathan raised his eyebrow and grinned at her. "These are my children you're talking about."

Cindy found herself giggling. They did have a tendency to make a mess. "Well, then *when* it gets messy."

The twins didn't seem to hear them as they began decorating their cookies.

"Would you like a cookie and some coffee while you wait?" Cindy found herself asking Jonathan.

"I'd love some coffee," he answered. "Thank you."

He had the warmest brown eyes Cindy had ever seen, and the expression in them when he looked at her had her pulse racing.

"I'll be right back." Cindy wished she didn't sound so breathless. But there was something in the way Jonathan looked at her today that caught her off guard. *Or am I looking at him differently after the talk this morning of my needing a personal life?* Cindy wasn't sure, but something had her fingers trembling as she poured him a cup of coffee. She managed to take it to him along with a fresh gingersnap for him and for the twins.

"Thank you," Jonathan said as he took a seat at one of the grown-up tables nearby. "This has become their favorite place."

"You can't beat a good cookie."

He shook his head. "I don't think they like coming just for the cookies. They come to see you."

Cindy could feel the warmth flood her face. "They are pretty special to me, too."

Jonathan nodded and took a sip of his coffee. "You've all lost a parent. . .at the same time. I can see why they relate so well to you."

"You suffered your own loss. One I can't even imagine," Cindy said. "It must be very hard to be both mother and father to the twins."

"At times it is. But I don't know what I'd do without them. They are all I have left of Leslie." He glanced at her for a moment; then he cleared his throat and looked at the twins.

She could see the sorrow in his eyes. He must have loved his wife very much. He was a good man. Over the last year, Cindy had watched him with his children—at church and when they came into the shop. He was gentle and loving toward them, even when he must have been grieving.

"They're doing it again."

Understanding Jonathan's need to change the subject, Cindy asked, "Doing what?"

"Whispering like crazy. I am sure they're up to something. They always do a lot of whispering when they are."

Cindy chuckled. "Is this 'something' they're up to usually good or bad?"

Jonathan shrugged and laughed. "It just depends."

"Well, with Christmas right around the corner, it could be about that."

Jonathan's glance met hers, and he smiled. "You're right. It could well be about Christmas. In fact it probably is." He nodded and took another sip of coffee. "Maybe it's time I started thinking about it, too."

Cindy thought he would have already been thinking about Christmas with two children to buy for, but she didn't say so.

"Come see, Miss Morrow," Lydia said. "What do you think of my cookie?"

Cindy was impressed by how neatly the child had outlined the dress and apron of her pilgrim woman. "You did very well, Lydia. I don't think I could have done better."

The little girl beamed. "Thank you."

"You're welcome." Cindy looked at Landon's cookie. His wasn't quite as neat as Lydia's, but one could tell he had enjoyed piling the icing on it. "Yours is quite impressive too, Landon."

"Thanks. Lydia's looks prettier, but mine is goin' to taste a lot better," he said matter-of-factly.

She laughed and looked at Jonathan. Her heart did a tumble when he grinned and winked at her. "That's my boy."

Several customers came in just then, and Cindy hurried to wait on them. She was a little flustered by the way she was reacting to Jonathan today. He had been bringing in his children since she'd opened her shop. While she respected him and thought he was a great dad, a really nice man, and very good-looking, she'd never reacted quite like this around him before. It had to be Em's nudges. That's all it could be....

Still, as Jonathan gathered up his children and came to pay her for their cookies, she hated to see them go.

"Thank you, Miss Morrow!" Lydia said. "We love coming to your shop!"

"I love seeing you come in. We've become good friends for a while, haven't we?"

"Yes!" both children said.

"Then why don't you two call me Miss Cindy from now on?"

They looked at their daddy for permission, and he nodded.

"Thanks, Miss Cindy," Landon said. "We had fun!"

"I'm glad. I had fun watching you." She put the cookies they had iced in a box, along with the others Jonathan let them pick out. She'd tried long ago to give them their cookies for free, but Jonathan had nixed that right from the start. She rang them up and took his money. "Thanks for bringing Lydia and Landon in. It makes my day brighter just to see them."

"Thank you for making them feel special. They always leave here with a smile on their faces."

" 'Bye, Miss Cindy," Landon said.

Lydia echoed him.

" 'Bye, you two. See you soon."

Both Landon and Lydia had turned and waved. Jonathan nodded in her direction and mouthed, "Thank you."

Cindy waited on her next customer and the next, but she couldn't erase from her mind the vision of the tall, handsome man holding the hand of each twin as they walked away from the shop.

❧

It wasn't until bedtime that Jonathan found out what the twins had been whispering about all day. Usually Lydia started saying her prayers once he'd tucked the covers around her. But tonight she looked up at him with a somber expression on her face. "Daddy?"

"Yes, honey, what is it?"

"You know, you said Santa doesn't bring mommies and that we need to pray and you need to start dating someone we like and you like?"

She stopped to take a deep breath, but Jonathan waited. He had a feeling more was coming.

"Well, Landon and me really like Miss Cindy."

"Landon and *I*," Jonathan corrected.

"You do? Landon said you *do* like her, too!"

"No, sweetie, I was correcting your grammar."

She looked disappointed. "Oh. I thought you meant you like Miss Cindy, too."

"I do like h—"

"Oh, goody! Are you going to ask her for a date?"

"Honey, I don't know. . . . She's very nice and all, but I really haven't been thinking about dating anyone."

"But, Daddy, how are you going to get us a new mommy if you don't date?"

"I'm thinking about it, okay?"

Lydia was nothing if not persistent. "Thinking about Miss Cindy or getting us a new mommy?"

It was his turn to sigh. "Both." Surely that would satisfy her... for now.

"Okay, Daddy. I'm ready to say my prayers."

Thank You, Lord. Lydia knelt beside her bed, and Jonathan joined her to listen to her prayers.

"Dear God, thank You for all that You give us and how much You love us. And, God, please help Daddy think about dating Miss Cindy so he can ask her to be our mommy. In Jesus' name, amen."

Oh, wow, Lord. I don't know how to handle this. I—

"Daddy, you always say amen, too."

Jonathan nodded. "Amen."

Lydia scampered up into her bed, and Jonathan tucked her in, as always. He gave her a drink from the water glass on her bedside table and kissed her good night. "I love you, Daddy."

"I love you, sweetie."

"I feel better since I prayed."

Jonathan felt unsettled, but he answered, "Good. Sweet dreams and sleep tight."

Lydia was already half asleep. " 'Night, Daddy."

" 'Night, Lydia." He kissed her forehead once more, turned on her night light, and slipped out into the hall. He crossed the hall to Landon's room.

He was lying in bed looking up at the ceiling.

"Hi, son."

"Daddy, I've been thinking."

Jonathan groaned inwardly. He had a feeling he knew what Landon had been thinking about, but he had to ask anyway. "What about?"

Fifteen minutes later, after listening to Landon, hearing his prayers. and tucking him in, Jonathan kissed his forehead and made himself walk, not run out of the room and down the hall. He reached the kitchen and poured himself a cup of strong coffee.

Letting out a deep breath, he took a sip from his cup, thinking about the conversations with his twins. Sure enough, Landon and Lydia were on the same page. Almost word for word. He had to wonder if they'd practiced their speeches. And their prayers. Now what was he going to do?

Jonathan took his cup into the family room and sat down in his recliner. He picked up the picture frame on the side table and looked at it. It held a snapshot of Leslie and the twins only a month or so before her death. He missed her. He missed the love, the companionship, and the intimacy of their marriage. He missed Leslie with all his heart, but she had been gone over a year. Jonathan shook his head. Beautiful as it was, a picture could not capture the essence of who Leslie was. What a wonderful wife and mother she'd been. Some of that was beginning to fade from his memory, and he hated it. His children needed a mother. . .and he needed someone to love.

He needed a wife.

Yet how could he even think about it without feeling he was betraying the mother of his children? He'd told them both the truth. He hadn't been thinking about dating—not yet. But to say he hadn't been thinking about Cindy Morrow would be a lie. He had been thinking of her all afternoon and evening.

He felt it was natural that she and his children would feel close to each other after their mothers had been lost in the same accident. Although the twins were young, they understood Miss Cindy's mommy had died, too. They'd seemed to gravitate toward Cindy ever since. And Cindy, even through her grief, had reached out to his twins, giving them hugs, bringing them treats, just being extra nice to them. She was a Christian sister, and he appreciated her care of his children. When she'd opened her shop, he'd wanted to support her and had begun taking the twins to Carly's Cookie Jar every Saturday. It had become a habit he enjoyed almost as much as they did.

And he hadn't thought of Cindy as anything more than a very good friend to the twins. . .until today. Something about her today had him thinking differently. She'd looked very pretty as she always did. . .but it was more. She had seemed a little flustered when they were talking, and whatever had made her blush brought such luscious color to her cheeks, which in turn seemed to make her blue eyes shine brighter. She was lovely. Looking at her, something had happened, and he'd felt his pulse speed up. For the first time, he'd become aware she was a single woman and he was a single man. And he just wasn't sure how he felt about that. No, he wasn't sure at all.

Chapter 3

C indy couldn't complain about business; it was picking up more each day. She was thankful her aunt had convinced her to call the two high school girls who'd worked part-time during the summer, to see if they could help during the next month. They were both happy to be asked back so they could earn some Christmas money. Since they had already been trained, they would start work the day after Thanksgiving.

The days were speeding by. Cindy found it hard to believe it was Thanksgiving week. On Monday night, she realized she'd better get organized. She had only two more days to get her shop decorated for Christmas. At home that night, she pulled out her mother's Christmas cookie jars and found that two were cracked. Blaming herself for her carelessness in packing them the year before, Cindy burst into tears. One thought led to another, and in minutes she was bawling. She missed her parents terribly, especially this time of year. And to top things off, she'd missed seeing Jonathan and the twins earlier in the day. She'd run to the post office to mail several boxes of cookies to customers who had ordered online, and then she got caught in traffic. By the time she'd arrived back at the shop, they had just left. That Em had said the twins looked very disappointed did not help her mood. She felt she'd let them down, too. Thinking about that brought on even more tears, and it took what seemed like forever to get them under control.

Jonathan had been bringing them in several times a week lately, and she looked forward to seeing them. The last time they were in the shop, they mentioned they were going to see their aunt in New York City for Thanksgiving, and Cindy was afraid she wouldn't get to wish them a happy Thanksgiving now.

Well, crying isn't going to help. It won't bring Mom and Dad back, and the twins don't know how attached I've become to them. So it's not as if I was going to get to spend the day with them or anything like that. Cindy sniffed and wiped her eyes. She put the cracked cookie jars aside to try to fix them later and then put other jars in her car to take to the shop the next day.

By the time she got ready for bed, she'd stopped crying and felt bad for giving in to the loneliness she was feeling more each day. She knelt beside her bed and prayed. "Dear Lord, if Jonathan, Lydia, and Landon have left for New York, please just watch over them and let them get there and back safely. And, Lord, thank You for Aunt Addie and Em and the rest of my family. At least I have them to spend the holidays with. I'm sorry I've been having such a pity party tonight. Please forgive me, and thank You for all my blessings. In Jesus' name, amen."

The next day, she found time to run across to Deck the

Hall to look for new cookie jars to finish decorating her shop. Just stepping into the shop made her feel like a kid again. They had decorations of all kinds and colors and the most beautiful nativity scenes she'd ever seen. She could spend hours in here—if she had them to spend. She didn't, though, and she would have to come in again when she could spend more time. Today she had to find cookie jars, and the best way to do that was to ask for help.

The shop owner led her to the back wall of the shop, where Cindy found the biggest selection of cookie jars and Christmas dishes she'd ever seen. She grinned. "Thank you. I'm sure I'll find what I'm looking for here," she said to the middle-aged woman.

"Good. Take your time."

Cindy was barely aware of the woman leaving and going back to the front of the store. She was simply amazed at how many different cookie jars lined the floor-to-ceiling shelves. It didn't take long to pick out two jars to replace the ones that were cracked. She was thrilled to find two that looked very much like them. One was of a snowman, a Santa, and a reindeer all together; and the other was of Santa's sleigh. She took her finds to the checkout counter and paid for them. "You have a wonderful selection. I run Carly's Cookie Jar across the way, so I'll be sure to tell anyone who asks about cookie jars to come see you."

"Thank you so much. I appreciate any business you can send me."

Cindy left the shop with a lighter heart. "Thank You, Lord," she whispered on her way back to the shop.

With Aunt Addie taking care of the customers, she and Em began decorating the shop, putting the cookie-jar collection on the shelves and counters. Cindy filled the space between them with lighted garland and put her mother's small kitchen tree, decorated with gingerbread and cookie ornaments, on top of the display case.

She was up on a ladder, adding garland to the high archway leading into the kitchen, when she heard Lydia's familiar voice. "Oh look, Daddy! Miss Cindy is decorating for Christmas!"

"So she is."

Cindy turned so quickly the ladder wobbled precariously.

"Whoa, there," Jonathan said, rushing to steady it for her.

She came down slowly and turned at the bottom to find his arms almost encircling her. She'd never been this close to him before. His eyes were warm brown flecked with gold, and his lashes were long and thick. "Hi." She sounded a little breathless to her own ears.

"Hi," Jonathan said, looking into her eyes. His gaze held hers for a moment before he cleared his throat and dropped his hands to his sides. "We came by yesterday, but you weren't here. The twins wanted to tell you 'bye before we head to my sister's today."

"My cousin Em said you'd been by." She smiled at the twins. "Hi, Lydia and Landon. I'm sorry I wasn't here yesterday."

"We wanted to tell you to have a happy Thanksgiving," Landon said.

"But it's okay. We can tell you now," Lydia said.

"And I can tell you. Have a happy Thanksgiving!"

"We will. We like going to Aunt Bev's. And we'll be back this weekend," Lydia said.

"We thought it would be nice to take her some of your cookies," Landon added.

"That's thoughtful of you."

"Well, Daddy said it's the least we can do. He's a good cook. He makes great macaroni and cheese and grilled cheese sandwiches—"

"And hamburgers and bacon and eggs," Landon interrupted his sister.

"I manage, but I don't know how to make any of the traditional Thanksgiving dishes," Jonathan explained with a shrug. "I didn't want to go empty handed. I'm sure her boys will like your cookies as much as Landon and Lydia do."

"Well, let's go pick them out," Cindy said. She turned to move the ladder, but Jonathan was a step ahead of her.

"Where do you want this?"

"In the back of the kitchen will be fine."

"Give me about three dozen total of a mix of whatever they pick out, please." Jonathan folded the ladder and took it through the archway into the kitchen while Cindy helped the twins select cookies.

"How many are three dozen?" Landon asked.

"It's thirty-six cookies," Cindy said.

"Thirty-six? Wow! That's a lot," Lydia said.

"Yes it is. Which ones do you like best?"

"Oh, the pilgrims are still my favorites," Lydia answered.

"Mine, too," Landon added. "But if we can have that many, we could have some pumpkins, too, couldn't we? I really like the icing on them."

"Why don't we get some of all the Thanksgiving ones?" Jonathan asked, standing behind them now.

"Oh yes!" Lydia clapped her hands. "Let's do that."

"Yes!" Landon said, his hand in a fist as he pulled his arm back.

Cindy had to laugh. She had seen teens do that, but not a five-year-old. "I think that's a wonderful idea." She carefully boxed the cookies.

"What are you doing for Thanksgiving, Miss Cindy?" Landon asked.

"I'm going to have dinner with my aunt Addie and Em and their family."

"That's good," Lydia said.

"We're glad you aren't going to be alone."

Cindy fought the tears that threatened at their sweet concern. She managed a smile. "I'm glad you all are going to be with family, too."

She taped the box shut and handed it to Jonathan.

"How much do I owe you?"

She looked him in the eye. "Nothing. Let this be my treat for the twins and your family."

"That's very kind of you, but I'll let you buy their cookies the next time we come in. I promise. But—"

"All right. But I'm going to hold you to it." She rang up the cookies and told him the amount.

Jonathan pulled out some bills and paid her. "Thank you. I know everyone will enjoy them. I hope you have a very nice Thanksgiving."

"I hope you all do, too." She came around the counter and gave the twins each a hug. "Have a good time, okay?"

"Okay," they said in unison.

Cindy looked up at Jonathan. "Drive safely."

"I will. We'll see you sometime next week."

Watching them walk out of the shop, she thought next week seemed a long way off.

Chapter 4

C indy had been dreading Thanksgiving almost as much as she had last year. But after helping set the table for eight, she was glad she'd come. She would have been awfully lonesome by herself.

Continuing in the traditions she'd shared with her parents brought back memories of them for sure; they were warm and good ones, though, and she let herself enjoy the memories instead of trying to block them. Now that she was in her aunt's kitchen taking orders, she was thankful to be there.

Aunt Addie turned from the turkey gravy she was stirring. "Add a little more butter to those mashed potatoes, Cindy, dear."

Cindy did as asked, adding another half stick to the potatoes she was mashing. She smiled, knowing her mother would have said the exact same thing.

"That pecan pie you made looks wonderful, Cindy," Em said from across the kitchen island where she was preparing the relish tray. "I never have been able to make one without its sticking to the pie pan. I don't think I inherited that baker's gene the rest of the women in our family have." She grinned and lowered her voice. "Don't tell Brent, though."

"Brent is going to be well taken care of, dear. You are a wonderful cook," her mother said.

"Mom, that's an understatement. I'm just going to depend on you and Cindy to keep me in baked goods."

"Well, you know, I'm awfully thankful to have Aunt Addie in the kitchen at the shop. I can bake, but I don't know that it's my favorite thing to do. Still, Mom had a wonderful idea. I think the cookie shop is going to turn out to be a great business, thanks to her recipes—and the two of you."

Her aunt gave her a quick hug and handed her a serving bowl to put the potatoes in. "That's what we're hoping for, too, dear. But remember—you have to have a life beyond the cookie shop."

"Aunt Addie, we've talked about this." Cindy filled the bowl to the rim. "You know I don't have time—"

"You just don't want to take the time."

Cindy shook her head. "Even if I did, no one is breaking down my door to ask me out."

"Maybe you don't give them a chance."

"That's for sure." Emily had to add her two cents. "Mom, don't waste your time. I tried to get her to meet the new manager at Jarvis Jewelers, but she wasn't fast enough, because I heard he's already dating someone."

Her aunt poured the gravy into a dish. "It sounds as if he might move a little too quickly anyway. He's only been at this store about a month, hasn't he?"

Cindy had been thinking along the same lines.

"What about that good-looking Jonathan Griffin?" Aunt Addie said. "I didn't realize how handsome he was until he brought the ladder into the kitchen the other day. He's been coming in the shop a lot lately."

"He just brings his twins in. They love coming to the shop."

"How do they seem to be doing?" her aunt asked.

"Well, I think. They're crazy about their dad and are very well behaved."

"It can't be easy for him. . .he should find a wife."

For some reason, that thought didn't sit well with Cindy. "I—"

The doorbell rang then, and her aunt rushed to greet Cindy's cousin Mark and his family. She breathed a sigh of relief that their timely arrival saved her from saying any more about Jonathan's finding a wife. What would she have said anyway? *"I hope not"*? Because that had been her first thought. For some reason, she liked thinking they were both too busy to date.

It was late when Cindy got home. Knowing what a busy day she was facing on Friday, she told herself she should have left earlier. But the thought of coming back to an empty house didn't appeal to her—especially after the discussion about how she needed to find someone and have a personal life. It had only served to make her aware of how lonely she was.

But relationships took time and effort, and she was using all her energy on the business. She didn't have time to think about a personal life, and that was best for her at present. Her goal was to make Carly's Cookie Jar a success, because it was her mother's dream. Still, she had to admit seeing her aunt and uncle's loving relationship after so many years together and watching Em and Brent's brand-new relationship blossom more each day made her want the same thing for herself. . . someday.

❧

Jonathan woke to the sound of sweet laughter in his sister's house. He pulled on his clothes and hurried out of his room to the kitchen. He stood at the doorway and watched the twins help his sister, Bev, crumble corn bread for the dressing she'd be making soon. They loved every minute of it. They'd clung to his sister ever since they'd arrived. That they missed having a nurturing woman in their lives had never been more apparent.

"Good morning!"

"Hi, Daddy! Aunt Bev said to let you sleep," Landon said.

"Yes, she wanted some, uh, 'one-on-one time' with us. Isn't that right, Aunt Bev?" Lydia asked.

"That is right, Lydia. I don't get to see you two enough."

"We already had breakfast, and now we're helping make the dressing," Landon said. "But Aunt Bev left you some biscuits."

Jonathan dropped a kiss on each of his children's heads then gave his sister a kiss on the cheek. "Thanks, Bev. Where are Ben and the boys?"

"The boys are bringing in some firewood. I sent Ben to the store for some sage." Bev shook her head. "I can't believe I forgot it! Oh, the Macy's Thanksgiving Day parade is coming on in a few minutes. I thought the twins might want to watch it."

"Oh yes!" the twins exclaimed together.

"Are we done here?" Landon asked.

"You are. Thank you both so much for helping me. It's going to be the best dressing ever."

They each brushed their hands together to get rid of the corn bread crumbs and ran into the family room.

Jonathan poured himself some coffee from his sister's coffeepot and helped himself to a couple of biscuits. He took a seat at the kitchen table. "It's good to be here, sis."

"I wish you'd come more often."

"I know. There is so much to keep up with at home. Weekends are the only times I can come close to catching up on things."

"You need a wife." His sister brought her coffee to the table and sat down across from him.

Jonathan sighed. "Have the twins been talking to you about that?"

"No. Why?"

"They want a new mommy."

"Oh, Jonathan." Bev patted his hand, and he could see the tears in her eyes as she continued. "They need a mother."

"I know. But how do I. . .it seems so. . .disloyal to Leslie's memory."

Bev shook her head. "Jonathan, don't you see? It is really just the opposite. You had a happy marriage. You liked being a husband. It's actually a compliment to Leslie that you are thinking of marrying again."

"I didn't say I'd been thinking about it. The twins want a

mommy, and you think I need a wife."

"You haven't thought of it at all?"

"Well, not really. Not until the twins brought it up. They wanted Santa to bring them a mommy for Christmas."

"What did you tell them?"

"That he couldn't do that."

"Did that satisfy them?"

"No. Landon wanted to know what to do if Santa wasn't going to bring them one. Lydia told him they needed to pray."

"Oh. Smart girl you have there."

"You really think I ought to—"

"Find someone to love? I really do. I think it's what Leslie would want, too."

Jonathan remembered bits and pieces of conversations he and Leslie had had before she died. After the twins were born, when Leslie and Jonathan traveled without them, she'd insisted they take different flights. She was afraid of flying and wanted to be sure that at least one of them would survive should there be a plane crash. That way the twins would have at least one parent.

Then the Christmas before she died, they'd been talking about taking a trip to Disney World when the twins got a little older. They had decided to do as they always had and take two different flights, but they would each take a twin on their flight. If the unthinkable happened, part of the family would survive.

Leslie had turned to him with tears in her eyes and made him promise that if anything happened to her, he *would* find a good Christian woman to love him and the twins and remarry.

How had he blocked that out until now?

"Surely you've thought of someone you might like to know better," Bev said, interrupting his thoughts.

Jonathan took a moment to gather his thoughts back to the present. He shrugged and took another sip of coffee. A month ago, he would have said no, but not now. He'd been doing a lot of thinking about Cindy Morrow lately, especially since the twins asked for a mommy for Christmas. "I'll think on it."

And he did—through the rest of the day when he watched Landon or Lydia interact with his sister. They did need a woman in their lives—on a daily basis. They needed a woman who would love them and nurture them. Someone who could give them what he could not. And he needed someone to love, to share his life with.

That night after he'd listened to the twins' prayers and tucked them in, he did a little praying on his own. "Dear Lord, please guide me in this. I miss being married, having someone to talk to at the end of a long day, someone to love. The twins want a mom, but You know it has to be the right kind of woman. Cindy Morrow may be that woman. I'd like to get to know her better. It's been so long since I dated that I'm nervous just thinking about it. Please help me know if this is Your will for us. In Jesus' name, amen."

Chapter 5

The day after Thanksgiving was indeed the busiest day of the year. Cindy was thankful she'd hired extra help. Aunt Addie needed her in the kitchen, and Em needed the two girls out front. The day went by in a blur of mixing and rolling cookie dough, cutting out cookies, baking them, and taking them out front where they were snapped up almost as soon as they were put in the cases.

By the close of the day, it looked as if this season would find her books in the black at long last. As she pulled the gate down over the entrance and locked it, she turned to her aunt and her cousin and the two high school girls. "I can't thank you all enough. I know today was rough, and I couldn't have gotten through it without you. Pam, Amy, thank you so much. I hope today hasn't scared you away."

"Oh no, ma'am," Amy said. "I like staying busy. It makes the time go by much faster."

"And we need the money for Christmas," Pam added. "Thank you for hiring us again."

They all walked out to their cars together, and Cindy gave her aunt and Em a hug before heading home. She was so tired she could barely remember the drive across town. She let herself in the house and locked the door. After taking a shower and saying her prayers, Cindy thought she would fall right to sleep, but she was surprised that sleep didn't come easily. Tired as she was, she found it hard to turn off her thoughts and drift into dreamland. Finally she got up and made herself some hot chocolate, hoping it would help her relax. She took her chocolate into the family room and sat down in her favorite chair. Sipping the warm liquid, she wished she had someone there to talk to about her day. . . someone to cuddle with and kiss good night.

What is wrong with me? I've never spent this much time thinking about wanting someone in my life. Besides, I don't have time for a relationship—and I don't even have anyone wanting a relationship with me. She sighed and took another sip of hot chocolate. *It must be all that talk about dating yesterday that had me looking for Jonathan and the twins all day. They wouldn't be back this early. Yet each time I heard a child's voice that sounded like Lydia's or Landon's, I found myself hoping they were.*

Cindy shook her head. She wasn't likely to fall asleep thinking about when the Griffins would be back. She took her cup to the kitchen. She had to get some sleep. Tomorrow promised to be another very busy day. She went back to bed and forced her thoughts to the next day. She mentally checked off the supplies she knew she had on hand at the shop—from the baking ingredients to the different-sized boxes to put all those cookies in. She hoped she had enough to get them through until delivery day on Monday. Cindy yawned and wondered if she needed to hire one more person. She yawned again...closed her eyes...and fell asleep.

The next day was not quite as hectic, probably because of the snowstorm that had come through early that morning. Still, it was plenty busy enough. She kept hoping the Griffins would come in, and she was a little frustrated at how aware she was that they didn't, in spite of how busy she was.

❧

Jonathan was glad he had taken the twins to his sister's for Thanksgiving. It had proved to be a good family time for all of them. He'd planned on going back home on Saturday, but it was easy for his sister and the twins to talk him into staying until Sunday afternoon.

Even though they only watched the Macy's Thanksgiving Day parade on television, they did make a special trip to see the display windows at Macy's and other big department stores on Friday. The twins loved it all.

On Saturday they took in the Radio City Christmas Spectacular, and Jonathan found himself wishing Cindy could see it. He wondered if she ever had and with whom. Did she date? Was there someone in her life? He didn't like the thought that she might be seeing someone—not at all. Her weekend had probably been very hectic. And she'd be busy all through the month of December. But that didn't mean he couldn't find out if she was seeing anyone. And he'd be taking the twins into her shop. Suddenly he was anxious to be back home.

Sunday they went to church with his sister and her family and then out to eat. By the time they loaded the car and said their good-byes, Jonathan was more than ready to get back. He hugged his sister. "Thanks, sis. I think it's what we all needed."

Bev nodded. "We need to get together more often. You're doing a great job of raising those two, Jonathan, but I hope you think about dating again. They really do want a mom, and you need a wife."

"What did they say?"

"They made sure they told us to pray for you to find someone you all like." Bev grinned. "They're serious about wanting a mom. And you've convinced them Santa can't bring them one. But since you're their 'Santa,' maybe you ought to think about it."

Jonathan chuckled. "I know. I'm just not sure the Lord is ready to send me one yet."

"He might expect you to do your part, too."

"Maybe."

"They seem to like this Cindy person they keep talking about."

"Not much they haven't told you, is there?"

Bev laughed. "Not on this trip."

Jonathan shook his head and got in the car. Bev leaned in and told Landon and Lydia good-bye; then she gave Jonathan a kiss on the cheek. "Drive carefully, okay?"

"I will."

"And keep me posted on the mommy hunt," she whispered. She was still laughing when he backed out of the drive.

❧

By Monday, the after-Thanksgiving rush had slowed somewhat, and Cindy was relieved. Otherwise she wasn't sure they could have kept up. She might have to plan a little differently for the next year.

She was disappointed Jonathan and the twins hadn't come into the shop. She wanted to know how their Thanksgiving went and what they did in New York City. She'd been there several times when she was younger but never at Christmas. She would love to see the city lit up at this time of year.

"Here are the candy canes." Aunt Addie came out of the kitchen with a loaded tray. "I'll be bringing out the wreaths next."

Those two cookies were proving very popular, along with Christmas trees and colored-sugar ornament cookies. "Thanks. I hope this will hold us for a while. Do you think we can handle it without more help?"

"I think we'll be all right," her aunt answered. "Amy is doing a good job in the kitchen. Once she gets here after school, we can make extras for the next day. If we can keep that up, I'm okay with you and Em taking turns helping in the mornings."

They'd decided to train one of the girls in the kitchen so Cindy could take turns being wherever she was needed most. It was working out very well so far. Amy had hinted that she'd like to work again after Christmas whenever Cindy could use her, and it looked as if she would need her often.

"I'm glad it's all working out. Looks like Mom's dream is

coming true, doesn't it—"

Em burst into the shop from her lunch break. "Have you seen the guy they hired to play Santa? I just saw him, and he looks like the real thing! Honest."

Aunt Addie laughed. "Now, Emily, you know there is no real Santa. I thought we went over that long ago."

"Oh, Mom, you know what I mean."

"He does look a little like everyone thinks Santa should look like," Cindy said. "You know who he is, don't you?"

Emily shook her head. "Do you?"

"He used to date Delia, the mall manager."

"You're kidding, right? What—"

"I don't know anything about it. I just know they used to date."

"Well, he must look a lot different under all that costume, 'cause he looks like Santa to me," Em said.

Aunt Addie shook her head at Cindy. "I tried to tell her."

"I know. She just won't give up, will she?" Cindy teased.

"Well, just wait until you see him up close. He's the best mall Santa I've ever seen."

"I'll be sure to make a special trip to tell him what I want for Christmas, dear." Aunt Addie chuckled and went back to the kitchen.

"And when she does," Em whispered to Cindy, "she'll know exactly what I'm talking about."

Cindy chuckled. "Nick does make a good one. I just wish he and Delia would get back together. They made a really cute couple."

"Well, if he's single—"

"Don't start, Em. I'm not—"

"I know. You don't have time, and you aren't looking for anyone—"

Well, not Santa anyway. "Why do people in love want everyone else to be, too?"

"Aww, Cindy, it's just so wonderful. I can't explain it. But I just want you to have the same feeling."

"Maybe someday. . ." *Why did I say that? Now she won't let up on me. Next she'll be trying to pair me up with the newest single male manager of any store in the mall.* "But not now." Cindy tried to sound firm, but she had a feeling Em wasn't buying it.

The brief lull in business soon ended as several customers entered the shop. It stayed busy until just before Amy came in after school at three thirty. Then at about five o'clock, business usually picked up again. Cindy had come to look forward to the break. It served to give them a breather and a chance to restock the cases again.

Her aunt and Em usually left for the day around four o'clock, and she knew they were more than ready after the busy weekend they'd just had.

"I wish you'd hired an assistant manager, Cindy," Aunt Addie said as she pulled on her coat.

"Business is really good," Em added. "Surely you can afford to hire someone so you can have some freedom."

She'd thought of offering the position to Em, but with her being newly engaged, Cindy was sure she wouldn't want the job. "It's too late in the season to find someone who qualifies as a manager now. Besides I'd need to train them, and it's just too busy for that right now. Maybe I'll hire someone after the first of the year—if business holds up."

"All right," Aunt Addie said. "But maybe we can rotate evenings a little bit so you have some downtime. You could still hire another part-time helper, too."

"We'll see. I'm fine for now. Honest." She gave them both a hug. "You go take care of the men in your lives, or they'll be demanding you quit working here. Go on now. I'll see you both tomorrow."

Emily's cell phone rang just then, and her side of the conversation proved Cindy's point more than anything else she could say. "I'm on my way," Em said smiling. "Okay. Love you, too."

Cindy waved to the two women as they headed out of the shop. They were wonderful, and they cared about her. But they both had their own lives to live with men who loved them.

What she hadn't told them was that the last thing she needed was time alone at night. She was feeling quite lonely this time of year. Everyone seemed to have someone they wanted to share their time, their lives, and the joy of the season with. All they would tell her was she could have the same thing. But she couldn't. She had to make a go of this business—it was her mother's dream. And that meant she had to work as hard and as long as she needed to, to see that it did come true—even if at times she wished she had someone to share her life with. . . someone who could help fill those lonely hours. . .someone to love.

Chapter 6

B y Monday afternoon, if the twins had asked him once to go see Miss Cindy, they'd asked him fifty times. Jonathan didn't need any more reason than that to take them. He decided to feed them at the food court then visit the shop. He hoped the after-Thanksgiving shopping rush had slowed so they'd be able to visit with Cindy. Of course she might not be there. Surely she'd hired extra help so she didn't have to be there around the clock. But this evening, he hoped she would be working.

He'd been thinking about her for days. Once he remembered promising Leslie he would remarry if anything happened to her, it was as though he finally felt free to think about dating again. And the only woman who came to mind was Cindy Morrow. Yet she might be seeing someone else. She was very pretty and sweet, and he would be surprised if she wasn't seeing anyone. He hoped—no, he prayed—she wasn't dating anyone and that she might be open to going out with him.

They entered the mall through the doors closest to the

food court. The lines were long, so the twins had plenty of time to decide what they wanted. Getting their food, leading them to a table, and settling them down to eat left Jonathan no time to notice anything that was going on around him.

"Look, Dad! Isn't that Miss Cindy over there?"

Jonathan looked in the direction Landon was pointing, and sure enough, it was Cindy. She was on the other side of the food court, emptying her tray into a trash bin. If they'd been here a little earlier, maybe they could have joined her for supper. "I think it is."

"Well, if she ate here, maybe she's going back to work," Lydia said in her matter-of-fact way.

Jonathan resisted the urge to chuckle. She really did remind him so much of Leslie at times. "You're right. I think she's just going back to work." He certainly hoped so. Otherwise the twins would be very disappointed. . .and they weren't the only ones.

❧

Cindy hurried back to the shop after a quick bite to eat. It was a good thing she hadn't taken any longer. Pam and Amy were keeping up with the customers, but barely.

A quick look at the inventory sent Cindy heading into the kitchen. "I have two trays of cookies cooling and two more ready to go into the oven, Miss Morrow," Amy called to her.

"Thanks, Amy. I'll take care of them." Cindy plopped the two waiting trays into the oven. Then she took the cookies Amy had baked and iced from the cooling racks and brought them out. She relieved Amy at the counter so she could get back to the kitchen, and for the next half hour, they had a steady stream of customers. Cindy had just turned to put on a fresh pot of coffee when she heard "She *is* here, Daddy!"

Cindy turned to find Lydia and Landon looking up at her with the most beautiful smiles she'd ever seen. They seemed as happy to see her as she was to see them. She glanced at Jonathan, but he was looking at the twins. When he raised his eyes to meet hers, he had a half smile on his face. She had no way of knowing what he was thinking, but the expression in his eyes sent her pulse racing.

"We saw you leave the food court," Landon said. "We was hoping you would be here when we got through eating!"

"Were, Landon. We *were* hoping," Jonathan said.

Landon didn't appear to notice the correction. He just nodded. "We were all hoping you would be here."

"Well, I'm certainly glad I didn't miss you this time," Cindy said. She caught Jonathan's gaze once more. "Is it all right if they have some dessert? I'd like to treat them to a Christmas cookie if it's okay with you."

"It's fine," he said. "As long as I can have a cup of that coffee when it's finished." His grin was quite engaging and did nothing to slow her heartbeat.

"You certainly can—and a cookie, too."

She turned to the twins. "Do you want a cookie out of the display case, or do you want to ice your own?"

"I don't think I could make mine as pretty as these. I'd like one of the Christmas trees, please," Lydia said.

Landon took a little longer to choose before saying, "I like the candy cane, please."

"And which one would you like, Jonathan?" Cindy asked. She glanced up to see him looking at her instead of the cookies.

"Oh—I think I'd just like one of your old-fashioned oatmeal cookies, please."

Cindy handed the twins their paper-wrapped cookies then handed Jonathan his. She wasn't prepared for the electric shock that sent tingles all the way up her arm when her hand brushed his. She was relieved when he led the children over to a table and couldn't see how badly her hands shook as she poured his coffee. She couldn't remember when she'd been so nervous. Taking a deep breath, she carried the coffee to his table.

"Can you sit with us, Miss Cindy?" Landon asked

"Yes, please. We haven't seen you in *forever*," Lydia said.

Things had slowed enough that Amy had returned to the kitchen, and Pam was waiting on the only other customer in the store. "I think I can take a break."

She took a seat at the table and found herself looking straight into Jonathan's eyes once more. Her breath caught in her throat. Why hadn't she realized before just how good-looking he was before? When he didn't drop his gaze, she felt her face flush. And why was she suddenly so aware of him as. . .a single male. . .instead of the twins' dad? Until a week or so ago, he'd been a widower with twins. It had to be all that matchmaking talk her family had been doing.

"Did you have a good Thanksgiving?" Jonathan asked.

"I did. I spent the day with my aunt and her family, and we had a great time," Cindy replied.

"Did you have turkey?" Landon asked before taking a big bite out of his cookie.

"I did have turkey and ham. How was your Thanksgiving?"

"We had turkey and ham, too!" Landon said.

"It was wonderful," Lydia answered Cindy's question. Then she went on to describe all they had seen and done in New York City. "You would have liked the Spectacular."

"Spectacular?" Cindy wasn't sure what she was talking about.

"The Radio City Christmas Spectacular," Jonathan said. "We went to see it with my sister and her family on Saturday night."

"Oh, I'm sure that was something to see. I've never been to New York at Christmastime."

"You haven't?" the twins said in unison.

"No. And I was a lot younger when I did go."

"Oh, I'm sorry. We get to go lots 'cause our aunt Bev lives there," Lydia said.

"And we have cousins and everything there," Landon said. "Maybe you can go next time we go."

They really were adorable. With a business to run, Cindy doubted she'd be going anywhere this time of year, but she didn't want to dampen their enthusiasm. "That would be nice."

"And we saw the windows at Macy's and other stores. Oh, they were so pretty!" Lydia added.

"Daddy's gonna take us to see the lights in downtown Snowbound one night, aren't you, Daddy?"

"I am. Once we get caught up at home."

"I've heard they're beautiful." Cindy hadn't seen them;

she'd only heard about them. She went from work to home and back again these days.

"You haven't seen them *either*?" Lydia asked, her brown eyes opened wide.

"Not yet," Cindy said.

"Maybe you can come with us—"

Cindy would like nothing better—if she had the time. But looking around the shop, she quickly realized she was dreaming if she thought she was going to be able to do that. She'd been so caught up in talking to the twins and their daddy that she hadn't realized a line of customers was waiting to be helped.

"Oh, I guess I'd better go to work." She hurried back to the counter and tried to tamp down the frustration she felt at having to get up when all she wanted to do was sit there with Jonathan and his twins.

❧

Jonathan watched Cindy go back to work and tried to hide his disappointment from his children.

"Miss Cindy works hard, doesn't she, Daddy?"

"Yes she does, Lydia." For the first time, Jonathan seemed to realize what long days she put in. The shop was open late, and she was here most of the time. It was her business, not just somewhere she worked. "This is her busiest time of the year, I would imagine."

He watched as a man about his age walked up to the counter. Cindy was waiting on someone in front of him, but Jonathan could tell the man was giving her an appraising look that indicated he was interested in her. When it was the man's turn to give his order, Jonathan could tell he'd said something that made Cindy blush by the way color flooded her face. She smiled and said something to the man that made him chuckle, and Jonathan couldn't help but wonder if he was someone she knew and what they were saying.

As his children ate their cookies and whispered between themselves, Jonathan sipped his coffee and watched Cindy wait on customers. A few times, she looked over at him and the twins and smiled. Once she shrugged, and though Jonathan hoped she was trying to tell him she'd rather be sitting there with him and his children, he had only a smile on which to base his wish.

"Daddy, do you think Miss Cindy could go look at the lights with us?" Landon asked.

"I don't know, son. She stays pretty busy this time of year."

"But you can ask her, huh, Daddy?" Lydia prodded him.

Jonathan looked over at Cindy again. Another man had taken the first one's place, and he, too, appeared to be quite interested in the cookie-store owner. And why not? She was a very attractive woman, and it struck him that she had one of the most beautiful smiles he'd ever seen.

"Daddy? You can ask her, can't you?" It was Landon this time.

"I'll think about it, but she might not be able to, so don't get your hopes up, okay?" But after watching several men try to flirt with Cindy, Jonathan decided maybe it *was* time he acted. . .if he could remember how. He hadn't flirted with a woman in years, but maybe it was time to start.

Chapter 7

After what seemed like hours, but in reality was only about fifteen minutes, Cindy came back over to them. She brought Jonathan a fresh cup of coffee and sat back down at the table.

She looked at Landon and Lydia with a sweet smile. "I'm sorry I had to leave. It's just been very busy today."

"Yeah, Daddy said you were really busy this time of year," Landon said.

"But you need to take some time off, don't you?" Lydia asked, looking at Cindy with big brown eyes.

"It would be nice, but—"

"Daddy, ask her," Landon said.

"Ask me what?" Cindy looked from Landon to Jonathan.

Jonathan didn't think he was this nervous the first time he asked Leslie for a date. While he fully intended to ask Cindy out, he wasn't quite sure how to go about it. But by the way his children were looking at him, it seemed he would just have to dive in. "We'd like to take you to look at the lights in historical

Snowbound. Do you think you might be able to go?"

Before she could answer, Lydia added her plea. "Oh, please, Miss Cindy. We want you to go. The lights will be so beautiful!"

Cindy smiled at his daughter. "I'm sure they will be. And I'd like to go, bu—"

"I told them you might not be able to," Jonathan said quickly, sure she was going to say no and fearing the out-and-out rejection if she did.

"It would be so much fun!" Landon said. "Please, Miss Cindy!"

Cindy looked from one child to the other and then glanced at Jonathan. "What night did you want to go?"

Jonathan's heart thumped in his chest, and he began to hope. "We'll go whatever night you can go with us."

"I'm not sure right now. I need to see if my aunt or cousin could work a night for me. Could I let you know tomorrow?"

Jonathan was surprised at the surge of relief he felt that she was even thinking about going out with him. "Of course you can. I'll call you tomorrow if that's all right."

"That's fine. I'll ask them first thing in the morning."

"Good. I hope you can go with us."

"We do, too!" Landon took it upon himself to speak for his sister, too.

"I'll try." She smiled at the twins and then looked at Jonathan. "Thank you for asking me."

"You're welcome. I've heard it's a very nice display." He wasn't sure what to say next. He felt like a tongue-tied teenager. He could have kissed Lydia when she gave out a big yawn. He chuckled. "I guess I'd better get these two home."

"They do look a little tired." Cindy stood. "I've got to start getting ready for tomorrow, too," she said as he and the children stood and prepared to leave. "Thanks for coming in to see me."

"Thank you for the cookies," Lydia said. "Don't forget to ask for time off, okay?"

Cindy chuckled and assured the child. "I won't forget."

"I'll call you tomorrow," Jonathan said once more before leading the twins out into the mall. She was really thinking about going out with him—with them. He didn't know if she would have even thought about it if it weren't for the twins. But he'd take what he could get and be thankful to them for giving him a chance to get to know Cindy better. He sent up a silent prayer that the Lord would help her find a way to take the time off and go with them. Otherwise he didn't know who would be more disappointed—the twins or him.

❧

Cindy was surprised at how pleased she was that Jonathan had asked her to go see the lights with him and the twins. She didn't know whose idea it was, but still it gave her a warm feeling inside. After all, it *was* Christmastime. She had to admit she wanted to see the downtown display and something besides the mall—and she didn't want to go alone.

Once Cindy mentioned the next morning that Jonathan and the twins had asked her to go with them to see the town lights, she had no choice but to go. Not that she didn't want to, but her aunt and cousin were so thrilled she was even thinking about it that they both volunteered to work.

"Oh, you need to go. The lights are lovely, and you need a break from this place," Aunt Addie said. "What night? I'll be glad to come in late that day and work until closing."

"Or I can," Em said. "I'll even come in early and work late the way you do if you'll go. And it doesn't matter what night."

"I don't need the whole day to get ready, Em."

"That's true. I just wanted you to know how happy I am for you."

"Just because I'm going to see the Christmas lights?"

"No. It's because you're going to see them with a very good-looking man. And maybe, just maybe, you might begin to have a life."

Cindy was reminded of the life she'd chosen—to see her mother's dream come true. Maybe she shouldn't go. This was her busiest season and—

"Cindy, I can tell from the look on your face that you're thinking about backing out," her aunt said. "Don't you dare!"

"Well, we don't have an actual date set yet." As soon as the words were out of her mouth, the shop phone rang. She was relieved to end the conversation until she heard the voice on the other end.

"May I speak to Cindy?"

Her heart did a double flip when she recognized Jonathan's deep voice. "This is Cindy."

"Hi. How is your day going? I hope I didn't call at a bad time."

"No, it's fine." She wished her voice didn't sound quite so. . .nervous.

"I just wanted to ask if you've found out which evening would be good for you to see the lights with us."

"I'm working on it now. Can you hold on a moment?"

"I'll be glad to," Jonathan said. "And remember that any night is good for us."

"Okay." Cindy put her hand over the receiver. "This is Jonathan. He wants to know which night would be good for me."

"He's leaving it up to you?" Em looked impressed.

"Yes."

"Well, pick a night, girl!" Aunt Addie said.

"Well, maybe tonight or Thursday night. What would work for whoever is going to fill in for me?"

"I am," her aunt said. "And Thursday will work fine. That will give you a rest going into the weekend."

"Thanks, Aunt Addie." Cindy took her hand away from the receiver. "Jonathan, are you still there?"

"I'm still here."

"Will Thursday evening work?"

"That will be fine. Will you have dinner with us, too?"

"I. . .well, yes, I can do that."

"Good. I have your address in the church directory. Can you be ready by six thirty?"

"Sure."

"We'll see you then. The twins are going to be so excited. They reminded me several times to call you before I dropped them off at preschool."

Picturing them telling him to call her made Cindy smile, but she couldn't help wondering if it was only for them that Jonathan had asked her out. "Tell them I'm looking forward to it."

"I will. Cindy?"

"Yes?"

"I'm looking forward to it, too. See you Thursday."

Cindy's heart was beating so loud she barely heard the *click* on his end of the phone. Suddenly she was a ball of nerves. *What am I thinking? I haven't had a date in a long, long time. I don't have a clue why I am doing this now. Like I really have time for it.* But deep down she felt like a teenager again, and she found herself looking forward to Thursday night more than she wanted to.

"Honey, don't look so scared." Aunt Addie gave her a quick hug. "You'll have a good time. How could you not?"

Cindy could think of many ways. "For starters I haven't dated in so long I'm not sure how to act or dress—"

"You're going to be outside after dark. Wear jeans, a sweater, boots, and a warm coat," Em said. "If you need something new, you can take a few extra minutes at lunch, you know."

Cindy acted as if she didn't hear her. "And what if Jonathan asked me to go just because the twins like me?"

"I know he loves his children, dear, but I can't see him dating you just for them—not if he isn't attracted to you," Aunt Addie said.

"Well, what if we can't think of anything to talk about?"

"Not likely with those two adorable five-year-old twins in tow." Em shook her head. "I don't think you'll have a lull in conversation."

"I just don't know why I said yes. I don't have time for this and—"

"You probably said yes because of Landon and Lydia. Maybe you said yes because you are a tiny bit attracted to their dad, too. You need to take time to have a life, Cindy. You really do," Em said. "Besides, I know those twins would be very disappointed if you'd said no. And I think their daddy would be, too."

Chapter 8

By Thursday evening, what began as a couple of butter-flies in her stomach seemed to have exploded into a butterfly garden. She had asked herself a hundred times what she was thinking when she accepted Jonathan's invitation. The truth was, she'd reacted to her feelings and not used her head. Still, she hadn't been able to cancel.

Jonathan and the twins arrived right on time. Cindy had made sure she was ready to go when he came to the door so the twins wouldn't have to wait in the car but a minute. Jonathan looked wonderful in jeans and a leather jacket. Landon and Lydia were dressed warmly, too, and Cindy was glad she'd gone with Em's advice. She'd chosen jeans, bought a new red sweater, and topped it all with a leather and suede jacket.

She slid into the car after Jonathan opened the door for her, and the twins' excitement seemed to overflow from the backseat to the front.

"Hi, Miss Cindy!" Landon said.

"We're going to eat first, Daddy said. And then we're going

to see all the lights and listen to the caroling," Lydia informed her. "It's going to be great!"

"They're a little wound up." Jonathan grinned at her. "They've been looking forward to this ever since I told them you said yes."

Cindy smiled back. It felt wonderful that they wanted to spend time with her. "So have I," she answered honestly.

Jonathan parked the car not far from the center of town, and they walked to the town square, he and Cindy in back and the twins in front of them. She'd never seen so much hopping and skipping in her life. Their excitement was contagious, and she found herself getting caught up in their joy of the season.

They went to a beautiful Victorian house right off the square that had been turned into a restaurant called The Laurel House. It was lovely inside and felt homey in that the proprietors welcomed families. They also had a menu full of items that appealed to both adults and children.

Jonathan ordered the twins' favorite, macaroni and cheese, and then turned to her. "I'm having a rib eye, but their filet mignons are very good, too. They just usually aren't quite enough for me."

"I'll have the filet mignon then. Medium well, please," she told the waiter.

The twins noticed all the decorations and informed her they'd put up their tree the night before. "It's beautiful," Lydia said.

Landon nodded. "It's prettier than that tree over there." He pointed to the large, brightly lit tree in the corner of the room.

"We have all colors of lights and decorations."

"I'm sure it is really gorgeous then," Cindy said. She'd put hers up the night before, too. Tired as she was, she wanted the lights at home, also.

"Last year I didn't put up a tree. We weren't going to be here for Christmas, and I didn't bother," Jonathan said. "But I should have. The twins really missed it."

"Are you going to be gone this year?" The twins hadn't mentioned it, and the way they were shaking their heads she wasn't surprised at Jonathan's answer.

"No," Jonathan said. "We decided we don't like being away at Christmastime."

"At all," Landon added.

"So Daddy promised us we wouldn't have to go," Lydia said.

Their meal came just then, and after Jonathan said a prayer, they began eating and talking. Conversation flowed easily, and Cindy found her worries about long silences to be groundless. By the time they left the restaurant and headed out to look at the beautiful displays, she felt completely comfortable with all three of them.

"Oh, look at Baby Jesus," Lydia said softly, calling their attention to the beautiful nativity scene in the middle of the town square. Displays were set up everywhere. And every business or home was lit from the front door to the rooftop. Historic Snowbound never looked lovelier. They walked around enjoying the different groups that were singing Christmas carols, and they waved at the people taking carriage rides around the town. Cindy couldn't remember when she'd had a better time.

"This is wonderful. Thank you so much for asking me," she said to Jonathan.

"Thank you for coming." He reached for her hand and pulled it through his arm. "You've made it better for all of us."

Cindy looked down at the twins, who were looking back at her and their dad and whispering. "Think they're up to something?"

"Oh, without a doubt they are." Jonathan chuckled. "I just don't know what."

❧

It didn't take Jonathan long to have an idea of what his twins were up to with all their whispering that evening. When they took Cindy home, he pulled up in her drive, got out, and hurried around to open the door for her while she told the twins good night.

He peeked into the backseat. "I'm just going to walk Cindy to the door. I'll be right back, okay?"

"Okay, Daddy," Lydia said as he shut the door.

He'd left the car running to keep it warm, and before he and Cindy had rounded the front of the car, Landon rolled his window down. "Daddy!"

Jonathan turned to him. "What, son?"

Landon motioned him over to the car and whispered loudly, "Don't forget to kiss her good night. That's what you're 'posed to do on a date."

"Roll up that window," Jonathan said sternly to his son. He

wasn't sure what to say. He just grasped Cindy's elbow as he walked her to her door. He took her key from her and unlocked the door then turned to find Cindy looking a bit bemused. . . and trying not to laugh. "I'm sorry," he said. "You just never know what's going to come out of a five-year-old's mouth, especially the two of mine. What I'd really like to know is how they learned so much about dating?"

Cindy's laughter broke free. "I wondered about that, too."

Jonathan shook his head and chuckled. "Thank you for being such a good sport. I. . .ah. . .I would like to kiss you, though."

Her eyes opened wide, and her lips curved up into a half smile. "You would?"

"Of course I would. I wanted to kiss you even before Landon spoke up. You are a beautiful woman, and I had a wonderful time tonight. I'd be crazy not to take my son's advice, don't you think?"

Her smile widened, seeming to give him permission. Jonathan started to lower his head then paused. "But I'm not going to let him know I did." He led Cindy a little closer to her door and turned her so she couldn't be seen from the car. Only then did he bring his lips down to touch hers briefly. . . once. . .then to linger a moment the second time. He thought she responded slightly, but he wasn't pushing his luck. He raised his head and looked into her eyes. "Have a good day tomorrow. I'll be talking to you."

Cindy nodded. "You have a good day, too. Tell the twins I said good night."

"I will. Thank you for tonight."

"You're welcome. Thank you," Cindy said before she disappeared into her home.

Jonathan hurried back to his car. For some reason, neither twin asked if he'd kissed Cindy, but they were both smiling from ear to ear and whispering to each other again. He chuckled to himself. There was no way he could be angry with them—not after that sweet kiss he'd just experienced.

❧

Cindy watched until Jonathan pulled out of her drive; then she locked the front door and stood there, touching her lips. She hadn't been kissed in a long time, and she couldn't remember one any sweeter than tonight's.

On autopilot she showered and got ready for bed, but she couldn't stop thinking about Jonathan's kiss. She went through to the kitchen and made herself a cup of hot chocolate. She took it upstairs into her bedroom where she sat down in her comfortable bedside chair. She could see out the window that it was snowing again. She was thankful it had waited until after her evening with Jonathan and the twins. She was sure, though, that Landon and Lydia would have loved it.

She couldn't remember when she'd had such a wonderful time. Had it been because she hadn't taken any time off in what seemed forever? Or was it because of the company? Cindy took a sip of hot chocolate. It was most likely a bit of both. . .and those kisses at the very end.

Cindy sat there awhile longer, reliving the evening. . .and

the kisses. Now what? Was she just to live on memories? She had no business letting Jonathan kiss her. She didn't have time for this; she really didn't. But she very much wanted to make time.

Tired of trying to figure it all out, she turned to the Lord for guidance. "Lord, I don't know what I'm doing. I really do like Jonathan and his twins. I want to spend more time with them. But I have so many responsibilities and don't need to be daydreaming as I have been. Please help me know what to do—how to say no if Jonathan asks me out again or how to say yes if it's what I should do. Thank You for the wonderful time I had tonight. Thank You for all my many blessings. And, Lord, please guide me in this. I don't want anyone to get hurt—not the twins or Jonathan or me. Help me know what to do. In Jesus' name, amen."

Chapter 9

Cindy woke with a feeling of expectation—of what, she didn't know. But she was in a wonderful mood in spite of staying up late and thinking about the evening with Jonathan and his children. . .and the private moment at her door. She'd told herself over and over that she shouldn't have let him kiss her. But her lips had tingled for hours after she got home, and she couldn't bring herself to regret the kisses. She'd just have to make sure it didn't happen again. She didn't have time for a relationship. She just did not.

But all that newfound determination seemed to fly out the window when she arrived at work.

"Oh, you had a good time. I can see it in your eyes," her aunt said first thing.

"It was fun," Cindy admitted. "The lights were beautiful, and the twins were so excited. I couldn't help but have a good time."

"And you enjoyed Jonathan's company?"

More than I'm willing to say. "I did. You were right. We didn't have any problem talking. With the twins filling in the gaps, it wasn't possible to have a lull." Cindy chuckled and darted into the kitchen, hoping her aunt wouldn't comment on the warmth she could feel inching up her cheeks.

But when Jonathan called the cookie shop around noon, Cindy found it almost impossible to hide how pleased she was to hear his voice. Her first instinct was to smile, and she turned to keep her aunt and cousin from seeing just how wide that smile became as she listened to Jonathan.

"I was wondering if you would mind if the twins and I join you for your supper hour at the food court. I promised to take them Christmas shopping for my sister and her family after we eat."

Cindy's heart turned to mush that he wanted to see her again. "I'd love that. I usually try to go about five thirty or six. Will that be okay for you?"

"I know you have to work, so any time you say is fine with me."

She didn't want to rush him and the twins. "How about six?"

"That's great. We'll see you this evening then."

Her pulse raced at the deep sweetness of his voice. It was only after they'd hung up that she realized she didn't know if they were going to meet her at the shop or in the food court.

They met her at the shop at fifteen minutes before six. "I forgot to find out where you wanted to meet," Jonathan said. "We figured if we got here early there wouldn't be any mix-up."

His smile and the warm look in his eyes had Cindy's heart thudding against her ribs. It felt wonderful to have someone be so considerate of her. She turned to Pam. "I have my cell if you need me."

Jonathan led the way out of her shop, and Cindy never gave it a backward glance. For the next half hour or so, she was going to enjoy herself.

❧

During the next week, Cindy experienced more fun than she had in several years. Jonathan and the twins had met her on Saturday evening for supper before going Christmas shopping again. They had teachers to buy for this time. They'd come back in for cookies before leaving the mall. On Monday night around ten o'clock, her phone rang. She thought something must be wrong with her aunt or cousin since she received few calls that late at night, so she answered quickly.

But it wasn't her family.

"Cindy? This is Jonathan."

As if I don't recognize his voice. The husky sound had her pulse racing. "Hi, Jonathan."

"I just wanted to make sure you got home all right. I know it's a little slick out there."

It had been snowing off and on most of the evening, but the streets weren't too bad. Still, Cindy's heart warmed at his concern. "I did. Thank you for checking."

"I was wondering if you'd have supper with us at the mall tomorrow night. The twins are hammering me to take them to see the Santa, and I told them I would. But I'll take them to eat first, and we'd sure like your company."

"I think that can be arranged," Cindy said. She kept telling herself she shouldn't be with them so much, but she just couldn't bring herself to say no each time they asked her to do something.

When they arrived at the cookie shop the next day, Cindy greeted them with a smile.

"Hi! What are the plans tonight? Your daddy said you talked him into bringing you."

"Dad said he would take us to see Santa. Could you come too, Miss Cindy?" By the look on Landon's face, Cindy knew she couldn't turn him down.

"I told them you'd probably have to get right back to work—"

"No," Cindy said. "I think it will be all right. This time of day, there usually aren't long lines to see him, at least not yet. Pam and Amy, do you think you two can hold things down for a little later than usual?"

"Yes, ma'am," Amy said.

"Of course we can," Pam added.

The two teenage girls beamed. They'd been trying to convince her they could cover for her if she needed to shop or take some time off. Cindy figured her aunt and cousin had been talking to them about her personal life, or the lack thereof until just recently.

"I'll have my cell phone if you need me," Cindy said before heading out the door with Jonathan and the twins. Children were standing in line waiting to see the mall Santa, but by the time they ordered and ate, the line had thinned out. She started to stand outside the line while Jonathan walked with his children, but Landon and Lydia insisted she come with them. As they made their way along, Jonathan bent his head and whispered in her ear, "I'm not sure why they insisted on coming to see this Santa. They know he's not real. But they said they wanted to talk to him anyway."

Cindy wasn't sure what to say. She'd always thought that when she had children, she would want them to know what the season was about—not the material aspect but the giving—to remind everyone of what God gave to mankind. But she didn't have children of her own, so she didn't know how she'd go about teaching them Santa wasn't real.

The twins reached the end of the line, and Santa, evidently because they were twins, motioned for them to come and sit on his lap at the same time. They were adorable as they sat there taking turns whispering in his ear. He nodded and whispered back. Landon looked at Jonathan and Cindy and pointed.

Santa whispered to the twins again, and they both gave him a hug before running back to their dad and Cindy.

"Thanks, Daddy! He's a really *real*-looking Santa!" Landon said.

"Thanks for taking us to see him, Daddy," Lydia added.

"You're welcome. Just remember—"

"We know he can't give us what we want, but it was fun, Daddy," Landon said.

"What did you ask him for?" Jonathan asked.

"To pray," Landon said.

"What for?"

"*You* know, Daddy!" Lydia said and giggled.

"They asked Santa to *pray* for something?" Cindy asked.

"Evidently they did," Jonathan said, but he didn't elaborate.

Cindy wasn't sure what to say. "Well, I hope their prayers are answered."

Jonathan smiled at her. "Oh, believe me, so do I."

❧

Cindy had decided to hold a drawing for a cookie jar full of cookies the last two weeks before Christmas. She wanted a cookie jar to put the entries in, but she hadn't had time to go to Deck the Hall to find one. It was when the twins finished talking with Santa that she mentioned it.

"We'll go help you, Miss Cindy. It will be fun."

Jonathan looked at his watch. "Do you have time? We'd love to help you, but if tonight isn't good, we can come back tomorrow."

She looked across the way at her shop. Several customers were inside the shop, but it was nothing Amy and Pam couldn't handle. "I think it will be fine. Let's go."

They entered the shop, and the twins immediately started exclaiming over everything they saw. Cindy let herself relax and enjoy the displays of nativity sets, snow globes, and ornaments.

"Where are the cookie jars?" Jonathan asked.

"Along the back wall," Cindy said. "But let the twins look—"

"I can bring them back in later. You'll want to get back to the shop soon, and we came in here to help you. They won't mind."

"Twins," he called to them. Cindy had found he addressed them that way when he wanted the attention of both of them.

They quickly turned to him. "Let's go look at cookie jars."

They immediately fell into step behind him as he led the way to the back of the store. Cindy smiled at the way they obeyed their father. He truly was a wonderful man, and she was in danger of falling in love with him. She couldn't let herself do that, but she was afraid she already had.

Cindy shook that thought away and focused her attention on the cookie jars the twins were pointing out to her. She found one she wanted, a precious jar with two children painted on the front that reminded her of the twins. Each child had a hand up as if they were lifting the lid of the cookie jar.

"Oh, look at this one, Miss Cindy!" Lydia was pointing to the same cookie jar.

"Oh, I like that one," Landon said.

"So do I, but for my own collection. I wouldn't be able to give it away. I'll have to keep looking."

Jonathan pointed out another jar farther up. It was a Christmas tree, and they all liked it a lot.

"I'm having two drawings. Should I get two different ones or another like this one?"

"Two alike," Jonathan said. "Then no one can complain that they didn't get the prettiest one."

"Okay. Can you reach those, or do we need to get someone?"

Jonathan answered her question by reaching up and bringing down one of the cookie jars. He handed it to her then reached for another just like it.

"Think these will work?" Cindy turned to ask the twins and found them whispering to each other. They quickly stopped and smiled at her, both nodding at the same time, then went back to their whispering. Their closeness never failed to warm her heart.

She looked at Jonathan, and he just shook his head and chuckled. "That's life with these two. I don't think there is much they don't discuss or share with each other. Sometimes I even feel left out."

Cindy's heart went out to him. How hard it must be to raise the twins alone and not have anyone to share it with at the end of the day. She knew how lonely she was, and she had never been married. How much more lonely must Jonathan be?

❧

On Tuesday Jonathan decided just to show up and see if Cindy would have supper with him and the twins. He'd planned to feed them at home, but they both had seemed a little downcast ever since he got there. Even their sitter had mentioned they didn't seem their normal selves. When he quizzed them, they just shrugged. When he asked what they wanted for supper, they begged to go see Cindy. Since Jonathan could think of nothing he'd rather do, he bundled them up, and they headed for the mall.

When they arrived at the shop, even Cindy could apparently see something was wrong. She didn't have many customers then, and Jonathan was glad she could take some time for the twins. She came around the counter and bent down to their eye level. "What's wrong?" she asked, placing one hand on Lydia's forehead and the other on Landon's. "You don't have a fever, but are you feeling sick?"

Both twins shook their heads.

"Can you tell me what's upset you?"

Tears welled up in Lydia's eyes and in Landon's, too. He sniffed. "We had a party at school today, and the other kids' moms were there, and—" His tears began to fall.

"We—we're missing our mommy," Lydia said as her own tears streamed down her face.

Cindy's eyes filled with moisture as she gathered them both close and hugged them. "I understand. I miss mine, too."

Feeling helpless, Jonathan watched as Cindy comforted his children, kissing them each on the cheek.

He should have known they were missing Leslie. Why hadn't they told him? Then it came to him—they didn't tell him because they didn't want to upset him. They'd seen him sad enough over the past year. And possibly because they needed a woman's arms to comfort them. He watched Cindy pull napkins from a dispenser and hand one to each child, once their tears seemed to subside. She wiped her own eyes and smiled down at the twins. "Sometimes it just helps to cry, doesn't it?"

Wiping their eyes and mustering smiles, both children nodded.

"We knew you'd understand," Lydia said.

Cindy nodded. "I know you do, too."

Jonathan watched as she hugged them again. He wasn't jealous of the bond they had formed. He welcomed it instead. Because in that one moment, he knew he'd fallen totally in love with Cindy Morrow.

Chapter 10

C indy's heart jumped when the phone rang after she arrived home that night. The last time anyone had called her at this time it was Jonathan, and hope rose that it was him now. She wanted to know how the twins were, and she especially wanted to hear Jonathan's voice one more time that day.

"Hello," Cindy said.

"Hi, it's Jonathan. I hope it's not too late for me to call."

Her heart sang at the sound of his deep voice. She could get used to talking to him every night. "No, it's fine. I have to unwind when I get home. How are Landon and Lydia?"

"That's one of the reasons I called. They are much better. In fact, they seem more like themselves than they have in several days. I wanted to thank you for being there for them."

"You're welcome, but no thanks are needed. I'm glad I could help. I"—she paused to ward off the tears that gathered just thinking of the twins—"do understand. Only they are so young."

"Yes, they are." Jonathan's voice broke, and he cleared his voice. Cindy could tell he was having a little trouble talking about his children, too. Then he sounded normal as he continued. "You've been more help to them than you imagine."

"Well, believe it or not, they help me, too."

"I'm glad. I did call you for another reason, as well."

"Oh?"

"Yes, I'd like to take you out to dinner. . .just the two of us. . . if you can get a night off."

Cindy's heart did a complete somersault that he wanted the two of them to spend time together. She loved being with the twins and Jonathan, but it would be wonderful to be just with Jonathan. She really shouldn't. But, oh, how she wanted to. "I don't know. I'll have to see. Can I let you know?"

"Of course, and any night you can do it is fine. I've already cleared it with my sitter. She said she can keep them any evening."

Cindy's heart warmed at his thoughtfulness, and she ignored the voice in her head. "You know, Pam and Amy are such good employees. I'm sure I can leave things in their hands for one evening. Would Thursday work?"

"Thursday will work great! I'll pick you up at six if that's all right."

"That will be fine."

"Good. I'll see you then. 'Night, Cindy."

"Good night, Jonathan." Cindy hit the END button on her phone and set it in its cradle. She looked at her Christmas tree and felt such joy that she could share this season with people she cared about. "Dear Lord, thank You for letting me enjoy this time of year once more. I hope I'm doing the right thing by going out with Jonathan. I'm not sure how I feel. I think I may be falling in love with him, and yet I don't have the time to give a relationship. Oh please, Lord, help me know what to do."

By Thursday evening, she still wasn't sure what direction the Lord wanted her to go in, but she had faith that at some point He would make it clear to her.

When Jonathan picked her up, he was wearing slacks, a dress shirt, and his leather jacket. Cindy had chosen pants and a sparkly top that made her feel dressy casual. He helped her with her jacket, and they were off.

She hadn't asked where he was taking her and was a little surprised when he headed out of town. "Where are we going?"

"I heard about a new place in New Haven. I hope it's all right."

"It's fine." It was only a twenty to thirty-minute drive; she used to make it often when she could. By the time they'd discussed the weather and the possibilities of a white Christmas and the advantages of living in Snowbound instead of a larger city, he was pulling into the parking lot.

It was a steak and seafood restaurant with a warm and cozy atmosphere. Once seated, they took their time looking at the menu. Jonathan ordered steak and fried shrimp, and Cindy chose the steak and lobster tail. She was quite pleased when, after the waiter left the table, conversation flowed easily between them. They talked about what they were doing for Christmas.

"We're going to have Christmas Eve and Christmas morning at our house, but we may go to my sister's for Christmas dinner," Jonathan said. "It's not that far of a drive. I'm not sure— I'd like to stay home. But after all the presents are unwrapped and Lydia and Landon are playing with their new toys, it gets a little lonesome."

Cindy's heart went out to him, and she couldn't help but blurt out, "You'd be more than welcome to spend Christmas with my family. We'll be at Aunt Addie's, and you know her." She knew her aunt would be more than glad to have Jonathan and the twins join them. But when Jonathan cocked his head to the side and his gaze met hers, she wasn't sure she'd done the right thing by asking.

"You don't think she'd mind three more mouths to feed?"

"I know she wouldn't. Besides, we all chip in. You could bring something like a salad. They sell them practically made at the grocery store. Of course, your sister might be disappointed. . . ."

"I think she'd understand. Thank you for the offer." Jonathan nodded his head. "I think we might like to do that, but you check with your aunt first, okay?"

That he would pick Christmas with her and her family over going to his sister's had Cindy's heart pounding. But she didn't want to read too much into it. It didn't mean he wanted to be with *her*—it just meant he wouldn't have to spend the major part of the day with no adult to talk to, only children.

Their meal came, and conversation continued to flow as they talked about her workday and his law practice. She hadn't had a chance to hear much about it before because they were usually focused on the children. On the way home, Jonathan entertained her with the Christmas list the twins had made out.

"They know they aren't getting everything they ask for, and they know I'm the one putting it under the tree, but they will still set out cookies and milk for Santa."

"I'd be glad to furnish the cookies for them. Old-fashioned oatmeal is your favorite, right?"

He grinned at her. "Right, and I'll take you up on that offer."

By the time they pulled into her drive, Cindy's fear of long lulls in the conversation had been put to rest. She'd been afraid they couldn't find anything to talk about if the twins weren't with them. She was more than a little pleased that hadn't been a problem.

Jonathan walked her to her door and took her keys from her. He unlocked the door and then turned to Cindy.

It was very cold out, and Cindy found herself asking, "Would you like to come in for a minute? I could make some hot chocolate—"

"No need for that, but I would like to come in for a minute."

As they entered her warm living room, Jonathan turned her toward him and looked deep into her eyes. "Thank you for going tonight. I..."

He lowered his head, and Cindy's heart began to pound so hard she was sure he could hear it as his lips touched hers. She'd been waiting for this moment since the last time. She found herself responding, and he deepened the kiss.

When she broke it off and looked up at him, Jonathan

smiled and leaned his forehead against hers. "You are one very special lady, Cindy Morrow. And. . .I'm in love with you."

Cindy blinked, and her heart felt as if it had short-circuited. "I—I think I love you, too. But"—she shook her head—"I. . ."

"We don't have to hurry into anything, Cindy. I just wanted you to know—that one day I'd like to ask you to marry me." He bent and kissed her again.

While she responded, Cindy's mind was whirling. What was she thinking? She didn't want the kiss to end, but she had to tell him. She pulled away. "Jonathan, I *do* love you, and I love the twins. I'm just not sure how good a wife and mother I can be, with all the responsibilities I have with the shop. I—"

He touched his fingers to her lips, stopping her from voicing her misgivings. "Cindy, I have no doubt you can be a wonderful wife and mother and still run your shop. I'm sure we can work out everything. The twins are at preschool. Maybe you could hire an assistant manager and work half days. Or maybe you could open a shop in the historic district where you could set your own hours and wouldn't have to work so hard. We can figure it out. I know we can. Just think about it."

Cindy didn't know how to answer him. She wanted nothing more than to be his wife and the twins' mother, but— Jonathan's lips covered hers once more, and her heart turned to mush. How could she give up him and his children? Yet how could she say yes? Falling in love wasn't in her plans. But in love, she was, and she didn't have the faintest idea of what she was going to do about it.

❦

For the next few days, Cindy did more praying and soul-searching than she'd ever done in her life, but she didn't seem to have any answers. She knew what she wanted. She wanted to be Jonathan's wife and Landon and Lydia's mom. Yet she had promised her own mother she would see her dream come true, and she just didn't know how she could combine the two.

She'd been running the store nonstop for over a year now, and she couldn't see that kind of schedule working with being newly married—with children.

"Cindy, dear." Aunt Addie put her arm around her. "Something is on your mind, and I think you need to talk. Em is going to hold down the fort. Let's go to lunch."

Only then did Cindy realize how badly she needed to talk to someone. She nodded and grabbed her purse. "Thanks, Em," she said as she and her aunt headed toward the food court.

They'd barely sat down with their food before she began spilling out the story to her aunt. When she finally finished, she realized Aunt Addie was grinning from ear to ear and had tears in her eyes.

"Oh, Cindy, you had better not come for Christmas unless you bring that wonderful man and his precious children with you! Honey, you aren't thinking clearly. Your mother's real dream was to see you married and happy. She didn't get to do that. But, Cindy, there is no way she would want you to give up the man you love to keep her other dream alive. Why, Carly loved being a wife and mother. She never worked outside the home until she took up this venture. And she only did that because she missed your dad so much."

Tears welled up in Cindy's eyes. This was what she'd needed, someone to affirm what she already knew but hadn't thought through. "Thank you for reminding me, Aunt Addie. I just don't want to see her dream die."

"There is no reason it has to. In fact, I was waiting until after Christmas to tell you Em and I would like to come in as partners if you'll have us. That way we could share the load. It has kind of turned into a family thing."

"Yes, it has. But—oh, Aunt Addie, are you sure?"

"I'm positive. You grab this chance for happiness, Cindy. We'll help you make it all work."

It *would* work. Jonathan was willing to make it work. Her family was willing to help. The Lord had answered her prayers! Cindy didn't know whether to laugh or cry—so she did a little of both.

❧

When Jonathan and the twins came in that evening, it was obvious they'd been doing some more shopping. Jonathan was carrying a beautifully wrapped Christmas present, and the twins seemed very excited.

"Hi, Miss Cindy!" Landon said.

"Can you go eat with us?" Lydia asked.

Cindy didn't hesitate. "Yes I can."

"Good," Jonathan said.

Cindy smiled at him, and the look in his eyes had her giddy

with excitement. She couldn't wait to tell him she'd figured things out.

Before she had a chance, the twins looked at their dad and asked at the same time, "Can we give it to her now, Daddy?"

"Give me what?" Cindy smiled down at the two children she'd come to love.

Jonathan looked around. He saw only one customer in the shop, and Amy was helping her. "I guess we can."

He handed the twins the present he was holding and then made sure they didn't drop it before they handed it to Cindy.

"This is for me?" At the twins' nod, she set the gift on a nearby table and began to unwrap it slowly.

"Hurry!" Landon insisted.

Cindy chuckled. "Why don't you two help me?"

They did just that, tearing into the paper and helping her open the box. Inside she saw the cookie jar she'd wanted. "Oh, thank you!"

"Open the lid and look inside," Lydia said.

Cindy did as she was asked. It was full of folded pieces of paper. At first she thought it was just packing.

"Read our notes!" Landon said.

Cindy opened one of the notes. It said, *"Please marry Daddy."* She was sure it was written by Jonathan, but Lydia had printed her name.

Next came a note with Landon's name at the bottom. *"Please be our mommy."*

Cindy was fighting tears as she picked up a third. *"Please marry me. I love you."* Jonathan had signed it. The next one gave all the reasons he loved her. One after another, each note told her how very much she was loved and wanted and that it was what the twins had been praying about. Cindy couldn't get through reading them all before tears of joy began to stream down her face. "Yes! Yes! I love you all, and I *will* marry you, Jonathan!"

"Well, dig down a little deeper then," he said, looking at her with the look she knew would never fail to send her pulse racing.

She dug down to the bottom of the jar, and her fingers closed around a small box. She pulled it out and opened it. It was the most beautiful engagement ring she'd ever seen. "Ohh!" she cried.

Jonathan took it from her and got down on one knee right there in her shop in the middle of the mall. "Cindy, I love you with all my heart. Will you marry me soon?"

"Oh yes, I will."

He slipped the ring on her finger, rose, and pulled her into his arms. She barely managed to say, "I love you," before he sealed their promise with a kiss.

It took a few moments before they realized Landon and Lydia were clapping and jumping up and down. As she and Jonathan gathered the twins into their arms, Cindy thanked the Lord for answering all their prayers and for her cookie jar full of love.

JANET LEE BARTON

After living all over the south, Janet now lives in Oklahoma where she and her husband and their daughter and son-in-law have bought a house together. They are finding that generational living can be much fun—especially with two granddaughters added to the mix! She and her family are active members in their church and feel blessed to be part of a large, loving church family.

Janet has written ten novels for Barbour's Heartsong Presents line—four historical and six contemporary—and she has three more Heartsong Presents historical romances coming out in 2009. She has written five novellas for Barbour Publishing. Since Janet began writing for Barbour, she has been voted one of Heartsong readers' favorite new authors and one of the top ten favorite historical authors. In 2006 she was a finalist in the short historical Book of the Year contest held by ACFW for her novel *A Place Called Home*. It was chosen for one of Barbour Publishing's first audio books. She is thrilled to be among the Heartsong top ten favorite authors for 2007. Janet loves being able to share her faith through her writing and is very happy that the kind of stories the Lord has called her to write can be read by and shared with women of all ages; teenagers and grandmothers alike.

You can visit Janet at www.janetleebarton.com.

Stuck on You

by Rhonda Gibson

Dedication

To my daughter, Stacy Baron. I love you, sis.

Chapter 1

"What do you see in these things?"

Sheila's gaze moved to the Christmas ornament her sister Samantha held up. A little brown
mouse held a sprig of mistletoe over its head; its lips were
puckered up and its eyes tightly closed. She loved that piece.
"What's not to like?" she countered. She bent back down and
carefully unwrapped another Woodland ornament.

"It's a rodent, Sheila!"

The wrapping paper revealed a little brown bunny pulling a
winter sled and two cute baby skunks under a blanket. "No, it's
a cute Foster's Woodland creature; it's a collectible."

"Just because the signature on the bottom says 'Foster's
Woodland Collectibles' does not make it cute." Samantha
placed the ornament on a low-hanging tree branch with two
fingers as if it carried some kind of disease.

"No, cute is in the eye of the beholder, and I say they are
cute."

Samantha's laughter tinkled throughout the room. She

flipped her blond hair over a slender shoulder, winked, and then teased, "Is that why you still don't have a boyfriend? No one's cute enough?"

Sheila took the ribbing in stride. She stuck out her tongue at her baby sister. "For your information, I haven't found a man who's nearly as sweet as these little critters." She hung the rabbit and baby skunks on the tree.

From the corner of her eye, Sheila watched her older sister, Sarah, waddle into the room. Sarah and her husband, Dave, were expecting their second child in two months.

"Well, maybe if you got your nose out of a book for a little while, you'd find a husband," Sarah snipped.

With her hands on her hips, Samantha confronted Sarah. "We were only joking. No need to get ugly."

"Who's getting ugly? I'm just thinking Sheila deserves to be as happy as you and I are." She patted her well-rounded stomach and smiled.

It was the same every year. Sheila shook her head. Samantha in her playful way would tease about the lack of a husband in her life, and then their sister Sarah would take it to a more serious level. She sighed. "Books are how I make a living, Sarah."

"I know, but do you have to become a recluse to be a writer?" Sarah lowered her body into a chair, all the while protecting her stomach with her right hand.

Unlike Samantha, Sarah had a bob-style haircut and dark brown hair. At the moment, with her rounded tummy, she reminded Sheila of the purple character from that movie where the boy ends up with the chocolate factory.

"Did the doctor say if the baby was going to arrive before Christmas?" Sheila hoped the change of subject would take her sister's mind off their current discussion.

Sarah sighed. "No, he insisted this baby is going to arrive around New Year's."

"I'm sorry, sis." Samantha knelt beside Sarah's chair and placed her hand on her sister's bulging belly.

A twinkle entered Sarah's eye. "I bet I'll have this baby before Sheila can find a date for the family Christmas Eve party." She winked at their youngest sister.

Samantha groaned.

Sheila answered in a dismissive voice. "You know I don't play those kinds of games." She set the box of ornaments to the side and stood. "How about a cup of hot chocolate, a nice fat sugar cookie, and a change of subject?"

❧

A couple of hours later, Sheila returned to the living room to finish decorating her Christmas tree. With both her sisters on their way home to their own homes, she could enjoy her collection and dream of the many stories they conjured up in her mind. Sheila's creativity seemed to explode with ideas when she unwrapped the ornaments she loved.

Sheila turned on the CD player and hummed along with "Away in a Manger" as she pulled a tiny squirrel decorating a Christmas tree from the brown wrapping paper. She smiled at the delightful sight within her hand. In her mind's eye, she could see the squirrel's little home. It stood behind the small

Christmas tree he worked to decorate. Colorful Christmas lights decorated the tiny window in the bark of the tall oak tree.

The sound track changed, and soft, whimsical music filled her ears as her mind continued to picture the scene. Tiny rabbits, mice, badgers, raccoons, and other forest animals joined the little squirrel, and they held hands and swayed to the tune of "Silent Night." The star on the top of the little tree shone brightly. She shook her head to clear it of the joyful scene.

"It's time to write the stories I have placed in your heart." Every year the same thought entered her mind. This year she sat down and looked up at the tree. All kinds of Woodland animals filled the branches. Over the years, she had thought up many stories for each ornament.

"I really should write stories about you guys." She spoke aloud to the tree and the many ornaments that covered it. Sheila picked up the phone and dialed her editor, Erin Walters, in New York.

"Hi, Erin. I hope I haven't caught you at a bad time." Sheila's gaze moved to the clock. In New York, it was 4:00 p.m.

"No, I have a few minutes. What can I do for you, Sheila?"

"Well, normally I'd put this in writing, but I wanted to run it by you first." Sheila and Erin had become good friends over the past five years. She was thankful she could call her on a moment's whim and discuss book ideas. Most editors were too busy for such phone calls.

"I'm all ears."

"I'd like to do a set of Christmas stories based on Foster's

Woodland Collectibles ornaments. You know the ornaments I collect?" She held her breath and waited.

"Sure, I bought you one last year. Tell me about your ideas."

Sheila was breathless when she hung up the phone. While talking to her editor, she'd gotten excited about the stories and what messages of faith she could impart in them. Her excitement had spilled over into the phone line. Erin told her she'd love to publish such stories, but Sheila had to get permission from the creator of the ornament collection and a synopsis with multiple stories sketched out to take to the pub board next week.

Sheila looked about her living room. The newly decorated Christmas tree with its warm lights and friendly forest creatures gave the room a homey feeling. Her gaze moved to the fireplace where she'd hung stockings for her sisters and herself. It, too, added warmth to her cozy home.

As she made her way to the kitchen, she thought about her life. Being the middle child in a three-girl family often had its drawbacks. Like today when Sarah demanded she find a husband by New Year's. Why couldn't her sisters understand that God hadn't blessed her with just the right man?

The smell of freshly baked sugar cookies greeted her as she entered her kitchen. A smile crossed her face at the many gingerbread men that decorated the room. They danced on the curtains, offered goodies from the canisters, and graced the faces of several plates that adorned one wall. Gingerbread-men-cookie figurines sat on the counters and ledges. The set of salt and pepper shakers on her stove even resembled the fanciful men.

Gingerbread-men plates were placed about the room holding sugar cookies that were decorated like Christmas trees, Santas, flowers, presents, and angels. Even a few gingerbread men filled the plates.

"What man would put up with my weird collections?" Sheila asked as she came into the room. A large tabby cat answered as she meowed and stretched in one of the chairs. She extended her claws and made paw prints on her plush pillow.

"That's what I think, too, Chrisy. Most men are too serious for my taste. They don't like cartoons, chocolate, sugar cookies, or fat cats." Sheila filled her teakettle with water and placed it on the back burner of the stove.

Chrisy sniffed and raised her tail up into the air. Her nose went up, as well, and she stalked out of the room.

"I wasn't calling *you* a fat cat," Sheila called after her. "And some men like cats, some like cookies, and some even enjoy cartoons, but I've yet to find one who likes everything I do." She shook a box of cat treats.

The cat stuck her head back around the corner.

Sheila poured a small pile of the treats into the cat's bowl. "Come on. I'm sorry. I didn't mean to imply you were a fat cat." She stroked the feline's back as Chrisy nibbled at her delicacies.

"I should probably check online and see if I can find information on how to get in touch with Mr. Foster." She stood and took a sugar cookie off one of the many plates that were sitting around. Sheila nibbled at the yellow frosting of a daisy-shaped flower.

The teakettle began to steam on the stove. She laid the cookie down on a small saucer, picked up her favorite Christmas mug, and added hot-chocolate mix to it. Then she added the water and stirred, all the while thinking about Morgan Foster.

He was probably an old man with a beard and round belly. She imagined he had a love for nature and spent long hours in the woods. Sheila pictured him petting a deer and feeding it an apple. As the scent of hot cocoa filled her nose, Sheila laughed. He sounded a lot like Santa Claus. She dropped six mini-marshmallows into the cup.

After adding a couple of more cookies to the saucer, she picked up her large mug of hot chocolate and headed for her office.

The room welcomed her like an old friend. The artificial fireplace warmed the room. She took a seat at the desk that faced a large, open window. The tree outside reminded her of the little squirrel. She rolled her mouse to make the computer screen come to life then typed in "Foster's Woodland Collectibles."

She knew stores carried the ornaments and figurines, but where did one look for the artist? Sheila put a plus symbol after COLLECTIBLES and added ARTIST. The screen flickered for several moments before pulling up several Web links.

Up popped www.Fosterswoodlandcollectibles.com onto the screen. She clicked on the link and was pleasantly surprised to see a picture of a man with unruly brown hair and smiling blue eyes appear on the screen. "Probably his grandson," she told a meowing Chrisy.

As she read aloud, her eyes grew round. "The creator of

Foster's Woodland Collectibles lives in Snowbound Village, Connecticut."

She looked over at Chrisy and whispered, "Oh, he lives here in Snowbound and is going to be at the mall today!"

Chapter 2

Sheila rushed into the mall. Thanks to bad weather, she was running late. The sign at the entry of the mall announced Morgan Foster would be signing his ornaments and figurines from 4:00 to 6:00 p.m. According to her watch, it was five thirty now.

She hurried through the crowds of shoppers. Sale signs stood in front of most stores; offers of half off the prices tempted her to stop as she moved toward the one store she really wanted to go to. If she could meet Mr. Foster and get his permission to use his ornaments, her trip out into the crowds of crazed shoppers would be successful.

A teenage girl in a red pinafore and matching Santa hat greeted her as she entered the store Deck the Hall. "Merry Christmas, can I help you?" Her voice sounded bored, and her gaze searched out something toward the back of the store.

Sheila took a deep breath. "I'm looking for Mr. Foster, the creator of Foster's Woodland Collectibles."

That got her attention. A genuine smile touched the girl's

lips and eyes. "He's dreamy, isn't he?"

Sheila didn't know what to think of the girl's whispered words. Either she stayed at home with her mom too much, or she was just out of the popular loop. She didn't think teens today would use the word *dreamy* to describe a man. "I do enjoy his ornaments. That's why I'm here."

"Sure. You and half of Snowbound came out just to see his collectibles."

Not liking the way the girl was looking her up and down, Sheila stood straighter and put a little authority into her voice. "Young lady, would you please direct me to where he is?" Was the girl a Morgan Foster stalker or what?

"In the back corner." She pointed in that direction.

Sheila passed a charming Victorian village, complete with festive carolers and tiny horse-drawn carriages. Then she walked by an array of cheerful Santa Clauses, Snowbabies, Christmas trees, and other collectibles. All were ignored as she made her way to the Foster's Woodland Collectibles display.

The girl wasn't lying; women of all shapes, sizes, and ages filled the back of the store. Sheila heard his voice but couldn't see him over the sea of heads that were all facing the same direction. She assumed Mr. Foster had given a talk about his art.

"Do you have any questions?" his warm voice asked.

Several hands shot up into the air.

"Is it true you'll no longer be making Christmas ornaments?"

Sheila leaned forward for his answer. Surely he wouldn't stop making the ornaments. They were her favorites! His figurines were nice, but they didn't hold the spirit of Christmas in them as the ornaments did.

"Yes, it's true. With the new line of Christmas figurines coming out, I really need to focus on them."

Sheila listened in shock as the artist continued answering questions. She couldn't believe there would be no more ornaments to collect. Her father had started her ornament collection the year before he died. She'd been collecting them for five years. How could she stop?

"What made you decide to give up the ornaments?" A woman's voice rose above the crowd.

"I want Foster's Woodland Collectibles to be the best they can, and I don't feel I can continue to keep up the quality of both the figurines and the ornaments. People seem to enjoy the figurines best so I made the painful decision to let the ornaments go."

Her thoughts moved to the ornaments on her tree at home. She loved them all. The knowledge that there wouldn't be any new ones saddened her. Sheila studied the cute Woodland figurines. She could write stories based on them, too.

While Morgan Foster finished signing figurines and ornaments for the women, Sheila moved about the room, looking at the other Christmas collectibles and mourning the loss of the ornaments.

❧

Morgan questioned his sense of sanity as the women pressed upon him to sign the bottoms of their figurines. A few had ornaments, and he put his initials in the small spaces they pointed out to him. He was thankful a table stood between them. He'd sat through most of his talk, but now that all the ladies had left but one, he felt the need to stand and stretch.

"I read somewhere that you're single."

He looked to the little gray-haired woman who'd wiggled around the table and now stood at his elbow. A smile touched his lips. "I am. Are you looking for a date?"

A soft pink filled her cheeks, and she giggled like a schoolgirl. Her hand came up over her mouth, and he barely caught the words. "Oh, not for me." She lowered her hand. "My granddaughter is single though. What are you? Twenty-two? Twenty-three?"

He signed his initials on the bottom of a little mouse's foot before answering. "I'm thirty."

"That's too bad. She's only twenty. Thanks anyway, son." She patted his hand and left.

He sighed. Now if he could get past the teenager by the front door, he'd be home free. But he knew that wasn't going to happen today. Normally the manager would walk him out, but she'd called in sick earlier and asked the teenager to take good care of him.

Morgan picked up his briefcase and looked toward the exit. The teenager no longer stood by the door. He glanced about and found her at the register, helping the woman who'd asked about his marital status. A smile touched his lips, and he hurried toward the door.

"Excuse me. Mr. Foster?"

Dread filled him. He'd been so close to escaping the store.

Morgan turned toward the soft-spoken voice. His gaze focused on her face. Hazel eyes beseeched him to stop. He did. "Yes."

The pretty woman extended her hand. "My name is Sheila Fisher. I'm a children's author, and I was wondering if I could have a few moments of your time." She brushed light brown bangs out of her eyes.

He glanced over his shoulder. The teenager was still helping the older woman. Morgan focused his attention back on Sheila. "What can I do for you?"

"I wanted to talk to you about turning Foster's Woodland Collectibles into children's stories."

Her words seemed to tumble over themselves as if she sensed he was in a hurry. It had been a long time since a woman had looked at him so full of hope. He enjoyed the way her eyes sparkled at him. His stomach growled loudly.

She smiled and ducked her head.

He laughed. "Okay, how about we go grab a bite to eat, and you can tell me what you have in mind?" He was surprised when she nodded.

"Mr. Foster!" The call came from the teenager at the register.

Morgan took Sheila's elbow and propelled her toward the door.

"I think she wants your attention," Sheila said as she looked over her shoulder.

He sighed. "I know."

The girl maneuvered around several displays. "Thank you for coming. Everyone seemed to have a good time. Do you think you'll be coming back soon?" she asked breathlessly.

"I'm not sure. Please have your manager call if she wants me to."

She looked from Sheila to him. Her eyes narrowed as she focused on his hand on Sheila's elbow, and she answered, "Sure."

Morgan hurried them out the door. When he was sure they were safely away from the store, he slowed down. "I was thinking we'd get something at the Golden Corral. They serve a wonderful steak and are right across the street from the mall."

"Sounds good to me."

❧

Half an hour later, they sat waiting for their order to arrive. Sheila knew it was time to tell Mr. Foster what she wanted to do with his Woodland collectibles. She just couldn't figure out how to begin.

She was thankful he broke the silence. "So you're an author?"

"Yes. I write Christian children's stories." She took a sip from her water glass.

He leaned forward and gave her his full attention. "And you want to use my characters to write new stories?"

She stared into his intense blue eyes. "Your characters? My father started giving me Woodland ornaments back when I was twenty." She paused and studied his handsome face. Not a wrinkle marred his smooth skin. "I thought you'd be older."

"I'm thirty. You know that's twice today I've told beautiful ladies my age." A momentary look of shock crossed his face.

Sheila felt the heat of embarrassment fill her cheeks.

Morgan reached across the table and took her hand. "I'm sorry. I didn't mean to embarrass you. Sometimes my mouth speaks before my brain thinks. I truly am sorry."

She pulled her hand away and tried to pretend his words hadn't affected her. "I know what you mean. It's one of the disadvantages of working alone."

A smile touched his lips. "I've never thought of it that way, but I guess you're right. Let's start over."

She nodded, grateful that moment had passed.

"You're asking permission to use my characters in your books. Is that right?"

"Yes. My editor requires I receive a written agreement from you since you hold the copyright on your collectibles."

He nodded. "Okay, but answer me this: Why do you want to use the Woodland collectible line?"

A smile broke across her face. "That's an easy one. Your ornaments stir up the creative juices in me, and my mind races with each one's story. Just this morning, I hung up the squirrel that was decorating a small Christmas tree." She paused and tried to remember the name of that piece, but it failed to come to mind. "I can't remember the name of it, but I could envision what his house must look like. A toasty fire and hot mug of chocolate were waiting for him inside beside his favorite chair. I could see other Woodland animals coming and singing around the tree and snow softly falling about them." She stopped talking. Her mind had entered an imaginary world, and for a few moments, Sheila had forgotten she was sitting at dinner with a handsome man.

He grinned across at her as the waiter placed a hot plate of food in front of him. "Please go on and tell me more," Morgan prompted after the waiter left the table.

"Well, each story will be based on a Bible story or something from the Bible that parents would want their kids to learn, such as not to lie, steal, talk back to your parents—that kind of thing." Sheila watched him lean forward with both hands face up on the table.

"Sounds good." He wiggled his fingers.

Sheila wasn't quite sure what he wanted her to do or say. She simply stared at him.

"Take my hands," he offered after several seconds.

"Why?"

Again his warm laughter washed over her. "In my family, we hold hands when we say grace."

"Oh." Sheila did as he asked. While he blessed their meal, she thought of all the ways he'd made her feel out of sorts. He'd called her beautiful, listened to her ramblings as if they really interested him, and now was holding her hands. Most men found her mousy looking; their eyes glazed over when she started talking about her books or ideas for books, and none of them had ever offered to pray over their food.

"Amen."

Sheila raised her head.

"Are you sure a salad is all you want?" he asked, cutting into a thick steak.

"After Thanksgiving. . .yes." She dipped her fork into the ranch salad dressing she'd requested on the side.

"Are you only going to focus on my characters? Or will you be creating other characters to go with mine?" Morgan asked.

Sheila finished chewing and swallowed. "I hope to add a few characters of my own. Each ornament whispers its own story; I'm going to tell that story. It may take just the one character or several. I'm not sure yet. Why? Will that be a problem?"

"I'm afraid so."

Chapter 3

Morgan watched her closely. He liked the way her eyes danced as she thought about her stories. Her face cloned that of a youthful teenager filled with joy. Her excitement matched his when she created her stories. He'd never met a woman like her and didn't like the idea of her walking out of his life once he signed over the copyright to her.

"What kind of problems do you see?" she asked.

He pushed his plate away and leaned back in his chair. "The idea of someone else creating characters like mine doesn't set well with me."

"What?" Disbelief filled her voice. "Anyone can create characters like yours."

"Really? I thought you'd already talked to your editor about this. If so, will he or she allow you to write characters that so closely resemble mine? Without my permission?" He crossed his arms and set his jaw in a stubborn line. For all appearances, he knew he resembled a stubborn man. His mother had told him so, many times after he'd given her this stance.

Sheila pushed back her salad. She stood slowly to her feet. "Well, then, Mr. Foster, I would say this business dinner is over." She picked up her purse and turned to leave.

"If you say so, but I had hoped we could discuss it further." Morgan watched her turn slowly to face him.

"What is there to discuss? I will have to create other characters to go into the stories. Without your permission, that can't happen." She straightened her spine and crossed her arms.

He took a sip from his iced tea. Over the rim of his glass, he watched her fidget. The desire to write her stories battled with her desire to leave the restaurant. "True. Maybe we can work something out that will satisfy both of us." Morgan motioned for her to return to her seat. Other diners stared in their direction as she sat down.

Sheila hugged her purse. "What do you have in mind?"

Morgan studied the hard set of her lips. She didn't like this one bit, and unshed tears filled her eyes. He hadn't realized how much she'd set her heart on doing this series of books. "Well, for starters I want to be included in the writing."

"How so?"

"I expect to meet once a week to go over your new characters and what you've written."

"What?"

Once more the other diners turned their attention to them. Color flooded her cheeks, and she ducked her head in embarrassment.

He ignored her outburst. "And I want a byline."

Sheila leaned across the table. "But you aren't writing the book. I am." Indignation dripped from her voice.

Morgan dug in his wallet and pulled out a business card. "Without my characters, you have no book. Here." He passed the card across the table to her. "Take this and think about what I've offered. If I don't hear from you in a couple of days, I'll take that as a no to my suggestion."

She grabbed the card and stood.

As she started to walk away, he said, "Who knows? Maybe I'll try my hand at writing if you decide not to do them."

❧

"Can you believe the gall of that man?" Sheila fumed into her cell phone.

"Calm down, Sheila. I'll come over. We'll watch a movie, eat a little popcorn, and drink hot chocolate. Then when you're all settled, we can discuss your Foster problem. Deal?" Samantha asked.

Sheila pulled into her driveway. "Sure. Come on over."

"I'll be there in a jiffy." Samantha hung up.

Sheila gathered her purse and headed inside. Going through the door off the garage, she entered her cozy kitchen. She fought the growing anger as she put water into the teakettle and set it on the stove to heat. Then she took a deep breath and bowed her head to pray.

Peace poured over her as she talked to the Lord. She admitted her love for the writing project she'd set her heart on and then told Him how frustrated she'd become over Morgan Foster's demands. By the time she said, "Amen," Sheila felt better.

Samantha arrived a few minutes later. Sheila offered her popcorn and hot cocoa.

"So what are you going to do?" Samantha asked, licking the salt off her fingers from the buttery treat.

Sheila leaned her hip against the counter and sipped at her hot chocolate. "Well, since he is discontinuing the ornaments, I think I'll go to the mall in the morning and buy all the ones I don't have."

"I meant about the books."

Sheila pushed away from the counter and sat down at the table. "I'm not sure. I want to do this project but hate the idea of every word being scrutinized."

Samantha studied her sister for several moments. "What about his wanting a byline? Are you going to allow that?" She munched on her bowl of popcorn.

"I'm still not too pleased with it, but Morgan is right. They were his characters first so that won't be a big deal." She picked up the movie Samantha had brought over. A chick flick. A big black dog sat between the couple on the cover.

Samantha grinned over her hot-chocolate mug. "I Googled your Mr. Foster before I came over."

Sheila inwardly groaned. "And?"

"He's easy on the eyes. I really don't understand why you'd protest spending time with him." Samantha stood, took the movie, and headed for the living room.

Well, Samantha did have the part about his being hand-some right. Sheila called to her sister as she gathered up cookies and popcorn and put them on a platter. "Don't even think about it, sis. I'm not interested in Morgan that way. I like him for his collectibles."

A laugh sounded from the other room. "Yeah, and that's why you call him Morgan and not Mr. Foster."

༄

Morgan sighed as he turned off the news and headed for his workshop. He'd had a restless night. His thoughts had returned over and over again to Sheila Fisher.

Maybe he'd pushed too hard. Sheila hadn't liked any of his suggestions of working together on her book idea. Why had he offered them anyway? Sure, she was cute and creative, but that didn't mean he should get involved with her romantically. Right?

Walking down the hall to his office, Morgan shook his head. He determined to put Sheila out of his thoughts and get to work on his latest project. As he walked past his desk, he picked up his sketch pad and pencil. The idea he'd been working on the night before was taking shape. Morgan sank into his favorite chair and began working on a little turtle that stood on the edge of a pond. He fashioned its legs so they appeared bowlegged. Next he placed a small snail on the turtle's back.

For the next hour, he worked. Finally he held up the drawing and admired the completed work. The turtle stood on the edge of the pond with one foot in the water, a small snail rested on its back, and a tiny ladybug perched on the shell of the snail. Each character wore a smile and a determined look on its face.

A smile touched his lips as he wrote in big letters above the drawing, "NEED A LIFT?"

The smile faded as thoughts of Sheila haunted him once more. Had he dashed her dreams by asking her to include him in the process of creating the book? If he were honest with himself, he'd admit he hadn't asked at all. As a matter of fact, he'd come close to threatening her. Well, maybe not her personally, but by telling her he'd think about writing the stories himself, he'd threatened her.

Morgan stood and stretched. What had he been thinking? He made his way to the kitchen. Maybe another hot cup of coffee would make him feel better. *Then again, maybe not.*

He poured the hot beverage into his favorite mug. The need to talk to Sheila bubbled within him. Since that wasn't possible, he went to the Lord in prayer.

"Lord, why is this woman affecting me so?" he prayed out loud. "You know a number of women have come across my path through the years, and I didn't give them a second thought. Now this one comes along, and she's in my thoughts constantly. After what I said to her yesterday, she probably hates my guts." He sighed and went for his running shoes. Maybe a brisk run in the falling snow would make him feel better.

A half hour later as he rounded the corner to reach his house, Morgan puffed out white clouds of air. The cold felt invigorating on his flesh. At least that's what he kept telling himself. His feet were freezing, his nose running, and still Sheila Fisher continued to come forward in his mind. He liked the way her nose turned up on the end and her eyes sparkled.

But he hated the last look she'd thrown over her shoulder at him. It had been a mixture of anger and disappointment.

Climbing the stairs to his back door zapped what remained of his energy. He dug in his pants pocket for the key. A whine drew his attention, and he turned toward the sound. A large basket rested on his porch, with a dark brown blanket tucked inside. Then he saw something wiggling underneath the blanket.

Morgan looked around his neighborhood; not a person or thing moved. Snow continued to fall softly to the ground.

The whine from the basket turned into a full-blown howl.

He whipped his head back around in time to see a big, sleek head pop out from under the covers. The color took him by surprise. It was silvery blue. Morgan smiled. The most soulful eyes he'd ever seen stared back at him.

"Now how did you get on my porch?" he asked, looking over his shoulder again.

The sound of the basket tipping over and spilling the puppy out onto the cold concrete porch pulled his attention back. The pup looked as surprised as Morgan felt. It wasn't what he considered a normal-size puppy. Large feet, long spindly looking legs, and a massive head told him this puppy was going to grow into a big dog.

Morgan knelt and offered his hand for the pup to smell. It came forward and licked his gloved fingers. "Come on. Let's get inside so I can decide what to do with you." He moved to the basket and scooped it up. The puppy followed him as he opened the door and went inside.

He pulled off his running shoes and set them beside the

door. Morgan moved through the washroom and into the kitchen. The sound of the puppy's nails hitting the floor alerted him to the fact that it had followed. He set the basket on the table and dug around inside.

Not seeing anything, Morgan pulled the blanket out and shook it. A white envelope fluttered to the floor. The puppy was on it in a second. He—or she—took off running and sliding, trying to toss the envelope into the air, but it fell flat.

Morgan scooped up the envelope and was rewarded with the puppy jumping on his legs. "Down," he ordered in a firm voice.

The puppy sat on his stocking feet.

"So now you're a foot warmer?" Morgan asked, pulling a Christmas card from the soggy envelope.

In answer the dog lay down on his feet.

A Christmas tree with gifts under it adorned the front of the card. Morgan opened it and read aloud.

May the season of giving continue throughout the year. Merry Christmas. I hope you enjoy Noel. She will make a perfect companion. Love, A fan.

At the mention of her name, Noel sat up and whined.

"So your name is Noel. That's very pretty, and it also indicates you're a girl." Morgan bent down and rubbed her ears. He couldn't decide what breed of dog Noel was. She looked to be part Labrador, Great Dane, or Saint Bernard—or maybe a mixture of all three. Since he'd never owned a dog before and usually thought of them as big dogs or little dogs, this one could be any breed.

He wondered which of his "fans" had given him the animal. What was he going to do with such a big dog? Morgan stood, put the blanket back inside the basket, then pulled Noel's basket from the table.

He carried it into the laundry room and set it down beside the washer. Noel followed. "Well, for now you're staying in here."

Noel clumsily climbed into it and looked up at him with questioning eyes. She tilted her head from side to side.

"Good girl." Morgan shut the door and headed to his bedroom. If he was going to keep the puppy, he'd have to make another trip to the mall for doggy supplies.

Chapter 4

Sheila juggled the packages she'd picked up at the mall. She'd stepped out of Deck the Hall, laden with more bags than she'd expected. Her credit card bill was going to be big, but she couldn't pass up the ornaments. Still, her mind was soaring with story ideas for her new purchases.

"Did you buy out the store?"

Sheila froze. She knew that voice. She raised her head and looked into the face of Morgan Foster. "It looks like it, doesn't it?"

"Sure does. Can I help you with some of those bags?" He reached out and took several without waiting for her agreement.

Sheila wanted to protest but felt grateful for the decrease in weight. "Thanks."

"You're welcome. I'm on my way to find a hot cup of coffee. Care to join me?" Morgan took a couple of more bags from her grasp.

"I'm not much of a coffee drinker, but I do need to talk to you for a few minutes. So, sure, did you have a particular shop in mind where you can get your coffee?"

Morgan began walking. "Not really. What is your drink of choice? Hot cider? Eggnog?"

Sheila smiled. "None of the above. I'm a dark-chocolate drinker."

"With marshmallows?" He spun on his heel and started walking back toward Deck the Hall.

She laughed, wondering where he was headed. "Is there any other way to drink cocoa?"

"Sure there is. My sister drinks hers with a peppermint stick poking out of whipped cream. She insists this technique makes the drink perfect." Morgan stopped in front of Carly's Cookie Jar. "How about here? I think they serve both chocolate and coffee."

"Perfect. I've been in here several times. They have the cutest gingerbread-men cookies."

He tilted his head to the side and studied her. "And this is important because—?"

She liked the way his eyebrow quirked up as he waited for her answer. "Because my kitchen is done in gingerbread men. Sometimes I buy cookies here to put on plates in my kitchen. I have a niece who loves them."

"So gingerbread men are something else you collect?" He proceeded into the store.

"Sort of. I like gingerbread men, and my family started adding pieces every year to go in my kitchen. So I have a collection, but I don't actively go out and look for pieces to add to it. My family does that for me." Sheila felt as if she were rambling. She decided to focus on her surroundings, even though she'd been in the store numerous times.

Carly's Cookie Jar wasn't very big, but it had a large glass display case full of cookies. Several tables and chairs served the customers, and in one corner were two smaller tables and chairs for children to sit on while decorating their own cookies. A sign with the words KIDS' CORNER distinguished that section as a child-friendly environment.

She noticed the shop was ready for Christmas. Lighted garlands, a small tree on the end of the counter where purchases were rung up, and a collection of Christmas cookie jars decorated the shelves around the shop. Sheila knew the tagless jars belonged to the owner's mother and weren't for sale. The store was called Carly's Cookie Jar, a place where customers could get their fill of cookies, coffee, and hot chocolate.

"What can I get for you?" the young woman at the register asked.

Morgan motioned for Sheila to order first.

Sheila smiled. "I'd like a large hot chocolate and a sugar cookie."

"Make that four sugar cookies and a cup of coffee, too," Morgan added from beside her. He shifted all the bags to one hand and pulled a wallet from his pocket with his free hand as their order was being rung up.

Sheila wasn't sure she wanted him paying for her morning treat. "You don't have to buy mine," she protested, reaching into her purse for her ever-elusive wallet.

"Oh, but I do. If you hadn't ordered a sugar cookie, I would have forgotten to order mine. So you see, I owe you a strong, hot mug and a delicate morsel to repay you for such kindness."

She found herself laughing once more. Morgan sounded like a knight of old. If he had used the words "my lady," Sheila felt sure she would have curtsied with the words "thank you, my lord" upon her lips. Instead she offered a simple, "Thanks."

"You're welcome." He handed her the bag of cookies and resituated the packages he'd been carrying. "I'll be right back for the drinks," Morgan told the girl at the counter.

She smiled sweetly at him. "Okay, they'll be here waiting for you."

Sheila led him to a table off to the side, placing them between the entryway and the children's center. "Is this okay?"

Morgan set the bags down. "Perfect. Be right back."

She watched as he moved between the tables. Under his coat, she could see the outline of his wide shoulders. His hair curled around his collar and looked windswept. He turned with a smile, revealing even white teeth. Her heart melted a little before she could stop it.

Morgan returned and slipped into the chair opposite her.

The sweet smell of hot chocolate drifted to her as he passed across her drink. "Have you given any thought to our conversation from the other day?"

Sheila pulled a cookie from the bag. "As a matter of fact, I have. I'm willing to share my stories with you, but I still don't like the idea of sharing the byline." She held her breath, hoping he'd say he'd reconsidered.

He pulled the bag of cookies to himself. "The byline is

necessary for us to work together."

She looked at him. It sounded as if he'd had trouble getting those words out. "Okay."

Morgan sat forward in his chair and leaned on the table. "Okay? That's it?"

An undercurrent of anger flowed through her. She felt her face flush but held her tongue. Why did he have to act so astonished? Was he expecting the worst from her? Or did he know how hard it was for her to share the byline, and this was his way of rubbing it in? Sheila sent a silent prayer heavenward for patience. "That's it."

"Good. I'm glad you decided to see reason." He leaned back and took a deep drink of his coffee then grimaced.

She hoped it scorched his tongue. Immediately she felt bad for the thought. Sheila took a sip of her chocolate and waited for him to say something she could respond to. Right now she didn't feel much like speaking to Morgan Foster at all.

He motioned toward the bags at their feet. "Christmas shopping?"

"A little, but mainly they're Christmas ornaments." She nibbled at her cookie.

"Foster ornaments?"

Sheila set her mug down and nodded. "Yes. Want to see which one I plan to write about first?"

She watched his eyes light up with what she hoped was excitement. "You already have one picked out to start with?"

"I had chosen one at home that I thought I'd write about first, but this one just spoke to me. I have to do its story first."

Sheila bent over and dug in the bags. She found the box she was looking for and pulled it free.

He leaned forward.

Carefully she unwrapped the chosen ornament. It was a small hedgehog with colorful bows stuck to its body. A red one on its head, a blue bow on its back, and a yellow one stuck to one of its paws. She flipped it over and read, "Stuck on You." Sheila was surprised to hear his voice blend with hers as she read.

"That's one of my favorites," he said.

Sheila held it close to her face and stared into the little eyes. Long eyelashes revealed the little hedgehog was a girl. "It's quite expressive. Do you remember what you were thinking when you drew it?"

A soft smile touched his lips. Sheila watched him closely as he answered. "Something silly, I'm sure."

She didn't push him for a better answer. If he didn't want to say, he didn't have to. But his smile had been nice to witness.

"What are you going to write about our friend there?" Morgan took a drink of his coffee and ate one of his cookies in two bites.

Sheila turned her attention back to the ornament. "I haven't really decided. I'll let you know in a few days."

❧

Morgan realized later he didn't have Sheila's contact information. He wondered if she was in the phone book and decided to check it out later. Right now he had to get this doggy stuff inside and let Noel out for some fresh air.

Looking at the boxed crate, he decided to take care of Noel's needs first and then wrestle the kennel out of the SUV. He entered the back door, carrying bags of puppy things. Noel greeted him with licks and whines.

He fished her new pink collar and matching leash from the bag. Kneeling down in front of her, he said, "Hey, girl, did you miss me?"

In answer Morgan received another wet kiss from the puppy. "No kisses!" he ordered, wiping puppy slobber off his cheek. He managed to get the collar around her neck. "Did you know you're a Great Dane?"

She wiggled about.

"Not just any ol' Great Dane either. You, little lady, are a blue Great Dane. See?"

He pulled the book on Great Danes from one of the many scattered shopping bags and held it up for her to see.

Noel studied the cover as if she understood every word he'd said.

Morgan laughed. Having Noel around might not be so bad after all. He attached the leash to the collar and stood. "Ready for a walk?"

Noel turned to the door and pulled on the leash.

"That's a good girl. But I warn you. It's cold out." He and the Great Dane puppy went around the block. She kept her nose close to the ground and smelled every little thing along the way.

Morgan enjoyed the fresh air. Snowbound Village had

grown in the last ten years. He enjoyed the quaintness of downtown but loved his neighborhood. It sat on the outskirts of the town. He was thankful he could still venture out into the woods with just a short walk as he had as a boy. Adventures in the woods had inspired the creation of Foster's Woodland Collectibles.

His thoughts turned to the hedgehog Christmas ornament. He'd created it on a day when he had felt prickly about his life. Morgan recalled telling the Lord how unsettled he felt. He'd confessed his desire for a wife, children, and a place farther away from town where he could be among the forest creatures.

Later that day, he'd drawn his little hedgehog and added the Christmas bows last. He hadn't thought of that day in a long time. At the time of its creation, the little hedgehog had represented his lack of love.

Her choosing to use the "Stuck on You" ornament made him wonder if this was God's way of telling him to pursue Sheila Fisher.

Chapter 5

Sheila sat in front of her fireplace. The embers crackled and popped. The Christmas ornament sat to her right, a hot cup of chocolate on her left. She placed the yellow legal pad on her lap desk and began to write.

Once upon a time, there lived a little hedgehog named Hannah.

Hannah and her mother, father, and two sisters lived in the woods. A small hole in the ground was the entrance to their home.

Hannah hurried through the earth door. She rushed through the kitchen, her nose twitching as the scent of mushroom soup on the stove caused her tummy to grumble. Hannah ignored the feeling.

She couldn't believe how pretty she looked today. Mr. Toad had told her a red Christmas bow adorned her head and a blue one rested on her back quills, and she could see the yellow one that was attached to her paw. She knew the red and blue were pretty because the yellow one was. Thanks to the human's carelessness, she'd rolled right into a bag of Christmas bows that had been discarded as trash.

"Mama, look at me," she squeaked, hurrying into the family room.

Mama Hedgehog sat in her favorite overstuffed chair. She held her latest knitting project on her lap. Hannah's two sisters played with their rag dolls on the floor at her feet. Mama laid down her knitting and stared at her oldest daughter. "Hannah, where did you get those?" She pointed with her needles at the bows.

"Aren't they beautiful? I rolled into them when I was escaping Mr. Morgan's mean old dog." Hannah turned around so her mother and sisters could get a good look at all three bows.

"I want one!" wailed her little sister Harley. The little hedge maid jumped up on her back paws.

Honey, the baby, squealed, "Me, too!"

Hannah put out her paws to ward off her sisters. "No! I found them. They're mine."

Mama looked from one daughter to the other. "Hannah, it would be nice if you shared with your sisters."

"I don't want to share with them. I always have to share. This time I want to keep the bows all to myself. I found them." She crossed her arms over her chest and thrust out her chin.

Harley and Baby Honey wailed their disappointment. Her mother tsked and shook her head. "Is that what

Jesus would do?" She pulled the two younger hedge children to her.

"I don't know," Hannah answered, knowing it wasn't true.

Jesus would share, but Hannah didn't want to.

Sheila looked over her story. So far, so good. But what would Hannah and Mama do next? Should she send Hannah on an adventure? Or simply allow Mama to talk some sense into her oldest daughter? Or would Mama think up a good solution? Sheila laid the pad and pencil to the side and picked up her hot chocolate.

She cradled the cup in her hands. Her gaze moved to the fire, and she allowed her thoughts to run wild. Hannah could go on an adventure and come across three other animals that showed her sharing was much more fun than being selfish. Sheila swirled a peppermint stick inside her chocolate.

Why had she given in to the temptation to try hot chocolate the way Morgan's sister liked it? She ignored the inner question and tried to focus on Hannah and her dilemma. Three bows, two sisters—Hannah could give her sisters each a bow and would still have one of her own. But she had to have a good reason to do so. What was that reason?

She stood up and walked to the window. Frost covered the outside pane of glass. The snowflakelike sparkles brought a smile to her face. The fire crackled behind her, and she enjoyed the coziness of her home.

The phone rang, breaking the quietness of the room. Sheila

allowed the answering machine to pick up. Her sister Samantha's voice filled the room. "Sheila, I'm heading to the hospital. Sarah is in labor."

Sheila grabbed her purse and coat. She closed up the fireplace and hurried to meet her family at the hospital.

❧

Morgan felt silly dressed as one of Santa's elves. His green and red costume with a matching hat and leggings was comfortable on his body. It was the jingly bell on the hat that felt ridiculous.

"Smile. Santa's elves are supposed to be happy," Carla, a fellow elf and church friend, whispered as she passed by. She carried a handful of candy canes.

Morgan followed. "Easy for you to say—you don't have to write down all these names and Christmas wishes," he teased as he followed her into the children's ward of the hospital.

"You volunteered, Foster. So stop being a whiny elf." She laughed.

Morgan stuck out his tongue at her. He liked Carla. She was easy to be around, and the fact that she was already married made it easy to joke with her. With Carla, he knew she wasn't flirting, simply having fun. She followed her husband, Santa Claus, down the long hallway. Santa was really Dennis Wheeler, his best friend and the one who'd called him thirty minutes earlier to come play elf.

"Come on, old buddy. We have children to visit," Dennis called back to him.

He hurried to catch up with his two friends. The bell on his hat jingled with each step.

When Morgan was even with them, Dennis asked, "How's it going with the lady author?"

"Good. We met yesterday, and she's already chosen an ornament to start writing about."

"Which one?" Carla asked, keeping in step with her husband.

"Stuck on You."

Dennis stopped. "That's the one with the bear and its cub. Right?"

"Wrong. It's the one with the mouse and the teacup," Carla answered with a giggle.

Morgan shook his head in mock sorrow, causing the bell to dance merrily beside his right ear. "You're both wrong. It's the little hedgehog with all the Christmas bows stuck to it."

"Oh," both Carla and Dennis said in unison.

"Look who's here!" A nurse opened double glass doors to allow them into the children's ward.

"It's Santa!" the children squealed.

Carla and Morgan fell into step behind Dennis. He entered the room with a merry "Ho! Ho! Ho!"

In a matter of minutes, the room was organized. Carla passed out candy canes, Dennis sat in a big chair at the back of the room, and Morgan stood by his side. As each child took a turn sitting on Santa's lap, Morgan jotted down the names and what they wanted for Christmas. He wrote them on what looked like a long scroll with a big feather pen.

"Hello, little girl, what's your name?"

"Sheila Lynn."

Morgan's head snapped up. He was surprised a young girl would carry the name *Sheila*. Even with *Lynn* stuck onto it, the name felt old-fashioned to him. He looked at the sweet-faced little girl who sat on Santa's lap. Her brown hair had been pulled up into a ponytail. Sparkling blue eyes looked up at Dennis with admiration. He'd guess her to be about four years old.

"What do you want Santa to bring you, Sheila Lynn?"

A hush fell over the room. Morgan grinned. It amazed him that all the children stopped what they were doing to hear what they each wanted for Christmas. Soft sounds of sucking on peppermint sticks could be heard in the stillness.

His gaze returned to Santa. He held his pen ready to write down what the child wanted to find under her tree on Christmas morning.

The little girl chewed on her finger for a moment then said, "Well, I'd like to have a buggy to put my baby in, but Mama says my aunt Sheila really needs a husband bad. Can you give Aunt Sheila a husband?"

A gasp filled the back of the room.

Morgan looked to the spot where the sound had emerged. He knew before his gaze locked with hers that Sheila Fisher stood at the back of the room. Her cheeks were rosy with embarrassment.

Santa laughed with a loud "Ho! Ho! Ho!" Then he tweaked her nose. "Well, Sheila Lynn. . .Santa's not very good at finding husbands for big girls, but I'll see if we have any buggies left in the workshop for your baby. How would that be?"

She wrapped her little arms around his neck and gave him a big kiss. "Thanks, Santa." As soon as her feet hit the floor, she skipped back to her aunt.

Morgan watched them leave, hand in hand. He wondered what they were doing at the hospital. The desire to follow them pulled at him, but so did his duty to Santa and the rest of the children at the hospital.

Chapter 6

Sheila still felt the sting of heat in her cheeks. "Samantha, how could Sarah tell Sheila Lynn such a thing?" She paced in the waiting area.

"I'm sure she didn't just tell Sheila Lynn. I'm sure our sister probably said it to Dave, and Little Ears probably overheard her."

"No, I wasn't," Sheila Lynn announced. She sat across the room and rocked her baby doll.

Samantha laughed. "You weren't?"

Sheila watched her niece shake her head. "Nope, I was in my car seat."

"What exactly did your mama say?" Sheila coaxed.

"Shame on you," Samantha scolded with a grin.

Sheila Lynn tucked a blanket more securely around her doll. "She said it wasn't fair the baby was coming this soon. She said she had hoped you would have a husband or at least a boyfriend by the time our baby came. Mama said you need a husband real bad." She looked up at her aunt with big eyes. "Do you need a husband real bad?"

Samantha turned her head away but not before Sheila saw her grab her mouth to keep laughter from pouring out. Her sister's shoulders shook with merriment.

On the one hand, Sheila wanted to say no, but to do so might make Sheila Lynn doubt her mama. The last thing Sheila wanted to do was make Sarah look bad in her daughter's eyes. On the other hand, there was no way she was going to say she needed a husband *real* bad.

She silently prayed for an escape from the question or a means to answer honestly and not make Sarah's daughter think her mother had lied.

"Do you, Aunt Sheila?"

Sheila studied her and frantically awaited an answer from God. "Do I what, sweetie?"

Samantha snickered.

The little girl stood up, put both hands on her hips, and said, "I told you. Need a man really bad."

She knelt down in front of her niece. "I don't think so, but your mama thinks I do."

"Oh, like when she thinks I need to eat all my carrots, and I don't think so?" Her face twisted in distaste.

Sheila sighed. "Exactly."

Samantha snorted and finally, unable to contain herself, laughed.

Dave entered the waiting room. His grin told them everything.

"Daddy!" Sheila Lynn rushed into her daddy's waiting arms.

"Congratulations, Sheila Lynn! You are the proud sister of

a little brother." He swung her up in the air.

Sheila Lynn squealed.

Dave hugged his little girl close and smiled at Sheila and Samantha. "Sarah did great. The baby was born about ten minutes ago. He weighs six pounds and three ounces, and best of all, he's healthy."

"What's his name?" Sheila and Samantha asked in unison.

"David James."

Sheila moved forward and hugged father and daughter together. "That is a wonderful name."

Sarah had refused to tell anyone the names she had chosen for this baby. It was fitting that he be named after his father, Dave, and his maternal grandfather, James. Tears filled Sheila's eyes. Her dad would have been so proud.

"Hey, let me hug them now," Samantha teased behind her.

Sheila moved out of the way and let her little sister in. "When can we see him?" she asked.

"They'll have him in the nursery here in a few minutes. I'm going back in to be with them. Do you mind taking Sheila Lynn home with you tonight, Sheila?"

Before Sheila could answer, Sheila Lynn protested. "But I want to see Mommy and DJ."

"You will, sweetheart, but Mommy and DJ have to stay all night at the hospital. So after you see them, I need you to go home with your aunt Sheila. Okay?"

She patted his jaw. "Okay, Daddy."

He looked over her head at Sheila, who nodded her consent to keep her. "Good. Now go with Aunt Sheila and Aunt Samantha.

They'll take you to the nursery to see the baby."

After he set her down on the ground, Sheila Lynn grabbed Samantha's hand and then Sheila's. Samantha scooped up the discarded doll. They swung their excited niece between them as they walked toward the nursery. Dave went back through two double doors to join his wife.

"DJ, huh?" Samantha asked.

"Uh-huh. Mama said if it was a boy she wanted to name him David James and if it was a girl she wanted to name her Donna Jo. So I told Mama and Daddy I wanted to call the baby DJ because I learned how to write that in preschool." She swung her legs out and kicked.

Samantha looked over her head. "Why didn't we ask *her* what they were going to name the baby? Here we've been trying to guess for months."

Sheila laughed. "I never dreamed they'd tell Little Ears for fear she'd tell us."

"Nah, Mama said it was a secret and not to tell you." She released their hands and ran ahead to the glass wall at the front of the nursery.

❧

Morgan carried the forgotten candy cane in his hand. He searched for the little girl named Sheila Lynn and her aunt. His bell jingled with each step he took, and for a moment, Morgan wished he'd brought extra clothes to change into after he and "Santa" had completed their visit.

Why would Sheila and her namesake be at the hospital?

The question had plagued him ever since the moment he saw her standing at the back of the room. Was one of the little girl's parents sick? And if so, where in the hospital would they be?

He'd just about given up on finding them when he heard a little girl's squeal of delight and the word "yea!" Morgan hurried down the hallway that led to the location the sound had come from.

As he rounded the corner, he saw Sheila standing in front of a large glass window. Morgan slowed his steps. What was it about this woman that attracted him like a painter to an easel?

Morgan leaned his hip against the wall and studied her. It wasn't her dishwater blond hair, her hazel eyes, or even her slim figure. Not that he didn't find her attractive, but though he'd met many women who were as attractive or even more so, they hadn't had the same effect on him as Sheila Fisher. Could it be that his soul could sense hers was his match?

He shook the thought away and walked up behind her. She was looking at a lone newborn whose name card read BABY GIRL HARRISON. He whispered close to her ear, "She's beautiful."

"Yes, she is," she whispered back. A smile touched her lips as their gazes met in the reflection of the window.

Still keeping his voice down to a whisper, he asked, "You saw me coming?"

"Yes." Her voice drifted to him like a petal on the breeze, soft and slow.

For a moment, she leaned into him. Then as if she realized what she was doing, Morgan felt her stiffen and straighten her spine.

"You two look awful cozy."

He turned to see a young blond-haired woman and the little girl, Sheila Lynn, standing a few feet away, staring at them. Morgan moved a little farther away from Sheila. He watched her cheeks take on a pink hue.

"Morgan Foster, this is my sister Samantha and my niece, Sheila Lynn."

He stepped forward and shook Samantha's hand. "Nice to meet you."

"I know you. You're Santa's elf," Sheila Lynn accused.

Morgan knelt down in front of her. "That's right, and you forgot your candy cane." He held the candy out to her.

A smile lit up her face. "Thank you." She took the candy.

"So, Morgan. . .are you going to escort Sheila to the family Christmas Eve party and help her win a bet with our sister?" Samantha asked.

Chapter 7

Just let the floor swallow me now, Sheila pleaded inwardly.

"You must be little Sheila's mother," Morgan said.

Samantha flipped her hair over her shoulder and grinned. "Nope, I'm her aunt. Sarah is Sheila Lynn's mother. And you didn't answer my question." She smiled and winked at Sheila.

"Samantha!" Sheila hissed, going from pink to red within moments.

"I'll be happy to escort Sheila to the party," Morgan answered. "If she will allow me to, that is." He turned and looked at Sheila.

Sheila looked at her feet. How could her sisters be so uncaring of her feelings? Didn't they realize how embarrassing this was for her? She saw his feet join hers. His hands felt cool against her hot cheeks as he lifted her face to meet his.

With his forehead resting against hers, Morgan whispered, "I'm wearing an elf outfit, and you're the one who's embarrassed?" He wiggled his head so the bell would tinkle. "Play along with me on this one."

She knew Samantha couldn't hear what he was saying. Out of the corner of her eye, she could see her little sister leaning in their direction and frowning with frustration. Sheila nodded and whispered back, "I'm sorry. I can't believe they are doing this to me."

"I have two older brothers. I understand." He took her hand and gave it a little squeeze. "Trust me. This can be fun."

"Okay." Her heart fluttered in her chest at his nearness. Morgan's breath smelled like peppermint.

He turned to Samantha and grinned. "Tell your sister I'll be there."

Sheila couldn't help but wonder why Morgan was being so nice. Didn't he realize her sisters were trying to set her up? Well, maybe Sarah wasn't; after all, she was more than likely focused on her newborn son. But Samantha was definitely up to mischief and matchmaking.

"Will do. She'll be thrilled," Samantha answered.

"Aunt Sheila, I can't see," Sheila Lynn whined. She stood on her tiptoes trying to see into the nursery.

Morgan squeezed Sheila's hand one last time then released her so he could lift Sheila Lynn onto his shoulders. "Can you see now?" he asked.

"There he is!" she squealed in answer. Sheila's gaze followed her niece's finger.

A bassinet had been pulled up alongside Baby Girl Harrison. A new baby boy lay wrapped up like a mummy in a blue blanket. He wore a blue stocking hat on his head, and the card on his bassinet read BABY BOY WAYNE.

"That's my baby," Sheila Lynn said, tapping Morgan on the head.

Sheila enjoyed the way he laughed. Warmth filled her at the sound.

"He sure is a handsome young man." His gaze joined Sheila's in the glass's reflection.

"I think so, too." She smiled up at Sheila Lynn. Morgan's warm fingers enclosed hers. A shiver ran up her arm.

Sheila Lynn yawned.

"I hate to break up this cozy scene, but I think Little Ears is getting sleepy and needs a nap," Samantha announced.

Sheila looked up at her niece. Another yawn followed the first. "It has been a long day. I should take her home."

"I'm not tired," Sheila Lynn said, pushing her lip out in a pout. "I want to stay here and watch my baby."

Morgan laughed. "Your baby is sleeping. If you went home and took a nap, I bet your aunt would bring you back tomorrow to see the baby."

Another yawn captured Sheila Lynn. "Okay."

"I'll carry her to the car for you," Morgan offered.

Sheila nodded.

"I'll see you tomorrow, sis," Samantha said.

Sheila gave her a stern look. "I'll call you after I get Little Ears to bed."

Samantha laughed, waved, and then turned, no doubt to go report to their older sister. She opened the door to return to the private rooms of the new mothers. "Okay," she called over her shoulder. "Nice to meet you, Morgan." And then she was gone.

Morgan's soft chuckle caught her attention. She turned back to him and saw that he now cradled Sheila Lynn next to his chest. The little girl was sleeping.

"Your sister is a mess, isn't she?"

Sheila smiled. "You have no idea."

❧

Sheila reread the last few paragraphs of her story.

> *Harley and Baby Honey wailed out their disappointment.*
>
> *Her mother tsked and shook her head. "Is that what Jesus would do?" She pulled the two younger hedge children to her.*
>
> *"I don't know," Hannah answered, knowing it wasn't true.*
>
> *Jesus would share, but Hannah didn't want to.*

Sheila began writing.

> *"May I go outside and think about it?" she asked, knowing Mama would let her.*
>
> *"Be back in time for supper," Mama said as Hannah turned to leave.*
>
> *Hannah walked down to the riverbank. She sat down in the dry grass and sighed. Why did Mama always want her to share with her sisters?*
>
> *"Those are pretty bows."*
>
> *Hannah turned toward the blade of grass where the*

voice had come from. A ladybug sat looking up at her.
"Thank you."

"Why do you look so sad?" the ladybug asked.

"My mama wants me to give my sisters my bows,"
Hannah answered, touching the yellow Christmas bow on
her paw.

"Oh, how many sisters do you have?"

Hannah answered, "Two."

"Let me see. You have one, two, three bows," the
ladybug counted. "And they are red, blue, and yellow."

Hannah smiled. "That's right."

"If you hid two of the bows, you wouldn't have to
share them, would you?" the ladybug asked, and then she
fluttered away before Hannah could answer.

Hannah picked the blade of grass the ladybug had been
sitting on. She thought about hiding the bows. If she did
that, which one of the bows would she keep? The red? The
blue? Or the yellow?

She walked to the water's edge and looked at her
reflection. A fish swam up. "I like your bows," the fish
offered sweetly.

"Thank you," Hannah answered. She tried to see the
bow on her head, but it was too far back for her to get a
good look at it. So she wiggled around until she could see
the one on her back. It was hard to see, too.

"What are you doing?" the fish asked.

"I'm trying to see the bows," Hannah answered.

The fish twisted its head sideways. "Why?"

Hannah sighed. "Because my sisters want them, and the ladybug told me I should hide two of them and then I wouldn't have to share them. I'm trying to see the red and the blue ones because I want to wear the prettiest one home." Even as she said the words, Hannah felt guilty.

"Oh, if you can't see all three of them, why don't you share them, and then you would be able to see all three?"

"I don't want to share!" Hannah yelled at him.

The fish shook his head and swam away.

She could feel the fish's disappointment in her, and she felt ashamed.

Sheila read over her words aloud and then muttered, "What should happen to make Hannah change her mind and share with her sisters?" She thumped the pencil gently against her chin.

She tried to think of a time with her own sisters that something like this had happened. Growing up, there had been a number of times when she and Samantha had wanted something Sarah had. Why had Sarah given in and shared with them?

A glance at the clock reminded Sheila that Morgan was expecting her at Carly's Cookie Jar at two o'clock. The face of the grandfather clock read eleven fifteen. She wondered if Sarah had eaten lunch yet. Picking up the phone, she dialed her sister's number.

Sarah answered on the second ring.

"Have you had lunch yet?" Sheila asked immediately.

Sarah hesitated. "As a matter of fact, I haven't. Why?"

"Care to have it with me?"

"I don't know, Sheila. I'd love to, but the baby is fussy, and Little Ears will need a nap soon. It would just be easier for me to stay home and take care of these kiddos." Her voice sounded tired.

Sheila felt sorry for her sister. "How about this? Have a pizza delivered, and I'll come over. We'll feed Little Ears, and I'll put her down for a nap."

Sarah laughed. "Only if you'll bring me a large diet cherry soda."

"Deal, and I'll pay for the pizza when I get there."

"Deal."

❧

The baby was asleep, and Sheila Lynn was tucked in for a nap. Sarah sipped on the diet cherry soda as if it were honey to a bear. Sheila admired her older sister. Her house was clean, the babies were happy, and Sarah still had her sense of humor.

"So tell me. What made you come running to me today?" Sarah asked, sitting up in her chair.

Sheila took a deep breath. "I'm stuck in my story, and I'm supposed to meet Morgan in an hour and tell him about my progress."

"I'm not a writer, Sheila. I can't imagine what I can do to help you." She set her cup down with a sigh.

Sheila smiled at her older sister. "No, but you are an older sister, and I know that when we were growing up, there were a lot of times you had to share with Samantha and me whether you liked it or not."

Sarah jerked her cup back up as if she thought Sheila was going to ask for some of it. "You got that right."

"What made you do it?"

"Do what?" Sarah frowned over her straw, not sure what Sheila was talking about.

"Share."

"That's easy."

Sheila watched her sister's eyes dance with glee as she sipped her drink. "Well, are you going to tell me?"

"Sure."

"Today?"

"Mama made me."

Chapter 8

Two days later, Sheila picked up her pencil and reread the last few paragraphs.

> *"Oh, if you can't see all three of them, why don't you share them, and then you would be able to see all three?"*
> *"I don't want to share!" Hannah yelled at him.*
> *The fish shook his head and swam away.*
> *She could feel the fish's disappointment in her, and she felt ashamed.*

Sheila tapped the pink eraser on the desk. Sarah had been no help at all. Her sister had simply teased with her about Mama making her always give up her favorite things. But the hug Sarah had given her as she'd left spoke louder than the teasing. The truth was, Sarah shared because she loved her little sisters.

Chrisy leaped from her lap when the phone rang. The sudden noise and movement caused Sheila to jump, too. She took a deep breath then answered the phone.

"May I speak with Sheila Fisher, please?"

Sheila recognized Morgan's voice, and her pulse did a little flutter. "Speaking," she answered.

"Sheila, would you mind meeting today instead of tomorrow?"

She wondered why he needed to change the date. Her gaze moved to the unfinished manuscript. "No. When and where do you want to meet?"

"In about a half hour. . .at Carly's Cookie Jar?" His voice sounded strained.

Sheila laid the pencil down and picked up her purse. "I'll see you there."

"Thanks." He hung up.

Her gaze moved to the irritated cat. "What do you think is wrong, Chrisy?"

As if she understood, Chrisy looked up and meowed.

"Yeah, I don't know either, but I'm going to find out." Sheila picked up the cat and carried her out of the office. She put the pet down in the hallway and shut the door.

᪥

Morgan set Sheila's hot chocolate down in front of her. "So how's the book coming?" He took the seat across from her.

"Pretty good. I'm about halfway through the first draft."

He watched her take a cautious sip of her drink. "Do you mind telling me about it?"

" 'Course not." She laid the cup down. "I named the hedgehog Hannah. She has two sisters. Her sisters want her to share the pretty bows she's stumbled upon." Sheila's words continued to tumble from her lips.

Morgan enjoyed the way her eyes lit up as she told him about the story.

"Hannah doesn't want to share her pretty bows. She's tired of giving her sisters everything. But I haven't decided yet how I'm going to make her change her mind." She picked up her cup and took another sip.

"You are what they call a seat-of-the-pants writer, aren't you?" Morgan asked, leaning forward in his chair.

Sheila smiled. "As a matter of fact, I am." She leaned forward and met him in the middle of the table. "On small books like these, I write strictly seat-of-the-pants. Meaning I don't bother plotting out the whole story. Now with my larger books, I do plot. I create a synopsis. Using that outline, I write the book."

With their faces so close together, Morgan felt as if they were in their own cozy corner of the world, even though the rest of the shop was full of mall shoppers. Two children stood at the table in the back corner, decorating cookies with their mother. "How are you going to make this book Christian?" Morgan asked. He inhaled the sweet scent of her perfume.

"I don't make them Christian. If I try to put Christianity into the books, they come off sounding preachy. So I write them and pray my faith comes through." She sat back.

The noise level in the store rose as a group of teenagers entered Carly's Cookie Jar. "I need to make another trip to the Pet Connection. Would you like to go with me?"

Her gaze moved to the noisy teens, and she nodded.

Morgan took her hand as they walked past the teens. He

felt her slim fingers intertwine with his. Walking toward the Pet Connection, he considered releasing her hand, but since she didn't seem to be in a rush to free his, Morgan decided to enjoy the sensation of feeling like a couple.

They walked around the long line of children and parents waiting to see Santa. Morgan felt her tug on his hand and for a second thought she was trying to remove hers from his. He loosened his fingers from hers. She continued to hold his.

He stopped to find out if she wanted to see something.

"Aren't they adorable?" Sheila asked, pointing to Santa, who held twin children in his lap.

He looked in the direction she pointed and observed Santa. They were close enough that he could see Santa's deep, laughter-filled blue eyes surrounded by wire-rimmed glasses. His red outfit seemed quite luxurious and authentic-looking, with thick white fur around the collar, down the front of the coat, and at the cuffs. His pants were tucked into black boots, and he wore a red hat with white fur that was generous enough to hide his hair. His beard could have been real; Morgan wasn't sure if it was or not. A big tummy and joyful laugh completed the illusion of old St. Nick.

Morgan watched as the twins took turns whispering in Santa's ears. They pointed back to their parents and then returned to whispering. "They are cute. But I'll bet they're full of mischief."

"All children are at that age."

A light pink filled her cheeks. He wondered if she were remembering Sheila Lynn's visit to Santa. "True." He lowered his voice and teased, "I do recall a certain young lady looking for a husband for her beautiful aunt."

More color joined the pink. She looked up, and a grin touched her face as she added to his playful banter, "And I remember a silly elf who didn't have nearly the class this one does. Remember him?"

Morgan pulled a shocked, wounded face and looked to the other elf in question. She wore a forest green tunic, tights with one green leg and one red leg, and red pointy-toed boots that had bells. Her hat was red and green striped with red fur. "Well, some elves wear their bells in all the wrong places."

Her laughter brightened his day. They watched the twins return to their parents, and then Sheila returned her attention to him. "What are you getting at the pet store?"

Still she didn't release his hand. He smiled. "I was given a new puppy for Christmas." They continued walking.

"This Christmas?" She tossed her empty hot-chocolate cup into a trash can as they passed.

"There's Santa!" the cry rang out as a family with several children hurried past them. One of the older children bumped into Sheila while trying to grab the one running toward Santa and his elf.

Sheila stumbled into Morgan. He held her close and looked down into her upturned face. "Yes. This Christmas."

"Oh." The sound came out rushed from between her slightly parted lips.

He fought the urge to kiss her right there in the middle of the mall. Morgan knew he wanted their first kiss to be special. The more he was around Sheila Fisher, the more he knew God had handpicked her just for him. Still, one kiss wouldn't hurt anything. He leaned forward.

A mother's voice broke into his thoughts of kissing. "I'm terribly sorry. At this time of year, it is so hard to contain their excitement."

Sheila stepped away from him and turned her attention to the woman. "No harm done," she assured her.

The family continued on in their wild dash through the crowded mall.

Morgan continued to hold on to her hand and led her the last few steps to the pet store. Had she realized he was going to kiss her and pulled away? Or had she just been polite and answered the woman, unaware of his intentions?

❧

Sheila followed him into the pet shop. He still grasped her hand tightly as if he were afraid he might lose her in the crowd. She liked the feeling of being a couple and for a moment thought he had been about to kiss her if the woman hadn't interrupted and reminded her they were standing in the middle of the mall.

He pulled her past the display window filled with colorful birds. "You never did say why we're here," she reminded him.

"Noel needs obedience classes." He answered, stopping by a glass wall that allowed customers to view the various puppies and kittens they had at the store without touching them.

She noted that his voice no longer held the teasing it had earlier. He seemed a little more standoffish, and she wondered if it had anything to do with their run-in with the family. "I'm assuming Noel is the puppy you got for Christmas?"

"Yes. She's a Great Dane, and according to the book I bought last week, she needs to be trained. So here we are." He indicated a sign-up sheet resting on a table beside the door that led into the glass room.

Sheila couldn't say he was rude, but he wasn't the fun-filled man of a few minutes earlier. She gently pulled her hand from his. "Okay. I'm going to see what kind of toys they have for cats." She walked away from the puppy section of the store in search of the cat items.

The store felt festive like the rest of the mall. Decorations hung from the ceiling and along poles throughout the store. Over the cash register, she noted several sprigs of mistletoe dangling over the cashier's head. A sign hung on the pole beside her read, BEWARE OF THE MISTLETOE—YOU NEVER KNOW WHERE IT MIGHT BE HANGING. The price tag on it was unreadable from where she stood.

Sheila shook her head. That sign didn't even make sense. She continued through the store. She couldn't believe all the Christmas items they had for animals. She saw Santa hats made just for dogs and cats. Sweaters for all kinds of animals hung on end caps. She ventured past a cage where little brown, raccoon-faced ferrets sported red, silver, and green jingle bell collars.

A smile touched her lips. Chrisy wouldn't be too happy with her if she brought home one of those.

She located the cat aisle. In search of a fun toy, Sheila walked past the colorful collars, food dishes, and various food and treat books until she came to the right section. This store had every kind of entertainment a cat lover could imagine, from climbing and scratching posts to little dangly toys.

Sheila picked up a peacock feather that had a bell tied to it with long ribbons. The jingling sound reminded her of Morgan's elf hat. She wondered briefly if he'd signed Noel up for the obedience class yet.

As if just thinking about him brought him to life, Morgan stepped around the corner and asked, "What kind of cat do you have? I saw a sweater back there that says, 'Merry Christmas.' The sales gal says if you have a mild cat it would make the perfect Christmas gift."

The twinkle was back in his eyes. Whatever had bothered him earlier seemed to have vanished like the scent of evergreen after Christmas morning. "Chrisy is not a sweater-wearing type of cat." She could just picture her feline ripping to shreds anyone who tried to put a sweater on her. Not a pretty picture.

"Not laid back enough, huh?" He picked up a mouse with a long tail.

"Afraid not. She's more of the 'I'm the queen, not now' type of cat." Sheila put the peacock feather away. "She's really not very playful at all."

Morgan came closer to her and grinned. He stood so close she could smell the earthy scent of his cologne. "What about you? Are you the playful type?"

"I think so. Why?"

A smile touched his lips, and he pointed up.

A sprig of mistletoe hung over her head. "Trapped by mistletoe, what's a girl to do but pucker up?" With that, Sheila pursed her lips, closed her eyes, and leaned toward him.

She let Morgan take her gently in his arms and kiss her, right in the middle of the Pet Connection. She'd read somewhere that a twenty-second kiss told a person how much you loved them. Sheila allowed herself the luxury of melting into his arms and kissed him back.

It might have been twenty seconds before he pulled away, but she couldn't be sure. Morgan looked into her wide eyes and smiled. "Thanks. I enjoyed that."

Heat filled her cheeks, and she confessed, "So did I."

A teasing glint entered his now smoky blue eyes. "Well enough to go to dinner with me tonight?"

Chapter 9

*S*o *this is what it feels like to date someone on a regular basis,* Sheila thought as she tossed another discarded outfit onto the bed. She and Morgan had been going out regularly every evening for the past week. He'd taken her to dinner one night, and a romantic carriage ride in downtown Snowbound another night. Last night they'd gone to a play rehearsal at his church then out for hot chocolate.

Tonight they were going Christmas caroling with the singles group she'd met the night before, and Sheila couldn't decide which sweater to wear. She stared at the remaining clothes in her closet. Knowing it would be really cold, she settled on a green wool pullover. It wasn't her prettiest, but it would be the warmest, she decided.

She finished dressing and moved into the bathroom to apply makeup and fix her hair. If her clothes couldn't be pretty, she'd make sure her face and hair looked nice. A smile touched her lips as she looked at her reflection. If anyone had told her three weeks ago how silly she'd act over a man today, Sheila

Fisher would have laughed. But now here she stood in front of the mirror, trying to make herself look as good as she could for Morgan.

Since their first kiss, he'd been nothing but a gentleman. He'd kissed her good night a couple of times. She'd forgotten how cold it was outside and just enjoyed spending a few minutes on the front porch with him.

As she applied a light layer of lip gloss, Sheila thought about her feelings for the artist. She loved when he called her on the phone "just to chat." His laughter warmed her insides as no one else's could. For the first time in her life, Sheila felt sure she was falling in love.

The ringing phone drew her from the romantic thoughts, and she laughed as she hurried to the living room and picked up the receiver. "Hello?"

"You sound happy." Morgan's warm voice filled her ear and sent a shiver of delight down her back.

She sat down in one of her plush armchairs. "I am."

"Because I called?"

One of the things she loved about him was his playful banter. "Well, honestly I was happy even before you called." She twisted the cord with her index finger and smiled.

"You were thinking of me, weren't you?"

"As a matter of a fact, I was. Are you wearing your elf outfit tonight?" she teased.

"Oh, you cut me to the core. You were only happy because you thought I'd be wearing that silly costume." He moaned into the receiver.

She laughed.

"No, seriously I called because I have to break our date tonight."

Disappointment filled her voice. "Oh?"

"My mother has invited me to come out for dinner, and I told her I would. I'm really sorry. I don't see my parents enough, and, well, you know how it is. Can we go out tomorrow night? I really am sorry."

Why couldn't he invite her to his parents' with him? Sheila wondered but didn't ask. "I can't go tomorrow night. I promised Sarah I'd watch the kids for her." She heard the sound of a beep on his end of the phone.

"I'm sorry, Sheila. That's Mom on the other line. I'll call you tomorrow, okay?"

"Okay."

They hung up with swift good-byes. Sheila dragged her feet as she walked slowly back to the bedroom and pulled off the wool sweater. She dressed in a pair of gray sweatpants and a long-sleeved, pink, oversized T-shirt.

She put the clothes back in her closet. Scooping up Chrisy, she walked back into the living room. "I guess it's just you and me tonight, Miss Chrisy." She set the cat down on the armchair.

It bothered her that Morgan hadn't invited her to his parents'. Didn't he feel the same way about her as she did him? She walked into her kitchen filled with gingerbread men. Turning on the teakettle, she pulled down her favorite mug and the container that held her hot chocolate.

Sheila didn't know how to answer her own question. It

wasn't as if they'd been dating for months. He may not have any feelings at all for her other than someone to have fun with. She sighed.

⟨❧⟩

Morgan hated letting her down like that. He could have kicked himself when his mother called to remind him dinner would be at seven. His parents wanted help putting up their Christmas tree. It was tradition, and he knew without asking that his mother didn't want a stranger coming along with him.

Sheila wasn't a stranger to him, but she was to his parents. He knew his mother would never have agreed to share what she called her "special evening" with him, so he hadn't even asked. Any other night, she would have welcomed Sheila, but not tonight. He sighed.

The more time he spent with Sheila, the more he wanted to spend with her. She was sunshine on a cold day to him. He pulled into his parents' driveway.

He noticed a new red car sitting in the drive and wondered when they'd purchased it. Morgan knew it didn't belong to either of his brothers, because neither one of them had mentioned the new wheels when he'd talked to them on the phone.

As he walked to the door, Morgan made the decision to tell his parents about Sheila. He wondered what they would think of him when he told them he'd fallen in love. They'd probably be shocked since he and Sheila hadn't known each other very long, just a few weeks, but when he told them God was in control, Morgan knew they'd accept Sheila into their family. He was thankful his two brothers were both out of town or he'd get the ribbing of his life. They would never understand love at first sight.

He laughed as he entered the house. It hadn't been love at first sight but was pretty close. Morgan closed the front door behind him and hung his coat on one of the hooks by the door. "Mom, Dad?"

"We're in here, son," his father called from the den. "Your mother has decided to put the tree up in the den."

"Well, I just think it will be cozier in here this year," his mother said.

Morgan saw that several boxes of decorations and the Christmas tree box had been brought down from the attic. "I thought I'd be bringing those down," he said, coming farther into the room.

"Your mother couldn't wait."

His mother ignored the sarcasm in his father's voice and pointed to the far corner of the room. "Would you move the tree over there, son? Your father refused to move it one inch more into the room. I don't know what's gotten into him lately. It's bad enough he bought that red monster out there without even consulting me, and now he's refusing to help out around here."

At the age of seventy-two, his father still got around very well. But Morgan hated the thought of his climbing up and down the ladder that ran to the attic. He decided not to get into the argument about the new car but wanted his mother to know he didn't like the fact they didn't wait for him. "Mom, you should have waited for me to help you and Dad," he said, pulling the heavy box into the corner she indicated.

"Nothing's gotten into me," his father grumbled as he stalked off to the kitchen.

His mother hugged Morgan. "Come on into the kitchen. I made pot roast for dinner. That ought to sweeten him up, and if that doesn't work, I made his favorite lemon pie."

Morgan shook his head as he followed his mother into the kitchen. His parents could argue with the best of them, but when it came time to go to bed, he knew they'd forgive each other and go to sleep content with the world once more.

After everyone had been served and grace had been spoken, Morgan's mother asked the question he'd been waiting for.

"What have you been up to, honey?"

He took a deep breath and plunged in. "I met the woman I'm going to marry."

His father dropped his fork; his mother sputtered and almost spit out the water she'd just drunk from her glass.

"You're both going to love her, too. I would have brought her with me tonight, but I know how you feel about Christmas tree night." He felt like a man standing in front of a freight train. Should he shut up and get out of the way of danger or continue to talk and stare like a deer in headlights?

His mother was the first to speak. "You met the woman you're going to marry?" She picked up his father's fork and handed it back to him.

Morgan nodded.

"Does this woman have a name, son?" his father asked,

forking a slice of roast and chewing it slowly.

"Her name is Sheila Fisher."

"The children's author?" his mother gasped.

Morgan looked at her in surprise. "You know her?"

"Not personally, no. But your niece and nephew have all of her books. I bought them for the kids last Christmas." His mother began to eat.

Morgan chewed his meat slowly and digested the fact that his family had seen Sheila's books and he hadn't. He decided to make a trip to the mall bookstore and see what her books looked like. He'd been so enthralled with the woman that he'd forgotten she had other books out.

"How did you meet?" his mother asked.

"She came to the signing right after Thanksgiving." He buttered a roll. "Sheila's using the Woodland characters in her next series of books."

"How exciting!" his mother proclaimed.

"Not to mention flattering," his father added before taking another bite of pot roast. "Think you'll be bringing her by soon so we can meet her?"

His mother looked at him with the same question in her eyes.

"I'll bring her over for one of Mom's wonderful dinners sometime. . .soon," he promised with a smile.

His mother grinned her approval. "That will be nice."

Morgan nodded and continued to eat. His thoughts were on Sheila and the book she was working on. She enjoyed talking about her story but didn't seem to appreciate when he asked questions unless she initiated the subject. It was as if she still held resentment toward him for requesting the byline.

"It's a good thing she needed you in order to write those stories, or you two might never have met," his mother interrupted his thoughts.

"What do you mean?" Morgan looked up and studied his mother's face.

She waved his concern away with her fork. "Nothing. I was just thinking that without your permission she couldn't write those books. Am I right?"

Morgan nodded. Sometimes he felt as if Sheila was beginning to care for him, but could it be she was just patronizing him so he'd continue to allow her to write the books?

Chapter 10

Sheila reread what she'd just written.

Hannah could feel the fish's disappointment in her and felt ashamed.

She knew she should share with her sisters, especially since she couldn't see the other two bows, but something inside her wouldn't let her.

"If you do like the ladybug says and hide the bows, then who will enjoy them? And if you do as the fish suggests and share, then who will enjoy them?" a little dog with a gray beard asked. He swished his tail from side to side in the grass.

Hannah thought about what he said. "If I hide the bows, no one will enjoy them because no one will see them. But if I give them to my sisters, then everyone will see them." She sighed. "And if I keep them and leave them on my paw, head, and back, then everyone will see them, too." She smiled at this new idea.

The dog nodded. "True, true. But won't your sisters be sad because you didn't let them have one to wear? And won't your mother be sad because you didn't obey her and share the way she wanted you to?"

It didn't seem fair to Hannah. If she kept the bows, she would be happy, but her sisters would be sad. And if she gave them to her sisters, then they would be happy and she would be sad. "But I will be sad to give them away," she answered, feeling sorry for herself.

"Yes, I'm sure the last time you shared with your sisters made you very sad, too, didn't it?" The dog lay down beside her and rested his nose on his outstretched paws.

Hannah remembered sharing her Christmas pudding with her sisters. It hadn't made her unhappy. She'd felt warm inside and cheerful. Her sisters had laughed and thanked her, and she'd felt good, not sad.

Just thinking about that happy time made Hannah want to share her bows. She could imagine her sisters' smiling faces. She imagined them wearing the pretty bows on their spikes and running about showing their parents. Her mother would stand and tell her how proud she was of her for making the right decision.

Jesus would be happy with her, too.

Hannah stood. She touched the dog's front paw. "Thank you, Mr. Dog."

She hurried home, ran through the earth door, and shouted for her sisters. "I've decided to share my bows with you!" Hannah called as she entered the den.

Honey and Harley ran to meet her at the doorway. Their laughter filled the house.

"Children, come in here." Mama called them back into the den.

They all hurried inside. Mama helped Hannah by removing the bows from her head and back. "This is a nice thing you are doing." She hugged Hannah.

"I want the red one," Honey said.

"May I have the blue one?" Harley twisted her little paws.

Hannah knelt down in front of her. "I'm sorry I was so mean earlier, Harley. You can have the blue or the yellow one."

Harley hugged her close. When she let her go, Mama held out the yellow and the blue one to her. Harley took the blue. "Thank you, Hannah." She stuck the blue bow on her front paw and looked down at it with awe.

Hannah watched her sisters dance around the room. They each wore a bow on their paws. Inside she felt warm and happy.

Just as she knew she would.

Sheila smiled as she wrote the words "The End." The story was finished and would be about the size of a Golden Book once the illustrator added the pictures. She knew editing would have to be done, but at least she had the story down. Setting it to the side, she stretched.

The story was good enough to show Morgan. "Maybe I'll

make Mr. Dog a Great Dane. Do you think Morgan will like that, Chrisy?"

She glanced at the clock. The cat purred contentedly. "Good. I have time for an hour nap before I have to meet him." She rubbed Chrisy's back and grinned.

The doorbell rang. "Just when I thought I could rest," she muttered to Chrisy. The cat yawned and looked up at her through slit eyes.

Sheila moved the cat to the floor then walked down the hall. Just as she reached the door, the bell sounded again. "I'm coming."

"Could you come a little faster, sis? It's cold out here," Samantha's voice called from the other side of the door.

She opened the door, and her sister stumbled inside.

"I don't feel so good," Samantha announced as she rushed past her and into the bathroom down the hall.

The sound of sickness came up the hall. Sheila hurried to her bedroom and grabbed a spare pillow and blanket. She made a quick bed for Samantha on the couch then returned to her bedroom for a fresh pair of pajamas.

Sheila knocked on the bathroom door. A white-faced Samantha answered the door. "Here—put these on. You'll feel a little better in comfy clothes."

A few minutes later, Samantha returned to the living room clad in flannel pj's and with a freshly washed face. "I'm sorry. Josh went out of town with work, and I didn't want to stay home alone."

"You know you are welcome here anytime." Sheila tucked the

blanket around Samantha. "How long have you been sick?"

"It started this morning. I just feel sick to my stomach. I'm not sure what's wrong with me." She sank further under the covers.

"Can I get you anything?"

"Not right now." Samantha's voice was muffled. "Thanks."

Sheila watched as Chrisy curled up at the foot of the couch. She rubbed the cat's ears and then headed to the kitchen.

"Well, maybe a cup of tea would soothe my tummy," Samantha called.

Sheila pulled a box of saltines from the shelf and set the teakettle on. "It will be ready in a jiffy." She looked at the clock on the microwave. In a half hour, she'd be meeting Morgan.

❦

Morgan sat at Carly's Cookie Jar nursing a cup of coffee and munching on a chocolate chip cookie shaped like a Santa Claus head. Sheila was ten minutes late. It wasn't like her, and he was starting to get worried.

His heart did a flip-flop as she bustled into the room.

She maneuvered around the tables and chairs. "Sorry I'm late. My sister showed up on my doorstep a little while ago and is very sick."

He stood. "I'm sorry to hear that. Is there anything I can do?"

"No, I just need to get back home. I hate leaving her like that." Sheila adjusted the shoulder strap on her purse.

"I brought the manuscript for you to look over. It's still a little rough, but I think the story is complete. I just need to make sure the grammar and punctuation are correct." She handed it to him. "I'm really sorry I have to go now. Let me know what you think about the story."

Morgan gathered his coat and bags then walked with her out to the parking lot. He slid the manuscript into one of the bags. As they turned to part ways, he said, "I'll read it this afternoon and let you know what I think."

"Thanks. As soon as Samantha is feeling better, I'll call you. Maybe we could have dinner and a movie at my house?"

"Sounds like fun."

She smiled. "Good. Talk to you later." And with that, Sheila got into her car and pulled out of the parking lot.

He smiled as she looked back at him in her rearview mirror and waved. Did she miss him as much as he did her when they were apart? Morgan drove home, glancing at the shopping bags on the seat beside him. Two of Sheila's books rested in one of those bags.

Noel met him at the door. She'd been to one obedience class and proved she was the smartest one there, at least in Morgan's eyes. "Hey, girl, it's cold out there." He laid his bags on the couch and gathered Noel's leash from the hook beside the door. "Are you sure you want to go for a quick walk?"

She answered by sitting down on his feet.

Morgan laughed. "Okay." He hooked the leash through the ring on her collar. "Come on then." He zipped his coat and opened the door.

It didn't take them long to get back inside. Noel wasn't a dog who liked the cold. She came in and burrowed under her favorite blanket. Morgan made a hot cup of coffee and sat back in his favorite chair in front of the fireplace to read Sheila's manuscript. While the fire crackled, he read.

A smile touched his lips. The story was both cute and taught a lesson. He liked it. His mind worked, and he thought of illustrations that he could put on each page. But he couldn't allow himself to keep his original agreement with Sheila.

❧

"You want to go back on our agreement?" Sheila felt tears stinging her eyes as she grasped the phone receiver in her hand. "But—"

Morgan interrupted her. "Look—maybe I shouldn't have done this on the phone. Would it be okay if I come over there?"

"No. My sister is still here, and she's still sick." The last thing she wanted Samantha to see was Morgan rejecting her story. She dropped into her office chair. A tear spilled down her cheek.

"How about tomorrow at Carly's in the mall?"

What choice did she have? She could refuse. If he wasn't going to allow her to use the Woodland characters, then why should she meet him again? *Other than the fact that you love him?*

"Please, Sheila, I really want to talk to you about this, and it's not coming out right over the phone." Desperation filled his voice.

"Okay. I'll be there. What time?" She knew her voice sounded as frosty as the windowpanes looked, but she didn't care.

"Is nine in the morning too early?"

"That will be fine." More tears trailed down her cheek.

❧

Sheila made her way through the semiquiet mall. Since it was just opening, a lot of people weren't present. All the night before, she'd cried and tossed and turned, and now she felt like a rag doll with no energy.

It wasn't that she had just lost a story, but Sheila also felt as if she'd lost Morgan. She thought he'd fallen in love with her, just as she had with him. He'd never said so with words; but the look in his eyes, the way he touched her as much as possible when they were together, and the fact that he'd seemed generally interested in every aspect of her life, including the book he'd rejected the night before, led her to believe he cared for her.

Had she wanted him to return her love so badly that she'd fabricated his emotions and actions to meet her purposes, much as she did the characters in her books?

Chapter 11

Morgan walked into Carly's feeling unsure. For the first time in his life, he worried things wouldn't go the way he'd planned. What if he'd misread Sheila? So much depended on how this meeting went. Not just businesswise but personally, as well.

His gaze found hers across the room. Her eyes appeared puffy, and the sparkle no longer filled them. Morgan felt like a heel. Why hadn't he just asked her to meet him here yesterday instead of calling her first? In his excitement of illustrating the book, he'd blurted out that he wasn't going to honor their original agreement. Now he had to patch things up.

He ordered a strong cup of coffee before moving to the table where she sat. Would she agree to his new proposition? Morgan patted the manuscript. He prayed silently, asking the Lord to give him the right words.

When he arrived at her table, he noticed she hadn't ordered anything. "Can I get you a drink or a cookie?"

"No, thank you." Her voice sounded hoarse.

Morgan pulled out a chair and sat down across from her. He looked about the empty cookie shop. He was thankful that if she declined his offer, there would be no witnesses. "How is your sister feeling today?"

"Much better, thank you."

He held out her manuscript and waited for her to take it from his hand. "I'm sorry I upset you over the phone. I wasn't thinking. I didn't mean to blurt it out like that."

"I don't understand why you don't want to continue with our arrangement." Her eyes pleaded with him to explain.

"Well, I have a better offer." When she continued to stare at him, this time he saw a spark in her eyes. But it wasn't joy; it was anger. Her jaw set.

Morgan pressed on. "I really like your story and don't feel it's fair of me to ask you for a byline since I didn't write a word of it."

"So you've decided to write your own stories." Bitterness laced each word.

He shook his head. "No. I want to illustrate yours."

Morgan watched another emotion cross her face, this one confusion.

"I don't understand."

He reached across the table and took her ice-cold hands in his. "I want to illustrate your books—if your editor will allow it, that is."

A smile brightened her face. "So you aren't going to stop me from writing the books?"

He shook his head no.

"And we will continue meeting and going over the stories?"

Morgan watched the light return to her eyes. "Well, I wanted to talk to you about that."

"Oh?"

He'd practiced this moment in his mind a hundred times, but now that it came time, Morgan felt clumsy. "I need you to look at the last page of your manuscript."

❧

Sheila heard the uneasiness in his voice. For a moment, she'd been thrilled. She'd thought he did care and wanted to keep working with her on their book projects. Now she worried he hadn't liked the story after all. Her fingers twitched on the pages as if they, too, feared what might be coming.

"Go on—open it." His voice trembled.

Sheila flipped to the last page. Her gaze met his. She didn't want to read what he'd written on the page. Rejection of her work from him would be very painful. Sheila put off that pain as long as possible. His blue gaze held hers in their grasp.

"Please, don't make me wait any longer. Read it." Morgan looked down at the page, breaking their connection.

She looked down. Drawn on the page was the hedgehog, covered in Christmas bows, just like the one in her story. In front of the girl hedgehog knelt a boy hedgehog. He held up a diamond ring. Only the ring wasn't a part of the drawing; it was real!

Sheila searched out Morgan. Her gaze met his over the drawing.

"Read the inscription above the drawing," he whispered.

She read the words aloud. " 'I'm stuck on you, Sheila. Will you marry me?' "

Tears of joy washed down Sheila's face. "I will."

Morgan came around the table and pulled her to her feet. He pulled the tape off the paper and took the ring from the page. Holding her hand, he slipped the ring onto her finger and then kissed her lips softly.

Sheila pulled away first. "I want a Christmas wedding."

"This Christmas?" Morgan asked. He sounded as breathless as she felt.

She smiled. "No, silly. Next Christmas."

"I love you, you know."

Sheila pulled his face down for another soft kiss and whispered against his lips, "I love you, too."

Rhonda Gibson

Rhonda resides in New Mexico with her husband, James, her dearest friend and greatest supporter. She is thrilled that God is using the talents He gave her to entertain and share her love for Him. Her novel, *To Trust an Outlaw*, was awarded favorite historical romance of the year in 2007 from the readers of the Heartsong Presents. She feels blessed to have achieved such an honorary award. When not sitting in front of her computer writing, Rhonda enjoys making cards and jewelry for her family and friends. She also enjoys taking day hikes with her husband. Rhonda loves hearing from her readers, so please feel free to write her at PO Box 835, Kirtland, NM 87417. No time to write a letter? Visit her Web site at www.rhondagibson.com or read her blog at www.rhondgibson.blogspot.com.

Snowbound for Christmas

by Gail Sattler

Chapter 1

"Isn't that a snowflake you'd just love to add to your collection?"

Rochelle McWilliams steadied the large box in her arms as she stepped around a puddle on the sidewalk then pushed her scarf back up over her shoulder. "Very funny."

Her friend snickered. "It might be a little big. Maybe."

Rochelle stopped walking and looked up at the two-story-size snowflake gracing the upper floors of the ten-story building, appropriately named Snowflake Tower.

Whoever designed it had spared nothing. Despite the changing of the seasons, through rain, snow, sleet, hail, and burning hot summer sun, the snowflake always retained its white color, and the embedded sparkles danced brilliantly all year long.

Or so she was told. She'd only just moved to the town of Snowbound Village in the fall, one short month ago.

The larger-than-life snowflake on the tallest building in town was the first thing she'd noticed when she'd arrived. Which was probably the point.

"I know it's big, but I like it."

Kristi snorted. "You would. But then you're the only one I know who collects snowflakes." Kristi gently shook the large box she carried—box two of Rochelle's collection—to make her point. "Is that why you moved to Snowbound Village?"

"No." Rochelle flexed her still-sore shoulder and resumed walking toward the building. "Hurry up. I can't be late for work. I haven't completed my three-month probationary period."

Kristi ran to catch up. "They're not going to fire you because you were late one morning. You're the best receptionist they've ever had."

"And I'd like to keep it that way," Rochelle muttered as she bent her knees then aimed her elbow at the button that opened the door for people with handicaps—and people with their arms full.

She'd barely stepped into the lobby when she saw Patricia, her supervisor, in the waiting area.

"Rochelle! Kristi!" Patricia called across the room. "I have good news!" Her eyes met Rochelle's. "Maybe not good news for you, but certainly good news for the rest of us."

Rochelle's stomach tightened as she gently lowered her box to the seat of one of the puffy chairs. She usually got only one end of good-news/bad-news scenarios. It was never the good part.

"The building superintendent asked me to find someone to decorate the lobby for Christmas." Patricia eagerly picked open the tape on the box Kristi had been carrying then pulled up the flaps, nodding in approval at the contents. "So I immediately thought of what you've done around your desk."

Rochelle suddenly wondered if she'd overdone it by decorating her desk and the area around it with the favorites out of her collection. She split the tape on the other box. "What's the bad news?"

Patricia straightened then swept her arm in the air, encompassing the large room. "You have to be finished by tomorrow at 10:00 a.m."

You. The word echoed in Rochelle's head.

"Me? What do you mean, me?"

"After you did such a nice job decorating our office, he wants you to do the lobby."

"I—thought you—just wanted to—see my collection," Rochelle stammered.

"I did, but now that we're under a deadline for time, since it's here, I hope you can loan it to the maintenance division. I know it's your personal collection, but we don't have time to approve a budget for such a large purchase before tomorrow. I got a small budget for you to buy supplies and a few items, though. Then you can keep what you bought in exchange for the use of your collection. So that's more good news!" Patricia clapped her hands. "Now let's get back to work, ladies, so Rochelle can do her best job for that group of potential new clients. Word has it they're looking at leasing the entire eighth floor. Mindy will take the switchboard today, so all you need to do is decorate."

Without giving Rochelle a chance to comment, the other ladies disappeared into the elevator, leaving Rochelle alone with the security guard.

She stared at the elderly gentleman. "Why exactly does an

office building in a place like Snowbound Village need a security guard anyway?" she asked, not really expecting an answer.

The gray-haired gent shrugged his shoulders and patted the brim of his hat. "Probably because I asked Mackie if he had a part-time job for me. The big buildings in downtown Hartford have security guards, so he said we should do the same."

Great. A token security guard would be a significant deterrent to any potential criminal.

He peeked down into one of the open boxes. "Want some help?"

Rochelle glanced up at the stark, empty ceiling then back at the security guard. He didn't look very imposing, but he was taller than she was.

"Sure," she muttered. "Why not?"

❧

Kade Guildford guided his visitors through the mall and into the open doorway of Carly's Cookie Jar. "Would you like to sit over there?" He pointed to a small table in the corner.

When his guests nodded, he left his briefcase on the table to reserve it and joined them at the front of the shop. "Hi, Cindy," he said to the woman behind the counter who owned the store but wasn't named Carly. "I see you've already started decorating for Christmas."

Cindy nodded. "All our turkey cookies are gone, and we're into the Christmas trees."

Bert, the principal investor, quirked his eyebrow. "Turkey cookies?"

Cindy pointed to the corner. "See those two small tables? I thought it was a great idea to let kids decorate their own cookies because it gives the moms more time to sit and relax. Before Thanksgiving we made cookies shaped like turkeys and let the kids decorate them. Now that Christmas is coming, we have Christmas tree cookies. We call it the Kids' Corner."

"Makes sense to me."

Cindy smiled and poised her hand above the till. "What can I get for you today? Five coffees and what kind of cookies? I have a nice batch of gingersnaps ready to come out of the oven soon."

Kade reached for his wallet in the breast pocket of his suit jacket. He didn't want to buy into the Christmas commercialism, but it was already starting to surround him. Still, he needed to be gracious in front of his guests, who were eager to be into the so-called "joy of the season." "We'll each have a coffee and an already-decorated Christmas tree cookie. Then I'm going to show them the rest of the town."

Gwen, the only woman in his group, smiled with approval as they took their seats at the table. "This place is so quaint. Some of the cookie jars on the shelves look like they're antiques. And the old lace curtains are just the right touch."

Kade nodded. "This is called Village Mall. It's within walking distance of Snowflake Tower and bustles with people from the industrial district at lunchtime. Our downtown area is even better. The town council voted to keep the city's core quaint and old-fashioned, retaining most of its old-time-type shops. We'll go there next. I'll give you the tour of

Snowflake Tower tomorrow morning."

"Before we go downtown, do you mind if I go there?" Gwen pointed to the Christmas collectibles shop, Deck the Hall, across from where they were seated. "I want to buy something for my niece. I see something from here that would be perfect."

"Of course."

As they drank their coffee and ate the ornately decorated cookies, Kade answered their questions about the amenities of Snowbound Village and the benefits of moving their business out of downtown Hartford to Snowflake Tower. He did have to give them some advice about where they could do their Christmas shopping, but he managed to fulfill his agenda.

He left a generous tip on the table as they slipped their coats back on and guided the group into Deck the Hall, a place he had always avoided.

The three other men seemed mildly entertained, but Gwen turned into a shopaholic, picking up and touching everything on her way to the one item she supposedly wanted to buy. But since she was a potential client, Kade stood to the side, near a wire tree decorated with every size and color of tacky acrylic snowflake known to man, and told himself to be patient.

A short woman with messy brown hair hustled toward him. "Excuse me. I need these."

As he moved over, the woman began removing every snowflake from the display and piling them all in her shopping basket. "I know you don't work here, but have you seen any more of these anywhere?"

"No."

She hesitated at his sharp reply then looked up at him. "Don't I know you from somewhere? Wait. You work at Snowflake Tower, don't you?"

He couldn't help but smirk. "I guess you could say that."

"Have you been there a long time?"

"Yes, I have."

"Is Snowflake Tower really the tallest building in Snowbound Village?"

"Yes, it is." When the building was still in blueprint stages, the town council offered him a deal—a permit for more height in exchange for the snowflake on the side as a larger-than-life town logo. They wanted free advertising once they decided what they wanted to advertise.

Kade hadn't cared about the height, but they'd pushed him, saying the two additional floors of office space to rent out would be a good profit for him. It would once he actually got some tenants versus the expense of maintaining two empty floors, which wasn't easy in a small community. Yet the agreement had good potential. He would have preferred his own business's logo on the building, but for the town to prosper was in everyone's best interest, including his own.

The woman dropped the last of the snowflakes into her basket. "I heard the guy who owns the building is a real hard-nosed old coot, and he badgered the town council until they approved the height of the building." As she opened her mouth to say more, something beeped inside her purse. "Oops. I've got to go. I guess I'll see you back at the office. It was nice meeting you. 'Bye."

Before he could defend himself, she was gone.

Kade gritted his teeth. Instead of quarreling with his existing tenants' employees, he had to impress the potential tenants he needed.

Unfortunately the woman with the basket of snowflakes arrived at the lineup before Gwen, forcing him to spend more time standing among the outrageous conglomerations of commercial Christmas curios.

From a distance, he studied the woman as she emptied enough snowflakes to fill a truck onto the counter. Kade didn't recognize her, but the building did have ten floors, eight of which were occupied—he hoped it would soon be nine if his meeting went well. The woman appeared to be in an incredible rush and didn't slow down to yak with the clerk. This led him to conclude she hadn't been born and raised in Snowbound Village—she was a transplant, moved into Snowbound Village from one of the bigger cities.

She would soon meld into the local habits and lifestyles. He hoped she wasn't listening to the locals who hated the limited amount of progress that helped the town to grow, especially since he was responsible for some of it and he knew what they were saying.

Kade was also a transplant, moved to Snowbound Village from a big city.

When he first arrived, with the help of some good financial advisors, he'd made a number of very profitable investments. Now he was here to stay.

He hoped to convince this small group of representatives to do the same.

He intended to show them the whole town, but the bottom line would be that his building and its ambience would meet their requirements.

Kade was a big believer that a happy employee was a good employee. He did all he could to encourage employee morale. Just today he'd requested that the lobby be decorated for Christmas. Already it was being done, with Jake helping to speed things up. The timing was perfect. This group was very concerned with atmosphere, both for their employees and visiting clients.

In his mind's eye, Kade pictured a tastefully decorated Christmas tree in the corner of the lobby, perhaps with wrapped empty boxes placed beneath it to give the impression of hearth and home.

Everything would be ready and waiting for their arrival in the morning.

Chapter 2

K ade smiled as he held the door of the lobby open for his guests. "Welcome to Snowflake Tower. I think you'll find. . ." His voice trailed off as an amassed choreography of color and tidal wave of multifaceted reflections assaulted his senses.

"Wow," Bert mumbled. "You really do keep in theme with that huge snowflake on the outside of the building, don't you?"

Kade opened his mouth, but no sound came out.

Snowflakes of every size and color and every variation of texture and density hung everywhere.

Everywhere.

From the ceiling. From corners of the furniture. From the valances. From the doorways. Even the doorknobs.

Snowflakes twinkled and sparkled, dazzling the room more brilliantly than the Waterford crystal ball that was lowered down the flagpole in Times Square on New Year's Eve.

Paper snowflakes, plastic snowflakes. Foil. Knitted ones like his grandmother used to make. Snowflakes made of glue and glitter. Many were constructed of compounds he couldn't identify. In every color of the rainbow and then some.

Gwen blinked then broke out into a big grin. "I've never seen anything like this! It's magnificent!"

It was probably a fire hazard.

Kade turned his head.

A snowflake even hung from the fire extinguisher on its cradle in the corner.

The men nodded, probably unable to find words.

Kade's feet refused to move.

"Uh. . .I. . ."

Bert cleared his throat. Almost in unison, all five of them turned their heads to the corner by the elevator, where there actually was a decorated Christmas tree.

It paled in comparison to the snowflakes.

"You certainly keep in the spirit of Christmas, decorating around here. I can hardly wait to see the rest of the place."

"I can assure you, it won't be like this."

He hoped it wasn't like this.

It wasn't like this when he'd left yesterday morning.

The elevator door opened. Four ladies stepped out. The second they saw the snowflakes, they giggled. They didn't stop giggling while they traveled from the elevator through the lobby, where they ducked under some snowflakes and flicked others. They continued past Kade and his guests then made their way outside, still giggling as the door closed behind them.

Kade gritted his teeth then forced himself to smile.

"Let me take you up to the eighth floor. I think you'll like what you see." Where nothing was decorated. The only people who had an access code for the still-vacant floor were the janitor, security, and him.

As they crossed the lobby, even though he tried to duck, too many snowflakes were hanging to avoid them all. A few times, the other men laughed as they knocked snowflakes out of their way, which sent the pretty projectiles flying into Kade's face as they swung back. After being touched, many of the snowflakes had sprinkled down showers of glitter.

Kade made a mental note to call maintenance to clean up the mess on the floor before someone fell and sued for injury.

By the time they reached the elevator, more swinging snowflakes than he cared to count had poked him in the nose. Once inside, adding insult to injury, he tried to be as discreet as possible while he swiped a layer of glitter out of his hair.

When the elevator began to move, something stabbed his left eye, making it stream with tears. He needed to excuse himself to run to the men's room before the stray piece of glitter made its way underneath his contact and blinded him permanently. But he couldn't leave his guests unattended.

One lone snowflake hung in the center of the elevator. Taunting him. It was all he could do not to tear it down.

"Excuse me," he muttered as he turned around. Trying to be fast, Kade used the reflective metal panels in the elevator as a mirror to take out his left contact, which left him able to see clearly out of only one eye.

He turned once again toward his guests while he swiped his

eye with the back of his hand and tucked his contact lens into his shirt pocket.

"Don't do that." Frank reached into his pocket and pulled out a lens container. "Put it in here until you can clean it properly."

When the door opened to the empty eighth floor, he was still fumbling with Frank's case.

He'd wanted to give this group the best professional presentation he could—to show them a small town lacked nothing the larger cities had, except population density. And here he was, fooling around with contact lenses and snowy decorations. They probably thought he was another flake.

Kade gave them the best tour he could, closing his left eye whenever he needed to foucs, even though that left him with no depth perception. It took him three attempts to hit the correct code to get into the dedicated computer room, and only after he covered his left eye with his hand. Fortunately they paid more attention to the features and amenities than his lack of coordination.

"For a treat and the last benefit, let me show you the view. Snowflake Tower is the tallest building in town. You can see most of Snowbound Village from here."

As expected, they oohed and aahed at the cityscape that stretched out into the distance beneath them, for as much as Snowbound Village covered.

Of course Kade's office was in the penthouse, which was on the tenth floor. His view was the best of all. When he could see properly.

"Thank you for the tour, Kade. We'll have our shareholders meeting on Monday and get back to you on Tuesday with our decision."

"Great. Either way it's been a pleasure meeting you. Let me take you back to your hotel." Which meant another foray through the acrylic snowstorm.

This time he kept his distance from anything that glittered.

Driving was difficult but not impossible with one eye. Fortunately the hotel where they were staying was close, and it wasn't long before Kade was back at Snowflake Tower. Within minutes he would have relief from the burning in his eye, and he could ward off the headache that was starting to take hold. He had some solution and a spare set of contacts up in his office, and he couldn't get there soon enough.

He parked the car and headed to the building, but he only got as far as the front patio when the chimes of the antique clock at city hall began to echo their metallic melody in the distance, indicating noon. As soon as it started, a flood of people began their exit from the building, most likely on their way to the mall to have a hot lunch and do a little Christmas shopping on their break.

"Kade! Kade!"

He closed his left eye and scanned the crowd. Patricia, one of the managers from the third floor, waved as she approached him.

He wanted to get to his office, but he stopped to be polite.

"Have you seen the decorating? Isn't it great? I'd like to introduce you to someone."

Even though he couldn't focus properly, he saw enough.

Standing at Patricia's side was the woman he'd spoken with briefly inside the Christmas store at the mall.

At least she'd been on a work-related errand and not skipping out to do her Christmas shopping.

"Kade, I'd like you to meet Rochelle, my new receptionist and the genius behind all this winter wonderland."

Once again he forced himself to smile, hoping he looked more gracious than he felt. "Hello, Rochelle," he said as he clasped her hand and returned her handshake. "It's a pleasure to meet you." He cleared his throat. "Again."

Chapter 3

Rochelle's hand went limp inside Kade's firm grip as they exchanged greetings.

The way his smile didn't quite meet his eyes told her he wasn't all that pleased to meet her officially.

Patricia smiled up at Kade, who towered over her. "I see you two have already met."

"Yes. At the mall," Rochelle said as she slipped her hand out of Kade's.

Kade's brown eyes bored into hers. Then he looked through the window at the myriad of snowflakes she'd spent all day and half the evening hanging from the ceiling.

Patricia smiled at Kade while he stared into the lobby. "I heard the people who are thinking about leasing the eighth floor were impressed."

His jaw clenched in such a way Rochelle almost thought he was biting his tongue. He cleared his throat. "I hope so. Please excuse me. I need to get back to my office."

Instead of continuing on their way, Rochelle and Patricia

turned and watched Kade enter the building and make his way through the lobby. Because he was so tall, he walked around some of the lower-hanging snowflakes and ducked his head for others on his way to the elevator.

With the movement of air when the elevator door opened, the lone snowflake she'd hung there swooped up. At the moment Kade stepped inside, it began its descent, striking him in the forehead. His right arm swung up, his hand open, just about to grab it; then his body stiffened, and he froze without capturing it. Instead with his shoulders slumped, he turned, his hand lowered to cover one eye, and pushed a button on the panel, and the door closed.

Beside her, Patricia sighed. "Can you believe he usually takes the stairs to his office? He claims it's because he's too cheap to go to a fitness club, but I think it's because he doesn't want to tie up the elevator going up when people are waiting to go down."

Rochelle had become winded the only time she'd used the stairs instead of the elevator. She didn't know which floor he was on, only that it was above hers. "I'm impressed."

Patricia crossed her arms. "I'm actually surprised he took the elevator. He also seems to be in a pretty bad mood."

Rochelle didn't know what, for him, was good or bad. The man was obviously her boss's friend, as Patricia had spoken very fondly of him. Rochelle thought back to her short conversation with Kade at Deck the Hall before she knew who he was. She hadn't said much, but she hoped the old coot who owned the building wasn't his boss or, worse, his friend. She'd only repeated what she'd heard, but that didn't make it any less gossip. God's Word was clear about gossiping. This was a vivid reminder that again God was right.

She put Kade out of her mind as they resumed their journey to the mall. After buying hot dogs at a concession, Rochelle and Patricia began their search for more snowflakes. They returned empty-handed. There had been a sudden rush for snowflakes, and every store had them on backorder.

Throughout the day, as Rochelle worked and people went in and out, she heard many stories about snowflake decorations appearing throughout the building. She smiled at the thought of the office tower being filled with her favorite decorations.

The second she arrived home, the phone rang. The call display feature showed it was Elsie, the head of the church's social committee.

"Hi, Rochelle. You probably didn't know I work at Snowflake Tower, too."

Rochelle grinned. "I moved here to get out of the big city and into a smaller world, and now it's gotten even smaller. We'll have to meet for lunch one day."

"Yes, but I'm not calling about that. I heard you're the one who decorated the lobby. A few others on the committee saw it, and we all love it. We'd like you to decorate the church foyer and meeting room for our missions meeting on Saturday."

"But today is Thursday."

"I know. But we thought some pretty decorations would lighten everyone's hearts and get them thinking about the joy of Christmas and what it means to the children."

"I guess I could—"

"Great! I'll see you there. Bye."

As she hung up the phone, Rochelle stared at her empty closet. She'd taken her entire snowflake collection to work. Nothing was left except the decorations for her Christmas tree. A major complication was that however she decorated the church, she couldn't use anything that looked expensive. The purpose of the meeting was to raise money. New or lavish decorations wouldn't encourage people to donate. People kind enough to reach into their already overburdened pocketbooks needed to know their money was going to be used wisely and for the intended purpose, which was to buy gifts for the underprivileged children, not decorations for the meeting room.

If she hadn't used everything at work, she had many in her collection that would have been perfect for a missions meeting. She'd loved snowflakes from the time she was in kindergarten, and that was when people started giving her snowflakes of all shapes and sizes for gifts. She'd received hundreds of snowflakes, maybe even more than a thousand. Her favorites were the ones either handmade by friends and relatives or purchased from craft fairs.

She picked up the phone to call Elsie back to tell her she couldn't provide the decorations, when an idea hit her.

Many of her snowflakes were handmade for craft fairs that were fund-raisers.

She could make only a limited number herself in one day. But she knew where to find many ladies, and even some men, just like her, who would be delighted to help a charitable organization at Christmastime.

First she would have to run her idea past the old coot on the top floor. After the things she'd heard, she hoped and prayed he wasn't as big a scrooge as people said. Many people who were tightwads all year round had even a small bit of charity in them at Christmastime. She hoped he would understand. She had a job to do, and she was going to do it.

❧

Kade pulled the door of his private office closed behind him and turned toward Jodi. "I'm gone for the day. I'll have my cell set to voice mail and—"The rest of his instructions froze in his throat. "What is hanging from the light ballast?"

Looking down at the floor beneath the fluttering monstrosity was also some familiar residue—which he'd already experienced as a new form of assault weaponry.

Jodi smiled at him, innocent as could be. "It's a snowflake. It was so much fun to make! I haven't used glitter since I was in grade school. Isn't it pretty?"

"When did you do this?" he sputtered.

"On my lunch break. Someone organized a bunch of tables in the cafeteria. You should have seen us; it was almost like an assembly line. We must have made more than a hundred in just an hour."

He looked down at the mess of glitter on the floor. "This should have been run by maintenance. I can only imagine the mess in the cafeteria. Why wasn't I notified this was happening?"

Jodi's smile faded. "When the call came in, you were on another line, so I okayed it. I didn't think you'd mind. It's for one of those organizations that gives gifts to needy children. Everyone who gives money or donates a gift gets to keep a snowflake as a thank-you."

Kade mentally drew an imaginary circle on the floor around the hanging defense mechanism to keep himself and his eyesight safe.

He didn't mind the idea of doing something to help needy children, but he liked to know what was going on in his building, especially if there could be liability issues.

"Please don't tell me I'm going to find more of these," he said, pointing to the latest snowflake to cross his path.

Jodi nodded. "Of course you are. Everyone who helped got to keep one."

He didn't know who was responsible for this latest snowflake fiasco. But he did know where the idea originated. Exactly seven floors beneath him.

"I was trying to say, before I got distracted, I'm not coming in this weekend. I have a meeting on Saturday afternoon, and of course I'll be at church on Sunday."

Jodi pushed the button to put the phone on night service. "Of course. I'll see you Monday. If you wouldn't mind, could you hold the elevator for me, unless you're doing the stairs?"

"Not today. Now let's get out of here before I do something to that snowflake I'm going to regret."

Chapter 4

Rochelle smiled as she walked in the sunshine. It should have been warm, but a cold snap that morning signaled the start of winter temperatures. Since it was nearly December, that wasn't unusual. A bit of snow covered the ground already, which helped put her in the mood for Christmas. At this time of year, the snow probably wouldn't last, but she intended to enjoy it anyway.

Rochelle lifted her chin into the cold breeze as she approached the small church. Even though Hartford wasn't polluted, the air was fresher and cleaner here in Snowbound Village. She inhaled deeply to enjoy the fresh air, one of many benefits of moving to a small town.

When the meeting started, she would be involved in a group so small she could actually remember everyone's name. And they would remember hers.

Her church back in Hartford had been huge, with attendance of more than nine hundred people in the service. Just like in the impersonal downtown rush hour, she'd been completely lost in the crowd. She'd never been shy—just unable to connect with any one special person, male or female, feeling overwhelmed in the large group.

Here in small Snowbound Village, she'd already made friends. A real person had invited her to participate in some church functions, rather than just reading an announcement in the Sunday bulletin.

"Good morning, Rochelle. Are you here for the missions meeting?"

Rochelle nearly tripped when she thought she heard Kade's voice behind her. "Yes," she said over her shoulder as she slowed her pace. But when she turned, he wasn't there. It was another man she didn't recognize.

The man ran a few steps to catch up with her. "I thought I saw you here last week, but we hadn't officially met then."

The voice. It was him. But it wasn't.

Instead of a suit and tie with tooled leather shoes and a formal knee-length wool coat, he wore a brightly colored nylon ski jacket with snug, faded jeans and running shoes that had seen better days. He was also wearing glasses, which meant at the office he wore contacts.

The difference was so striking that if he hadn't spoken, she wouldn't have recognized him. She still barely recognized him. But then just because at the office he looked as if he'd stepped out of the pages of *GQ* didn't mean he was required to be the same away from work. Of course he had a personal life. Since it was the first time she'd seen him like this, she didn't know which she preferred, but he was very good-looking both ways.

"Elsie invited me to join," she stammered, getting her thoughts back to where they should have been.

"That must mean you haven't been attending Village Community Fellowship for very long."

"This is only my third week." As she continued to study him, recognition began to set in. He had been at the other church services she'd attended. Now looking at him, she remembered her friend Nicole had told her, without mentioning his name, that he was a very eligible bachelor but was difficult to get to know, and she hadn't introduced them. It didn't matter. Rochelle wasn't interested in dating until she was more settled anyway.

"Then please allow me the pleasure of being the first to welcome you to our Missions Outreach Committee."

Rochelle bit back a grin. Despite the casual attire, the professional manners appeared to be an ingrained part of him.

"Thanks. I really like it here." And she did. Everyone was so warm and friendly.

They stopped at the entrance to the church. Automatically Rochelle extended her hand, but Kade was quicker. He pulled the door open and stepped back for her to enter first in a gentlemanly gesture. For as little as she knew about him, she hadn't expected any less, despite the fact that she was perfectly capable of opening the door for herself.

"We're a few minutes early," he said as she stepped in ahead of him. "I wonder if whoever opened the building made coffee and—" His mouth dropped open then snapped shut as he took in the scene before him. "Not here, too!"

With the door held open, the snowflakes fluttered in the

breeze. The bright sunlight catching the glitter made the ceiling of snowflakes sparkle in a rainbow of happy colors.

Rochelle stiffened. "It's cheery and wintery."

He stomped inside, letting the door bang shut behind him. He strode to the nativity scene set up in the center of the room. "This is so wrong!" He extended his arm in the air. "This is supposed to represent the area around Bethlehem, where Jesus was born. Bethlehem is a desert. It doesn't snow in the desert. You've got to take this down."

"But Elsie said the committee wanted the lobby decorated. She said they liked what I did at work. I thought you were on the committee."

"I missed the last meeting."

"There weren't any pine trees in Bethlehem either. But Christmas trees are a huge part of Christmas."

"I can't explain that. But that doesn't make snow over the nativity scene any less wrong. As if I haven't seen enough of this in the last few days, now it's invading my place of worship."

"Why do pretty decorations bother you so much? It's not meant to be historically or geographically accurate."

"It just does. Okay?"

Rochelle didn't know what to say, so she said nothing.

"Rochelle!" a female voice called from the hallway. "I'm so glad you could come. Everyone loves your decorating."

"Not everyone," she muttered to herself.

Kade turned to Elsie, who had just walked into sight. "This is wrong. This isn't a winter wonderland at the mall. We're supposed to be celebrating the birth of Jesus Christ."

Before Elsie could respond, Kade made a beeline to the table in the corner and poured himself a cup of coffee. He grumbled something about "holiday madness" then stormed into the meeting room.

"I've never seen him like that," Elsie said softly. "Maybe he's had a bad day at the office."

Rochelle thought he had a lot of bad days. Her cheery snowflake decorating at the office tower hadn't brought a smile to his face there either. He couldn't possibly hate snow, living in a place called Snowbound Village.

Perhaps as a child, he'd cut himself while making snowflakes, and he'd been carrying around a lot of personal baggage over the years. Although she hadn't noticed any big scars on his hands.

She was thankful someone called the meeting to order, which pushed her thoughts of Kade and his hang-ups aside.

Until she was paired up with him to work in a booth in the mall as part of the group's efforts to seek donations from the community.

Starting immediately after the meeting.

She could hardly wait.

Chapter 5

Kade couldn't shake the feeling he was being watched.
When he finished hanging bows on the cardboard display where Rochelle couldn't reach, he turned to see her staring at him.

"Have you always been such a scrooge?"

"Excuse me?"

"I've never seen anyone hang messages about the joy of Christmas and be so grumpy."

"I'm not grumpy."

Her eyes narrowed.

Okay, so maybe he was a little grumpy. He'd joined the missions committee to do administration, and just administration, because he was good at public relations in the corporate world. Now here he was, thrust out on display in the middle of the mall with a tacky Santa hat on his head.

Elsie and the rest of the committee thought he'd be pleased to do something in public, that it would be good for his corporate image—as if they were doing him a favor.

He did fine for his corporate image inside his office. Outside the office, he wanted to leave it all behind.

"Do you hate kids or something?"

"I don't hate kids. I was one once."

She continued to stare at him like a bug under a microscope. Just like the one he'd had as a kid.

"Then do you hate Christmas?"

"I don't hate Christmas." What he hated was the world's obsession with parties and celebrations and throwing caution and good sense out the window for the sake of the alleged joy of the season.

"Then what do you hate?"

He opened his mouth, ready to tell her he hated nosy people who asked too many questions, but he stopped himself. They were here on a goodwill mission. His bad mood wasn't helping their cause. He suspected some people had avoided their booth because they were arguing.

He let out a long sigh. "Why don't I get us a couple of mochas? I'll be right back." Before she could agree or disagree, he left the booth for the coffee concession.

He didn't want to argue. He just wanted to be left alone, away from the noise and lunacy. All the artificial holiday joy only reminded him of why he didn't have the real thing.

Since it was Saturday, the lineup for people buying coffee was long, giving Kade more time to settle his thoughts and numb himself to the activity around him. By the time he returned to Rochelle and their booth with two steaming Peppermint Snowfall Mocha Delights, he'd managed to close his mind to everything except what they were there to do—seek donations for needy children.

Rochelle thanked him politely for the coffee but otherwise didn't speak.

Guilt for his earlier mood poked at him. She'd done nothing; he was the one with the issues concerning the idiocy surrounding them.

To ease the heaviness that had developed, he thought the best thing would be to get her talking. Just not about anything to do with Christmas.

"How long have you lived in Snowbound Village?" he asked while sipping the frothy coffee.

She smiled pleasantly, which made him feel forgiven for his earlier surly behavior. "Just over a month. I used to live in Hartford. What about you? Have you always lived in Snowbound Village?"

"No. I used to live in Rochester."

"They get a lot of snow there, don't they?"

"Yes, that's why I moved."

"To a place called Snowbound Village? To avoid snow? That's rather ironic."

"There's less snow here than there. This is closer to the coast." And much smaller, where you could see, at least most of the time, what was coming at you and be able to do something about it before it was too late.

"I have to admit, I like snow but not too much. Snow is fun for a child, but I hate having to drive in it when I'm on my way to work."

Kade's gut tightened. That was something else he didn't want to talk about. He sipped his coffee again to feign a nonchalance he didn't feel. "So why did you move?"

She stiffened from head to toe. "I don't want to talk about where I came from. I want to talk about where I'm going. Can I ask you a few questions about Snowbound Village?"

"Sure. I know a lot about the city." Before he'd moved his business and built his office tower, he'd done a very detailed demographic study. He knew more about Snowbound Village than most people who had lived there all their lives.

"I saw a family of raccoons in the field by my house. Do you think they have a nest or a den nearby? Should I be concerned? I know in Hartford they were considered pests, but I like to let them do their thing and live together. Here both of us seem to have plenty of room. In Hartford, the pest-control people trapped them."

"Yes, they live here. If they're making a mess in your garbage, then enclose the container, and they'll just move on to easier pickings elsewhere. I don't believe in trapping them either."

"I also saw some birds, so I put out feeders. They're so pretty. They're a beautiful blue color with an orange blush on their chest, maybe even their wings. It was hard to tell; they flew away so fast. Do you know what they are? I'd like to look them up, but I don't know what they're called. I want to build them a birdhouse, but I don't know what kind to make."

Kade blinked. "I have no idea. I can tell you all about population growth and density and where they've zoned for urban renewal and what they have designated as heritage sites.

I can tell you what year the city hall building was constructed, where they're going to build a new rec center, the average-size single family dwelling in Snowbound Village, and the average number of residents per home. But I honestly can't say much about the wildlife."

"Oh. Never mind then."

Strangely he felt disappointed in himself, which was ridiculous. He was helping people feed themselves by providing jobs, which was more important than the sparrows. Yet God also remembered the sparrows and cared for them, too.

A family arriving with a donation saved him from having to be concerned about the ecosystem and economic liability within his realm of responsibility. The interruption allowed him simply to think of the joy of a child opening a gift on Christmas morning he or she otherwise would not have received.

A little girl with the cutest smile boldly lifted a box containing a new doll and set it on the table. "I have a dolly just like this at home. So I want to give the same dolly to someone who will love her as much as I do. I think that's a great present. And I helped pay with my allowance."

Kade leaned down so he didn't tower over the little girl when he spoke. "That's very nice and very generous. I know this doll will make someone very happy, all because of you."

He didn't know exactly how much the little girl contributed, but he was touched that she'd donated her own money and was happy to give something she considered special to someone less fortunate. Although he had never seen the family before, he wanted to take the parents aside to tell them how special their daughter was, but he was trapped behind the table where it was too far to speak privately.

The family watched Rochelle wrap the box in shiny pink paper, smiling as she scissor-curled the ribbon for a final touch.

"Thanks for your donation," Rochelle said as she gave them a snowflake, the same kind Jodi had hung outside his office. "These snowflakes were made exclusively as a thank-you for people who donated. Have a merry Christmas, and may God bless you and your loved ones."

The family walked away then stopped to talk to another family, pointing to their booth as they held up the snowflake for everyone in the group to see.

"You have a thing about snowflakes, don't you? I'm seeing them everywhere I turn around. Is that why you looked for a job in a place called Snowflake Tower?"

Rochelle laughed, and it was a delightful sound. "Indirectly, yes. My first day in town, when I drove into the industrial area, I couldn't resist going into the tallest building around with the snowflake on the side. The lady at the information counter said they were hiring on the third floor. Patricia interviewed me and hired me on the spot. The rest is history. I guess you know Patricia."

"Yes. I know most of the people in the building, by face if not by name."

Her smile faded. "Before I forget, I want to take back that 'old coot' comment I made the first time we met. I was just repeating what I'd heard, and that was wrong. I realized it was unfair of me to base my opinion on hearsay. It was wrong of me, and I'll never do that again."

He opened his mouth to tell her that her apology was accepted, but before the words came out, a little boy approached the table and pushed a toy truck toward him.

"Can you wrap this for a little boy who doesn't have any other presents?" Behind the boy, his parents smiled proudly.

Kade accepted the truck. "Of course I can." *Maybe.* He hadn't wrapped a gift for many years, perhaps not in his entire adult life. Rochelle made wrapping appear easy, but he found out the hard way it was tougher than it looked. His finished job looked like something a child had done. His cheeks grew warm as he passed it to Rochelle to fix, causing the donors to chuckle. As Rochelle worked, Kade graciously gave the family a snowflake, and they were on their way.

"Pardon me for saying this, but this is really bad," Rochelle said as she straightened his cut edge and refolded the paper. "I don't think what's under your tree on Christmas morning is a worthy photo op."

"I don't wrap gifts." The corporate gifts he gave, Jodi wrapped. The few personal gifts he gave were gift cards, which didn't require wrapping.

"Let me guess. You do all your shopping online with direct delivery or gift cards."

"It's efficient."

She paused in her final touch-ups to the wrapping and looked up at him with sad, soulful eyes.

"What?" he asked, seeing a conversation he didn't want to start.

"Nothing," she muttered and turned her concentration back to her wrapping, which was fine with him.

"I think people are starting to notice our booth. I see another couple of groups coming with toys for us."

Her face brightened, which was a relief. "Great! I hope we get so many donations we run out of wrapping paper."

"That would be nice. Tell you what. We'll save paper if you do the wrapping and I give out snowflakes."

"I have a better idea. Watch what I do, and when it's your turn, just do it slowly." She accepted another donation then explained every step as she measured paper, cut, folded, taped, and applied the ribbon as a finishing touch.

Kade had a bad feeling it was going to be a long day.

Chapter 6

R ochelle, Kade. Can I see you both for a minute?"
Rochelle turned and made her way around a couple of children who were sitting in the middle of the church's foyer comparing their Sunday school projects. Kade also broke away from a small group of people, heeding the pastor's request.

Rochelle took advantage of arriving first and spoke. "Pastor, I want to tell you the service was lovely. It's a joy to make this my new church home."

Pastor Harry returned her smile. "It's a pleasure having you. I wanted to tell you both that the donations we received yesterday were beyond expectations. Those handmade snowflakes are encouraging people to tell others, and donations are already ahead of last year. We expect to run out of snowflakes. In fact, I hope we run out."

Rochelle couldn't hold back her smile as she looked first at the pastor then at Kade. "It was fun making them. I had help from a very special group of people. I'd think they'd be more than happy to help make more." First thing Monday morning, Rochelle would phone Jodi and let her know how much the snowflakes helped and ask Jodi to thank her boss for allowing them to use the cafeteria for a workplace. "What do you think, Kade? Would you like to join us during the lunch break on Monday to make more?"

For a split second, he stiffened. "I'll pass. Now if you'll excuse me."

Before anyone had a chance to say more, Kade walked away and left the building.

"Is he always like this?" Rochelle asked.

Pastor Harry shook his head. "Not really."

"Meaning?"

The pastor sighed; then his shoulders sagged. "He's usually very pleasant, although he tends to be a bit distant. After knowing him for about four years, I've noticed he gets moody right after Thanksgiving. This year seems worse for him. I wish I could do something, but he won't talk about it."

Rochelle could certainly agree. They hadn't started out well. It wasn't difficult to figure out he was struggling with something deeply personal and painful. Yet he'd been much better when he came back with the mochas. A few times, she'd tried to reach out to him without being sappy, but he hadn't reached back. "He doesn't talk about much actually."

All through the service, Rochelle had become distracted, watching Kade. He wasn't unfriendly; he spoke when spoken to, but he seldom initiated a conversation. He seemed to join randomly with people he knew, but he never stayed long.

She hadn't found out if he was simply alone or lonely. She suspected it was a bit of both. She also knew it was worse during the Christmas season when a person didn't have family or a circle of close friends nearby.

Often all it took was for one person to reach out, but sometimes no one did.

"He knows a lot of people, and he does a lot," Pastor Harry said, "but he makes a lot of people nervous. They don't know what to say to him."

Rochelle nodded. "I can understand that." In addition to the fact that he didn't talk much, his secret-identity persona would be unnerving to many. He was almost two different people—the contacts with the power suit at the office, and outside work, the glasses and more-than-casual clothes to blend into the background like Mr. Joe Ordinary.

Except he could never be ordinary. He had an inner strength that set him apart; yet he cared deeply for people, especially the children. It was obvious he hadn't felt comfortable in the booth, for whatever reasons. But whenever a family with children came with a donation, he'd softened like the Pillsbury Doughboy. He'd even blushed.

Except he was in far better shape than the Pillsbury Doughboy. During the course of the afternoon, they'd bumped a few times while wrapping or reaching for the same thing. He didn't have an ounce of dough on him.

His habit of using the stairs instead of the elevator worked. She didn't know how many flights he climbed, but whatever the number, it did make him a superman.

"I wonder. He seems to know a lot about Snowbound Village, and I don't know anything. Maybe I should ask him to show me around."

"You were okay with him in the booth, weren't you?"

"Yes. He was very pleasant to talk to, even though it was difficult to get him started. But he did seem to enjoy talking about the town's history, and that's what I'd like to know."

"Then that's a great idea. You would get an education on our fair city better than anywhere else, and he won't be alone through the Christmas season. He's a busy man, but I suspect he spends most evenings home alone. That's not a good thing during the holiday season. I have an idea." Pastor Harry pulled his cell phone out of his pocket and hit one of the buttons.

Rochelle began to step away to give him some privacy, but he motioned her to stay. "I've got Kade on my speed dial. He's our treasurer, so I phone him a lot." He waited a few seconds. "Kade, it's me. I need a favor. Rochelle has been here a month, and no one has offered to take her around town. I was wondering if you could show her some highlights. Great. Thanks."

Pastor Harry flipped his phone shut. "He said he'd be more than happy to show you around. He suggested driving around town and showing you the historic buildings."

Rochelle liked that idea. Seeing the older area of town would be a good start. On Monday back at work, she'd keep a lookout for him, and they could decide which evening worked best.

The pastor checked his watch. "He said he'll be at your house in a half hour."

Chapter 7

There, just after that big tree, is the city hall. It's an historic building and declared a heritage site. Too bad it's Sunday, because it's closed today. It's got an atrium that's really spectacular. In a minute, we'll get to the town square. It's been all set up with Christmas lights and decorations, so you should like it."

"Look! A horse and carriage."

Kade nodded and slowed the car so Rochelle could see better. "This time of year, some of the locals who own a horse make a little extra money taking people through the quaint part of the historic area. Since it's the weekend, you'll see a lot of them out today. There will be even more as it gets closer to Christmas."

He hoped she wouldn't suggest they hire one and take a ride. Sitting behind the wheel of his car while she sat with her face nearly plastered to the passenger-side window was close enough for him.

He didn't know why he'd agreed to show her around except

that he liked going through the older part of town. He'd always been fascinated with the history and liked sharing what he had learned.

So he wouldn't tie up traffic behind him, Kade pulled off to the side of the road. "The city hall building used to be a library on the ground level with the chamber of commerce meeting room on the second floor. The story goes that one day, thirty-something years ago, the clock stopped. The council decided to fix the clock for the millennium celebration, but after being silent for three decades, the hourly chimes were suddenly disruptive to the silence of the library. So they packed up the books, and now the whole building is the city hall."

The clock had been fixed before he'd moved into town. Every day he'd listened to the familiar song—regular and predictable. The consistency had helped settle his spirit when he needed it. Since he was in the penthouse, most days he still stepped out onto the roof to stand alone on the pad next to the helicopter, eyes closed, temporarily removing himself from the rest of the world just to listen to the clock strike noon.

"What happened to the library?"

"It's a couple of blocks from the mall. Far away from the clock. In a brand-new building."

Kade was about to ask if she wanted to go there, when Rochelle turned and smiled at him. All his thoughts froze.

"Can we get out and watch the clock strike? It's nearly 2:00."

"It's not like a cuckoo clock. It doesn't do anything. It just makes noise."

"It's not the same from the car. Please?"

He couldn't refuse. Not only that, he didn't want to refuse.

After he parked, they waited beside one of the old-style globed lampposts. Snowbound Village wasn't exactly a tourist mecca, so he suspected they looked a little foolish standing in one spot, watching a clock that wasn't going to do anything but ring out.

Then she pulled a camera out of her purse.

Kade smiled. He'd done the same thing when he'd first moved to Snowbound Village. The historic building and its unique construction fascinated him. It still did.

"If you want to get a better angle, we can—"

She waved her hand in the air to hush him. "Shh. It's about to chime. I'm going to take a video, so I can record it. No talking, please."

He'd just taken pictures. One of which had won first place in a local photography contest.

He remained respectfully quiet until the music and the chimes were finished. "I don't think you got much background noise," he said as she lowered the camera.

"It doesn't matter. It's just for me. I often listen to the chimes from outside the office at lunchtime. I've never known where it came from."

He pictured Rochelle standing by the door of Snowflake Tower while he was on the roof, both listening to the same thing, just like an old cartoon he remembered from his childhood. As he recalled, two mice separated by miles both looked at the moon at the same time, thinking of each other.

Kade blinked. He didn't want to think of such sentimental nonsense.

He turned to Rochelle. "Since we're out of the car, would you like to walk past the old shops? Most of them are open. This is their busiest time of the year." Not that he wanted to go inside or even window-shop. He simply wanted to walk past then go home.

"Sure. I'd like that."

As they walked, he told bits of history and trivia on their way to the town square. Village Mall was closer to the office, but this was the area of town he loved.

"What's this place? It looks like an old house."

He smiled. "You're right. It's an old Victorian that's been converted into a restaurant called The Laurel House. A charming older couple own and operate it." He'd met Bob and Ellen Laurel years ago, just after they'd opened the restaurant. When he'd presented his proposal for the town's highest office tower, the majority of the chamber members simply agreed to give him what he wanted because he was the biggest employer in town. But Bob and Ellen stopped the discussion, suggesting he not put the tower on the edge of the historic older section as he wanted but in the growing industrial area. They'd been right, but what had impressed him the most was that they were the only ones with courage to confront him, even though at the time they were only a two-person operation and outnumbered in the crowd. "Do you want to go in for something to eat? They serve everything from macaroni and cheese to filet mignon. Something for everyone, at a reasonable price."

"No, thanks. It's midafternoon, and I'm not hungry. I'd much rather keep walking. Unless you're hungry."

"I'm good. Besides, that gives us more time at the town square. I read in the local paper that the nativity display is all set up." He'd wanted to see it, and taking Rochelle was a good excuse to go.

Sure enough, it was the highlight of their trip. In the center was the town's pride and joy of the Christmas season—a large and very beautiful nativity scene, created by local artists.

"It's magnificent!" Rochelle covered her mouth with one hand and giggled. "It's also surrounded by snow."

"This snow is real. This is Connecticut. It's December. It can't be helped."

He led her closer, toward the ceramic sheep that surrounded the manger where Baby Jesus lay. "Every year they add one more piece to the set. This year they added this sheep at the side. It was made by a guy who—"

Before he could explain further, a teen on a skateboard roared behind them. The boy jumped with the board then flung his arms to the side to land. When the skateboard touched the ground, one of the wheels skimmed a seam in the cement, causing it to dip to one side. The boy's elbow whacked Rochelle in the shoulder as he corrected his landing, and he sped onward.

"Rochelle? Are you. . ." His words trailed off. The boy hadn't appeared to hit her hard, but Rochelle hunched over, curled her shoulders, and pressed into her right shoulder with her left hand. Her face was nearly white, and she gritted her teeth so hard that lines formed around her mouth.

Kade curled his arm around her waist and held her against

his chest to support her. He didn't know whether he should move her to a nearby park bench or call an ambulance.

"What happened?" he whispered in her ear. "What can I do?"

"Nothing," she ground out between her teeth. "Just don't move for a minute."

Even through the layers of clothing, he felt her breath come in short gasps. He wanted to do more, but all he could do was hold her until it was over.

Gradually her breathing slowed and deepened to normal.

"What happened?" he asked, not wanting to release her until she confirmed she could stand.

"Just over a month ago, I had a shoulder separation. The doctor told me it could take two to three months to be back to normal. I'm finding out the hard way he was right."

He waited, but she didn't volunteer any more information. Maybe it was sports related, but maybe not. Either way he didn't like the thought of Rochelle being hurt. He couldn't help but like her, even if she did have a strange affinity for tacky snowflakes. What he liked most of all was that she was one of very few people with the strength of character to stand up to him and not be afraid to speak her mind.

Right now he wanted to speak his mind and grab the kid who bumped her and wring his scrawny neck. He would work on forgiveness later when he wasn't holding Rochelle and he could think more clearly. "Maybe I should take you home?"

"I hate to let this spoil the day. I'll be fine."

He didn't think she was, but he did know something that usually made anyone of the female gender feel better. "I don't mind if you want to do a little shopping as we go." As soon as the words came out of his mouth, he wondered if an alien had taken over his brain or at least his good sense. He hated shopping, and he hated it more at Christmas.

"I'm not in the mood for shopping. I'm in the mood for sightseeing."

Slowly he released her. "Okay, I'm good with that. But if you do want to stop, just make me one promise."

She looked up at him. "Maybe."

"Promise me you won't buy any more snowflakes."

"Ha. Never. Now let's go."

Chapter 8

Patricia slowed her step and poked at the new snowflake hanging in front of Rochelle's desk. "Another one? I thought you didn't have any left."

Rochelle nodded while she hit SAVE. "I didn't. Kade bought it for me yesterday."

Patricia stopped.

"Kade? This is a joke, right?"

If it was a joke, then the joke was on her.

"We were walking through that cute little area around the town square when I saw it hanging in one of the store windows. I wouldn't have stopped, but Kade saw me looking, and he bought it for me. Of course he didn't let me browse through the rest of the store, but I didn't need to. It was the only thing I wanted."

"What were you doing there with Kade?"

"We go to the same church. Pastor Harry asked him to show me around town, so he did."

"Just like that? I'm impressed."

"Don't be. It's not like it was his own idea."

Patricia didn't look convinced, but Rochelle knew otherwise. She wanted to tell her so, but the phone rang.

She answered with the company's rehearsed greeting and was shocked to hear Kade's voice respond.

Patricia was standing only a few feet away, obviously listening, so Rochelle turned her head for privacy.

"Hi, Rochelle. Pastor Harry just called me. Sasha and Jason just canceled what they were doing for the Christmas Eve service because they were invited out of town. Pastor Harry said you played the guitar. Maybe the two of us could do something."

"I'm flattered. But I'm not very good."

"Neither am I, but he's desperate. Everyone else is already doing something or won't be there."

"Doesn't that keep me humble?"

"Same. But we belong to a small church. If it were bigger, people like you and me wouldn't be asked."

Regardless of his claim, she suspected Kade was better than he let on. "Have you got anything in mind?"

"No. If you don't have any ideas, we could go through what's at the church."

She thought of her meager music collection. "That's a good idea. How does 7:00 sound?"

"Great. See you there."

❧

While she waited for the elevator, Rochelle glanced at the door to the stairs. The elevator had been waiting on the sixth floor for a long time, making her consider using the stairs as Kade often did.

She checked her watch. She had less than a half hour to go home, change, eat something, and get to the church to meet him.

Finally the elevator light indicated it had started again. Still, she was going to be late.

The elevator door swished open. Inside was a man with a handcart loaded high with boxes and a pile beside him.

And Kade. Wearing the power suit with the expensive coat—and his glasses.

She'd seen him briefly during her lunch break in the cafeteria. Thanks to Jodi, she'd organized another snowflake-making session. Kade had walked past, so she'd asked if he wanted to join them since a couple of men were in the group. Everyone had gone strangely silent; he'd politely declined and excused himself.

He quirked his eyebrow. "Now I don't have to worry about being late. You're just as late as I am."

"Patricia needed me to stay for something urgent. What about you?"

"Brad needed to talk to me, and we lost track of the time. Then when UPS arrived earlier than expected, he asked me to help pack some things he wanted to be shipped for the trade show."

Rochelle had never met Brad, but Patricia had told her all about him. Brad, the owner of the business on the sixth floor, had a bad reputation for requiring his employees to stay late often, especially his department managers.

She looked up into Kade's eyes. They were bloodshot, and he'd already taken out his contacts and put on his glasses, something she'd never seen him do at the office. He also wasn't standing quite as straight as usual.

Until now, she hadn't known exactly where Kade worked in the building, but now she knew why he put in such long hours. Patricia had said Brad was a hard boss, but he paid well when a person worked hard and met his expectations, which Kade obviously did.

She admired Kade's dedication, although she didn't like the way the job was wearing him down. Today had been another long day for him, because he was leaving at the same time; yet he always arrived much earlier every morning than she did.

When the door opened on the main floor, instead of walking to his car, Kade stepped to the back of the elevator and picked up a box from the stack, while the UPS man maneuvered his cart over the bump then continued outside. Seeing he intended to finish his job of getting the boxes in transit quickly, Rochelle stepped outside the elevator, set her purse on the floor, and held out her hands to help.

"You probably haven't eaten anything yet," Kade said as he handed her the first box. "How would you like to take one car and pick up a couple of burgers or something and go straight there?"

"But I have to go home and get my guitar, and so do you."

"I had a feeling I was going to be late tonight so my guitar is in my car. We can make a quick stop at your house to get yours and keep going."

"It's funny you know where I live, but I don't know where you live."

"I don't want my address to be public record in the church directory."

"I'm not in the directory. I'm too new to the church."

"I'm the treasurer. I see your address every week."

She wouldn't have agreed except she was low on gas, and filling up was one more thing that would take more time than she had. "Okay, let's do that," she said as she stacked the last box on top of the pile.

She didn't have to ask which car was his. Nor did she have to ask where he'd parked. On her way in this morning, she'd noticed it was parked in the very first space. She found it odd but rationalized it to small-town living. In a bigger city, the first spot would have been reserved for Jodi's boss. She'd also found out from Patricia that not only did MGE Enterprises own the building, but the same company also owned and ran the battery factory next door, which was now the biggest employer in town.

Apparently the owner was a financial genius. After relocating from a larger city nearby, he'd made a huge difference in the economy of the town in just a few years. One day she would meet this prodigy; the one time she'd gone up to the office he hadn't been there, and she couldn't stay because Kade had been waiting for her downstairs.

She strode back to the elevator and dragged a box into the path of the laser light that prevented the door from closing. "Come on. If we're too late, Pastor Harry will be gone, and we won't be able to get in."

Kade pulled his keys out of his pocket. "Did you forget? I'm the treasurer. I have my own key. We can stop for something to eat first. I know a great little place that has good food, and it's ready fast. I also know a shortcut, so I'll drive."

Chapter 9

Kade adjusted the tuning on his D string then strummed an A-major chord, letting it ring out in the empty room. He closed his eyes to enhance the sensation of the resonance around him.

His guitar was only of average quality and workmanship, but here it sounded better than anywhere or anytime he'd played. He didn't know why he'd never thought of this. After Christmas, when his life was back to normal, he would do this again many times until the floor was rented and the building was full. Or maybe he didn't have to be in such a rush to lease the last vacant level, now that the eighth floor was rented and awaiting its new tenants.

He opened his eyes and watched Rochelle in the chair beside him, also tuning her guitar. Because he was left-handed and his guitar flipped the opposite way from hers, they were sitting so close they were nearly touching.

The empty room was quite chilled, the thermostat turned down for energy conservation. Wearing a full suit, he wasn't uncomfortable. Rochelle, though, like most of the women in the building, wore just a blouse and pants. From her slightly jerky movements, he could see she was cold. He wanted to open his suit jacket, wrap it around her, and hold her close until the room warmed up. They wouldn't be able to practice all snuggled together, but he could dream.

In the past few weeks, something had changed. He didn't know what; he only knew he couldn't go back to the way things had been before. He wanted to keep seeing Rochelle, even though he didn't have a reason except that she worked in his building.

He lightly strummed an E7 then A major. "I'm all tuned up. You?"

Head lowered, Rochelle also lightly strummed the same two chords, listening closely.

She nodded, her head still bent. "I'm ready to rock 'n roll."

"I don't think 'O Holy Night' is quite rock 'n roll."

She raised her head and grinned at him. "I know. But I've always wanted to say that."

"Me, too. You should have seen the looks I got this morning, coming in with my guitar slung over my shoulder. Everyone looked at me as if I were cracking up."

Rochelle's grin dropped. "You know, the same thing happened to me, except it was really strange. People I've never met before stopped and stared at me, and I don't know why."

"Maybe because people don't usually go to work with a guitar?"

"Probably. Didn't Jodi have a great idea? The acoustics in

here are spectacular. Much better than my little living room. Jodi even got the security guy to bring us these chairs. I'm going to make an extraspecial snowflake to thank her."

And he would be giving Jodi a bigger Christmas bonus than originally planned. "Your living room isn't little. It's very nice. It suits you." Her whole house suited her. It was small but homey and, most important, comfortable.

His own house was too big and too looming. He'd been too easily convinced to contract a big executive-style home that was supposed to match his lifestyle and his position. But he didn't have a big family or a couple of large pedigreed dogs, nor did he ever entertain.

Most days he spent his time alone, using only a few rooms. The housekeeper who came in weekly spent more time in the rest of the house than he did. Besides the housekeeper, he didn't like having people over, because the house felt pretentious with the marble entryway and spiral staircase leading up to even more rooms no one used. The designer had insisted on a grand piano in the sitting room, and he'd bought one, intending to take lessons then never did. All he could play was "Chopsticks." Badly. Which was why they'd been practicing at Rochelle's house and not his.

"We've got to start," Rochelle said as she checked her tuning one last time. "I left for my lunch break a few minutes early so I could go up the elevator before everyone else started going down. What about you?"

"I'm flexible."

She leaned toward the music stand and pointed to the

section they'd had trouble counting out. With one finger resting on the page, she turned to him. "I've been meaning to ask you something. What's with the contacts and the glasses? Why do you switch like that?"

"I've got an astigmatism that's right at the point where my optometrist wasn't sure if I could wear contacts. I'm trying a new brand that's better. But my eyes still feel too dry after a while, and sometimes my vision gets blurry, so I don't like to drive with them. I wear the contacts at work then glasses when it's time to go home."

"And this has nothing to do with vanity?"

He cringed inwardly. "Ouch. You're subtle."

"If you have so much trouble with the contacts, why do you bother? Don't get a swelled head or anything, but you look good in glasses. In fact, I think the glasses make you look more distinguished."

"In other words, geeky."

"You say that like it's a bad thing. Geeks rule the world, you know."

"They didn't when I was a kid. I was teased mercilessly. I was the studious type who couldn't see two feet in front of me without my glasses, and the school bully wouldn't leave me alone. It only stopped when I got taller than everyone else and started lifting weights. But by then, I'd already made up my mind. No matter what, I was getting contacts." He leaned closer toward her. "Anything else you want to know?"

When her eyes widened, it made him realize how close they were.

Only six inches apart, there was nothing wrong with his vision now. Everything was crystal clear, maybe more clear than ever. Rochelle was the most beautiful person he'd ever met, inside and out.

Starting with her deep, sea green eyes. Along with soft, pretty lips, just right for kissing.

He wanted to kiss her. Right now. Before it was too late. Soon he wouldn't have a reason to see her multiple times a week. Even now he needed more than to be with her at the missions booth at the mall and practicing guitars twice a week. He wanted to see her every day and not just in the elevator.

Slowly he brushed his fingertips over the tender skin of her cheek. At his touch, her eyes began to flicker shut.

His heart pounded as if he were running up the stairs. He leaned forward, and their lips met.

They were as warm and soft as he imagined. Warmer. Better.

He tilted his head for more.

She jerked back. "I think we should play a C# minor seventh on that bar."

Kade stiffened. He didn't know what happened, other than he'd just been poleaxed.

Rochelle grabbed a pencil and changed the chord on the page, frantically scribbling out the old chord much more than necessary.

He reached and covered her hand with his before she tore a hole in the paper. "Rochelle. Stop. I shouldn't have done that."

She swiped her hand through her hair then turned to face

him. A thick pause hung between them. He struggled to think of something to say, but his mind was completely blank. He probably should have said he was sorry, but he wasn't.

He cleared his throat, hoping his voice would come out sounding normal but knowing it wouldn't. "Maybe we should start again. I know you enjoyed the tour of the historic district. Can I give you a tour of the rest of the town tonight? A lot of houses are set up with a galaxy of lights. Would you like that?"

"Uh. . .I guess so."

"Good. Let's leave your car here. We can pick up something quick for supper and go from there."

"Uh. . .I guess. . . ."

"Then it's settled. Now where were we? Let's pick it up from the top and nail down the intro."

Chapter 10

O f all the things Rochelle had imagined they would have done, this was not on the list.

Kade pointed to a smaller tree at the end of the row. "What about this one?"

Next to the huge trees in this lot, it looked as if it had been uprooted and bundled too soon, but for her, it was perfect. "I like it. It's a good size for my living room. I don't know how to thank you. I don't remember the last time I had a real tree for Christmas."

He shook off the fresh snow then picked up the tree to carry it to the gate. "Then consider it my treat."

Kade paid the lot attendant, and the two men hoisted the tree to the top of Kade's car.

He had taken more pleasure from the historic background of the downtown tour than the cheerful Christmas decorations. Likewise, he'd given a good tour of the homes in Snowbound Village that were elaborately decorated, but he'd been more fascinated with the newer LED lights and how much power they saved than the actual displays.

Now he'd bought her a live tree that after Christmas she would plant outside and it would last forever.

The live trees were far more expensive than the cut ones, which made her wonder even more why he'd bought it. In church he was quiet and reverent and truly celebrated Christmas for the birth of Jesus Christ. But once he left church, he didn't seem to like Christmas at all.

Yet he had just bought her a tree.

While the two men tied down the tree, Rochelle's attention wandered to the pristine layer of new snow in the empty lot beside the parking lot.

"What are you thinking?" Kade asked as he checked the knots. "You have a faraway look on your face."

"I was thinking of when I was a kid. My brother and I would go into the backyard and make snow angels. My parents have a half acre on the outside of town. When there was enough snow, we used to make a whole choir of angels."

"If you want to make one now for old times' sake, go ahead."

Rochelle automatically rubbed her sore shoulder. "Not this year. I'm not sure I should move my arm like that yet."

In an instant, Kade was at her side. He placed one hand on her shoulder and gently pushed into the sore spot, massaging it with his thumb. "I wish I could do something. What happened? I'd like to know."

Even though it was now nearly two months, she shrank inwardly at the memory. He must have felt her cringe, because both his arms wrapped around her, making her feel secure and protected.

If only he'd been with her that day. If she hadn't been alone, then it wouldn't have happened.

She kept her head down, not wanting to see his face as she spoke. "It was one of those bizarre things you read about in the paper, and it was in the paper. There had been a big traffic tie-up in the afternoon rush hour downtown. People were getting more and more impatient as we moved a few inches, stopped, then waited some more. I was at an intersection, and the light turned yellow. Since the traffic wasn't really moving, and I didn't want to be stuck in the middle of the intersection when the light turned red, I stopped."

"That's what you were supposed to do. Did you cause an accident?"

"No. But the guy behind me wanted me to go. He started honking his horn and making obscene motions, and when I didn't go, he lost it. He got out of the car and stormed up to me and was yelling and swearing. I started to roll up the window, but that made him even madder. He reached in and grabbed my shoulder and started shaking me. No one was getting out of their cars, and I was really scared. I couldn't get him to let go, so I started honking the horn. He flew into an unbelievable rage and grabbed my arm so I couldn't honk anymore.

"Then, just like something you see in a movie, he pulled out a knife. I froze. I thought he was going to slit my throat. He sliced through my seat belt, braced his foot on the door of my car, and pulled me through the window. That gave me a shoulder separation."

Kade's body stiffened from head to toe. "How badly were you hurt?"

"Besides the shoulder injury, I was pretty scraped up from landing on the pavement. I've never been so scared in my life. I thought he was going to kill me. Fortunately a bunch of people finally started getting out of their cars. God must have been watching out for me. One of the people was an off-duty police officer, and he had a gun. That made the guy back off really fast."

"What happened? Was he thrown in jail? Has he been stalking you? Is that why you moved?"

She shook her head. "He was charged with assault, but he had a good lawyer. Even though I had plenty of witnesses, they gave him a lower charge by calling it road rage. It was a first offense, so he got to serve his sentence on weekends if he took an anger management course. I went back to work, but every day when I got stuck in traffic, I relived it in my mind, over and over. The fear that he was going to find me for some kind of sick retribution was driving me crazy. I didn't see him, but rational or not, I couldn't take it. So I quit my job and moved to a place where there's no rush hour."

"The industrial area of Snowbound Village."

"Exactly."

He gave her a gentle squeeze in his arms. "I wish you would have told me sooner."

"Why? It's over. There's nothing you can do."

"Yes, there is." He glanced at the snow on the ground. "I can make a snow angel for you."

Before she could tell him that wasn't necessary, Kade released her. He stepped into the snowy area beside the parking lot and sat. He flopped flat on his back, all six foot one of him, stretched, and swished his arms and legs to make a snow angel, just as he said.

When he was finished, he stood carefully so as not to disturb his artwork and with a giant step leaped out.

He returned to her, grinning from ear to ear. "There. Done. Just for you. What do you think?"

Rochelle gulped, stared at the large economy-size angel and clamped her lips shut so she wouldn't say her thoughts out loud.

I think I'm falling in love.

Chapter 11

L ook, Kade! It's snowing."

"Yeah," he muttered. He looked out the window. Big, fat, fluffy flakes were coming down, coating the cars in the parking lot, which meant it would be slow leaving work tonight.

"Doesn't it make you feel like Christmas?"

"No."

He didn't want to feel like Christmas. Outside of church, the Christmas season meant only one thing. People forced themselves into an unnatural state of euphoria topped only by irresponsibility in the name of Christmas.

Right now, the week before Christmas, was always the worst for him. Before that, people were obsessed with decorating and shopping and parties, but in days leading up to Christmas, they concentrated more on what was truly important, which was being with family and loved ones.

He stood. "I don't feel like Christmas. In fact, I feel like going back to my office and getting some overdue work done."

He placed his guitar on the stand and turned to leave. Agreeing to play for the Christmas Eve service had been a mistake—an error in judgment he would never repeat.

"But. . ." Rochelle's voice trailed off. "What's wrong?" she asked as she followed him.

"Nothing." He knew he was being obtuse, but he couldn't help himself.

Before he could open the door, Rochelle whipped in front of him, blocking the doorknob. "Did I say something wrong? Are you angry at me? If so, I'm sorry."

He felt ten times a jerk, but knowing he was wrong didn't change how he felt.

"I'm not having a good day. Now if you'll excuse me."

Instead of moving to the side, she braced herself against the door. "Do you want to talk about it?"

"No." He waited for her to move, but she didn't.

He ran one hand down his face and sighed. "Are you going to get out of my way?"

Her gasp told him he'd been as rude as he thought. He let out another sigh. "I don't feel very sociable right now. I need to get back to my office." Where he would close the door and keep his phone on voice mail. Jodi would recognize he needed the downtime and respect it.

Rochelle reached out and rested her tiny hand on his forearm. "I'm a good listener."

"I'm not a good talker."

She moved closer and rested her other hand on his other forearm, completely blocking him unless he physically pushed her out of his way. "Ever since we met, I've known something was bothering you. I hoped you would tell me when you were ready. Maybe that's now."

He looked down at her pleading eyes. He'd never talked to anyone about his difficulty in dealing with it, not even Pastor Harry. The pastor wanted to help, but Kade never knew what to say. He still didn't.

Before he realized what she was doing, she had slipped her hands around his back. He stiffened from head to toe as he opened his mouth to protest, but she pressed herself against him, leaning her head into his chest under his chin. Slowly she moved her hand, rubbing his back in slow, soothing circles.

"Close your eyes if it helps. I want to know."

He closed his eyes, but no words came. Instead he put his arms around her and rested his chin on the top of her head.

"I'm here to listen."

"I don't really hate Christmas," he said, keeping his eyes closed.

"I know you don't."

He sucked in a deep breath. "All the artificial happiness and partying drives me crazy. The celebrating just for the sake of having parties, not caring about the reason. Every year more people just use Christmas as an excuse to party harder, not caring about anyone around them or the harm they're doing."

"I know."

"They just use Christmas as an excuse to drink and go wild."

Her hand stopped moving. "You lost someone special, didn't you? Was it a drunk driver?"

Kade squeezed his eyes even tighter. "Yes. We were out

walking around, looking at the Christmas lights. A drunk driver hit another car; then both cars spun on the fresh snow and skidded up the curb and plowed into us on the sidewalk. We couldn't get out of the way in time. I got a broken leg and some internal injuries, but I recovered. My mom, my dad, my kid brother, and the woman I was dating didn't. None of them made it."

He relived that day over and over, every detail, every moment. The impact, the screech of tires, the screams. He'd drifted in and out of consciousness; then he finally awakened in the hospital after surgery to be told his family and his girlfriend had all died.

Everyone he'd loved was gone.

Kade felt a burn in the back of his eyes. He blinked it away. He would take his contacts out later.

"Christmas in the hospital is a very lonely and depressing place." Then, after he was released, everything hit him even harder when he had to tie up all the loose ends and get on with his life.

"I'm so sorry. I don't know what to say."

He swallowed hard to give himself a moment to regain his composure. "There's nothing you can say. They're with Jesus, and I'll see them again one day in glory."

"Is that why you moved to Snowbound Village?"

"Yes. I needed a new start, with new surroundings. But this time of year, when I see all the lights and the hoopla, everything comes back."

"You know what? Let's forget about the music today and go

for a walk where it's quiet. No people, no lights, no traffic. Let's go where they've got the road finished but no buildings, where it's really empty, and have some quiet time. We don't have to talk. We can just go and be alone with God."

He almost refused, but as he looked into her eyes, he saw a shimmer; then she suddenly blinked rapidly a few times, and it was gone. The thought that she was moved so deeply at his pain tugged at his heartstrings. The few people who knew what had happened had expressed surface condolences then continued on as if he'd just repeated the weather report. But Rochelle wasn't backing off because she didn't know what to do; she still wanted to be with him, even though he was obviously carrying significant emotional baggage. Perhaps following her suggestion was what he needed.

"That sounds like a good idea. Let's go."

❧

Just as she'd suggested, they walked without the need to speak.

The silence between them was comfortable, which confirmed to Rochelle he needed it.

After his heartbreaking story, she knew he already spent a lot of time alone with God. But today he needed a friend.

Since they didn't have any destination in mind, their pace was slow. That was also a good thing, because the undeveloped industrial area in Snowbound Village was only two blocks long. But it was away from activity. What little construction had started was shut down, being less than a week before Christmas.

It was comfortable to walk with their hands in their pockets as they meandered along the edge of the road. To show him without words how she felt, Rochelle removed her hand from her pocket and tucked her fingers in the crook of his elbow, just like couples used to do in olden times.

They weren't exactly a couple, but she could dream.

"This is nice," he said softly as they continued walking. "Thank you."

She didn't know if he meant her idea to go outside to where it was quiet or something else. She chose not to ask, so she could let herself believe he was enjoying being together with no pressure or time constraints.

Except she did have one time constraint. She had less than fifteen minutes to get back to work. Being the receptionist, her absence was immediately noticed.

"We've got to turn around, or I'll be late."

Instead of turning, he rested his free hand on hers before she could pull it out of where it was so snugly nestled, giving her no option but to stop.

"Wait." In one motion, he released her hand then slipped both his hands to rest on her shoulders. "I have to apologize for losing it back there. I want you to know you've made this Christmas a lot better for me by doing things that really matter—the music and spending time with me as a friend."

She wished she could be more than a friend, but *friend* was better than *fellow church member*.

He stepped closer then moved his hands so his thumbs rested on her cheeks, and his fingers slipped through her hair to rest behind her ears.

Her heart picked up in double time.

He cleared his throat, and his voice came out softer and much deeper. "I was wondering if we could still see each other after Christmas."

Rochelle had to force herself to speak. "Yes," she said, her voice coming out far too breathy, like something out of a tacky old movie. "I'd like that."

He smiled. "I'd like that, too," he whispered then lowered his head and kissed her.

And she kissed him back. She heard as well as felt him sigh as she leaned into him, seeking his warmth and the intimacy of the contact, even though they were standing outside in the snowy, deserted street.

Slowly he lifted his head, then pressed her to him, making her feel loved and cherished. She wished he would say something, but at the same time, she didn't want to ruin the tender moment. No man had ever kissed her like this outside. She'd certainly never kissed a man on her lunch break.

Her lunch break.

Which was almost over.

Rochelle pushed herself away, knowing she was blushing. "I'm going to be late!"

He had the nerve to laugh. He extended his hand, inviting her to grasp it, which she did. "Then we'll just have to run."

So they ran, snow kicking up in all directions around them.

By the time they reached the main door, Rochelle was winded although Kade was not, telling her she ought to take the stairs instead of the elevator after all.

They thumped the snow off their boots, opened the door, and ran toward the elevator, which was starting to close. Kade sprinted forward, raising his arms over his head to protect himself from the hanging snowflakes. He made it just in time to press the button to make the doors reopen. Rochelle rushed inside and pushed the button for the third floor; then she pushed the button for the sixth floor for Kade.

He reached past her and hit the button for the ninth floor.

"What are you doing?" she asked as the elevator began to rise.

"I do need to talk to Brad, but first I want to get my guitar; otherwise I might forget. I can get yours, too, if you want. Since we didn't get anything done at lunchtime, it might be a good idea if we practiced together tonight. We probably won't have another chance before Christmas Eve, because I have a lunch meeting tomorrow. I think I have something also at lunch the day after, but I can't remember what right now."

The elevator slowed as they reached the third floor. "That's a good idea. Phone me later, and we'll set up a time."

As she turned, Kade reached forward and tipped her chin up with one finger. "I'll do that." Just as the door started to open, he brushed a light kiss on her lips then backed away. A couple of ladies who had helped make snowflakes for the missions outreach stepped in, making Kade step back. They looked at her as she stepped out of the elevator then at Kade standing in the corner, grinning like a Cheshire cat. Then the door closed.

Chapter 12

He probably should have felt nervous, but he didn't.

The church was small, usually about two hundred people in attendance. Tonight many members had brought friends and family for the special Christmas Eve service, making it standing room only—a first for Village Community Fellowship.

Positioned as they were, with him being left-handed, they stood side by side on the stage with the necks of their guitars extended in opposite directions, giving them a stage presence like many famous guitar duos. Their performance stance generated anticipation in the expressions of the people in the congregation as they waited for their cue to begin.

Kade adjusted his glasses; then he looked down at Rochelle to make sure she was ready. She nodded and smiled back.

His heart swelled. He was with the woman he loved, surrounded by a community of fellow believers, celebrating the birth of their Savior.

Life didn't get any better than that.

Pastor Harry stepped to the microphone. "Kade and Rochelle are going to play a series of duets for us, starting with 'O Holy Night.'"

As they'd practiced, Rochelle played the chorded accompaniment, while he played the haunting melody line. At the end, they let the final notes ring out then fade to silence, encompassing the sanctuary in a collective hush with the reverence of the song. Next they played "What Child Is This?" Kade strummed the accompaniment while Rochelle picked the melody. For the third song, "Angels We Have Heard on High," they both picked alternating counter-melody lines for the harmonic chorus. It was intricate playing; the congregation sat so enraptured it was as if no one were there, and they both made it through without a single mistake.

At the conclusion, as they'd agreed, they set their guitars in the stands and left the stage before anyone could applaud then quietly returned to their seats.

He wanted to talk to Rochelle privately after the service ended, but that was neither practical nor possible. People swarmed them.

Elsie, from the missions committee, was the first to speak. "I've never heard a more beautiful version of 'O Holy Night.'" She reached up to wipe her eyes, which had begun to tear. "It's my favorite carol, you know."

Rochelle smiled graciously. "We didn't know, but we do now."

Elsie patted Kade's arm. "You two will have to play more songs for our church. I should go. More people want to talk to you."

Kade felt as if half the congregation approached them to express their surprise and delight at their contribution to the service.

He grasped Rochelle's elbow to get her attention. "Let's go up on the stage to get our guitars. Then we can be alone even if it's in full view of anyone who cares to look."

Slowly they made their way through the crowd, stopping to speak to a few more people who wanted to thank them for the way they'd played.

Rochelle unplugged her patch cord from her guitar amp and began to wind it into a circle. "This is strange. I see more people who look as if they want to talk to us, but they're not."

Kade began to wind his cord. "That's because they won't come up onstage. Unless they're musicians, most people won't come up here, even when the service is over and everyone's packing up. Even to talk—they'd start a conversation if we went to the edge, but if we stay here at the back, no one will come."

"I need this break. I don't know what to say anymore."

Out of the corner of his eye, Kade watched the door as people departed, many starting to prepare for Christmas Day.

He didn't want to leave. He wanted to spend as much time with Rochelle as he could, but the evening was almost over. After they had finished cleaning up the sound equipment and putting their guitars into the cases, he would have no excuse for her to stay and talk to him.

"I guess you go to your parents' place in Hartford for Christmas, don't you?"

Rochelle nodded. "Yes. Everything is packed in my car, and

I'm ready to go as soon as I'm finished here." She picked up her guitar from the stand, put it in the case, and turned to him. "I'm so sorry. I didn't ask what you do for Christmas. I had assumed you'd go somewhere to be with family, but now that you told me what happened, I don't know. Do you have any other family?"

He shrugged his shoulders. "I have an aunt and uncle in California, but we only exchange cards."

She reached forward and rested her hand on his arm. "I should have asked sooner. I'm sure my parents would love to have you as a guest for Christmas."

The last Christmas he'd spent with his own family replayed in his mind's eye. Just like every other year, he'd spent most of the day playing Xbox with his brother, not truly appreciating what a special time it was to be alone with his family and have no other obligations or demands. He would never have another chance to sit and talk with his parents about nothing in particular, have a few good laughs, and just enjoy being together. Every year, as Christmas Day approached, he felt the gaping hole in his life, missing things he should have done with his family while they were together.

He wasn't sure he was ready to be on the sidelines of someone else's Christmas with their family, still missing his own family so much. But he did want to spend Christmas with Rochelle.

"I always go to the homeless shelter and help serve turkey dinners for Christmas Day. MGE sponsors it, so I know they'll have enough people, and I won't be putting anyone else out if I'm not there. I would just have to go back to the office and get the list of names off Jodi's desk and make a few phone calls."

Rochelle jerked her hand away. "Jodi's desk?"

"Yeah. It won't take long. I know where she keeps it."

"Which Jodi?"

Kade dropped the connector box into the pouch. "Jodi. My secretary. You've talked to her a number of times about making those snowflakes for the missions committee. But don't ever tell her I called her a secretary. I believe the new politically correct term is 'personal assistant.'" He turned to Rochelle, grinning at his own joke, except Rochelle didn't share the humor in knowing Jodi's reaction. The opposite. Her face had turned almost as white as the snow outside.

"Is something wrong? Do you feel sick?"

She backed up a step, bumping into his guitar amp and causing it to shake. "Who—who are you?"

"Excuse me? Is this a trick question?"

"Jodi's boss is the guy who owns MGE, who owns the building and the battery factory next door."

"That's right. I also own my home, and I'm not making any payments on my car. So what?"

She stepped backward again, around the amp, until her back was pressed against the wall. "*You're* MGE?"

"MacKade Guildford Enterprises. MGE."

"You're rich beyond anyone's wildest imagination. I thought you were old."

"Define old. I'm thirty-one." He stared at Rochelle, who was looking at him as if he'd sprouted a third eye. "Is something wrong?"

"What—what about Brad?"

"What about him? I have him do the business trade shows for the building committee on contract because he can be a very persuasive guy."

"I thought. . . ." Her voice trailed off. "I thought he was your boss."

He almost started to ask where she could possibly get such an idea but stopped with his mouth open. If she'd ever seen him talking with Brad, she wouldn't have known who was higher on the corporate ladder just by watching.

In hindsight, he'd once told her he didn't want to talk about work or business after he left the building because he didn't want to think of the issues he'd left behind until the next day. To her credit, that was exactly what she'd done. He had no idea she didn't know his position or his worth. Yet every time they rode the elevator together, she got out before he did, so she really didn't know his final destination was the top floor. She'd also never been to his pretentious house.

She squeezed her eyes shut. "I can't believe this is happening."

"Does it make a difference? I am who I am."

Her eyes widened. "Of course it makes a difference. Now I know why you never wanted to sit with me in the cafeteria. Why you never stopped to chat with me in the lobby. Why you didn't make snowflakes with everyone else. I'm not in your social circle except for church. I'm an embarrassment to you."

Kade felt as if he were being sucked into a black hole. He could see a wall going up around her, brick by brick. "That's not true. I don't even have a social circle."

She shuffled to the side, keeping her back to the wall, making sure she didn't come any closer to him. "Of course it's true. It's like you have two lives, the almighty superman executive with the power suit for what's important, and the average-guy stuff with the glasses as a disguise for church where everyone is the same in God's sight."

"It's not like that at all."

"Then why didn't we ever do anything with other people? Am I only good enough to be seen with you in church where you have to treat everyone as your equal?"

A million thoughts roared through his mind. It was true he had secluded himself when he was with her, but not for those reasons. "I didn't want you to become the victim of the rumor mill. You know how it gets."

"No, I don't. It doesn't matter to me what other people think or what they say. As long as I'm right with God, nothing else matters." She picked up her guitar, holding it between them like a shield. "I thought I loved you, but I don't know you at all. I have to go."

Just like Goldilocks escaping from the three bears, she ran down the stairs, dodged around groups of people who were standing around talking, and disappeared out the door.

Kade stood there with his mouth hanging open again.

She loved him.

She said she didn't know who he was.

But she did. He'd shared his deepest sorrows and his greatest joys with her. She knew him better than anyone else. She just hadn't known him long. Which was something he intended to change.

He needed to talk to her, but the longer he took, the wider the gap would become.

His first thought was to go after her, except she'd had a head start and he didn't know where she was going, except to Hartford. Even if he did chase her down the highway, she wouldn't stop. Besides, she'd been a victim of road rage. To chase her in the car would worsen the trauma, and he couldn't risk that.

All the strength drained out of him. He sank down to sit on his guitar amp. The next time he saw her had to be at a place she felt comfortable, which wouldn't happen if she saw him getting out of his car angry.

Kade slipped his guitar into the case and slowly left the building.

As he drove home, the top of Snowflake Tower showed above the flat city line. He couldn't make out details from so far, but the glow from the backlit snowflake was visible for miles.

Automatically he turned the car and drove toward his building.

On days when he felt drained, he would go up to the roof at noon and stand beside the helicopter to listen for the clock to strike noon.

It wasn't noon, but in a few hours, it would be midnight.

He didn't have anything better to do, and naturally he knew the security codes to give him access to anywhere in the building, including the roof.

The roof. Where the helicopter was parked.

Besides the light of the snowflake, another light went on in Kade's head.

Chapter 13

At nearly midnight, Rochelle pulled into her parents' driveway.

She was thankful the darkness would hide her red eyes and they wouldn't ask what was wrong.

She sucked in a deep breath, grabbed her backpack with her overnight things and gifts, and trudged up the sidewalk, not feeling the spirit of Christmas at all.

Only a few hours ago, she'd been happy. She'd thought she'd found her soul mate. A man she understood and who understood her. But she was wrong.

Rochelle wanted a partner who would be her equal—a man with a pure heart and simple needs. She thought Kade had been honest with her, especially when he shared his hurts about losing his family. But he wasn't as honest as she'd thought.

He'd lied about who he was. Not directly, but omission was equally deceitful.

When they were introduced she'd been told his name, not his business assets, which were considerable. She was new to

Snowbound Village. She couldn't have recognized him as the richest man in town any more than if she'd bumped into the mayor at the mall.

As she walked up the sidewalk, the front door began to move.

Despite her heavy heart, she smiled. Her father never could wait for her to knock; he liked to think he was surprising her by beating her to the door.

She opened her arms as she approached to give him a hug the second she made it up the steps. "Merry Christmas, Da—" Instead of her father, a much taller man greeted her. "Kade?" She dropped her arms to her sides and stepped back on the sidewalk. "What are you doing here?"

He opened his mouth, but before he could speak, a woman's voice called from across the street.

"Billy! Come back!"

Little Billy continued running from across the deserted street, past her, to stand in front of Kade.

"Mister! Mister! Can I have a helicopter ride?"

Rochelle blinked. "Helicopter?"

Billy grinned and pointed. "Right there. In the backyard."

Sure enough, the tail of a helicopter poked out from behind the house, illuminated by the security lights.

On the highway, she'd seen a helicopter fly overhead. She'd wondered what kind of moron would be flying late at night on Christmas Eve.

She glared at Kade. "Isn't that dangerous? What were you thinking? Didn't the pilot have something to say about this?"

"The pilot thought it was a good idea."

She glanced behind him, inside the open doorway. "Where is this irresponsible maniac?"

"You're looking at him. I'm the pilot. It's my helicopter."

She'd heard the roof of Snowflake Tower had a landing pad, but she didn't know it came with a helicopter. And apparently a pilot.

"How did you know where to go? And you just landed that thing in the backyard?"

He grinned. "I looked up your parents in the phone book. You told me they had a half acre on the edge of the city, so I knew the approximate area. When I confirmed they were your parents, I asked if they had any obstructions in the backyard. They liked my idea. Most people are fascinated when they see a helicopter land. Your parents have lots of nice neighbors. But I owe a lot of people a lot of rides for blasting in at this hour."

Kade squatted to lower himself closer to Billy's height. "You can have a ride in the morning. Now go home like your mother says, and look both ways before you cross the street this time."

Obediently Billy returned home.

Her mother's voice echoed from inside the house. "Will you two get in here and close the front door? You're heating up the outside!"

Rochelle frowned. "I see you've already met my parents."

"Yeah. I think they like me."

She didn't want them to like him. She didn't want to like him.

But she did.

Begrudgingly she followed him into the house and dutifully closed the door.

"We've invited your young man to stay for Christmas," her mother said, grinning as her father slipped his arm around her waist. "Especially since he went to so much trouble to get here."

Her father nodded then faked a huge yawn. "It's late, and we're tired. Turn off the lights when you go to bed."

Before she could say anything, including the greeting she'd missed, her parents disappeared.

Kade coughed. "I see where you learned the art of being subtle."

"It's a gift," she muttered as she slipped off her coat.

"Speaking of gifts, I have one for you." He reached into his pocket and pulled out a small, badly wrapped box. "No commenting on the wrapping skills, please. Don't say you won't accept it. I've come a long way to give this to you. Your parents said it was okay if you opened it before Christmas."

She didn't want to be obligated to take it, especially since it looked like a jeweler's box.

Her heart twisted. "I can't—"

He raised his hand to stop her protest. "It's okay. It's not an engagement ring."

She shook her head. "I'm so confused right now. I don't understand what you're doing here or why you went to all this trouble."

He stepped closer, extended his hand toward her, stopped, then rammed both hands into his pockets. "Because I love you. It's as simple as that."

"But you can't."

His voice softened. "I do. I thought about what you said the whole way here. I honestly had no idea you didn't know I owned MGE. I also thought I was doing the honorable thing, trying to protect you from the gossip."

"I don't care about gossip. I only care that you're embarrassed to be seen with me."

"But I'm not. When we were at church, it felt so good and so right to be with you in front of everyone. Which means that, regardless of what either of us wants, word is going to spread real fast now. Maybe I might even help it along by eating in the cafeteria instead of at my desk." He smirked. "That would really start people talking. I've never eaten in the cafeteria, even before we met. If I was hungry, Jodi went so I wouldn't have to wait in line."

"But I saw you in the cafeteria. The day I asked if you wanted to make snowflakes."

His ears reddened. "I'd gone down to ask if you wanted to go out with me for lunch, but you were busy. I didn't join the group because I know a lot of people get nervous around me. When I'm working, I can't just be one of the boys. I knew I would stifle your group, so I left."

Even though she wanted to tell him he would have been welcome, he was right. Everyone in the group had stopped talking when he approached. She'd heard people talk about him before she met him. Most of it wasn't complimentary.

She wanted so much to tell them how wrong they'd been. But she'd been just as bad. She'd listened and believed them, which was part of the reason she hadn't realized Kade was the "old coot." She suspected many of the cruel things people were saying were because of jealousy.

She looked up at Kade, waiting patiently while she sorted through her thoughts.

He didn't interact with people from the office tower because of the gossip. At church, people could have gotten to know him if they'd tried, but few did, probably because many worked for him or his company.

Knowing what they were saying about Kade, in her heart, she knew they would be equally cruel to her, maybe worse. In hindsight some people had already started avoiding her. She now had no doubt word was starting to spread that she was after his money, which until today she didn't know he had.

He was the victim here, trying to do the honorable thing to protect her from what he couldn't control.

"I believe you," she whispered. "I'm so sorry for jumping to conclusions. Will you forgive me?"

He replied without words, in an embrace so needy she nearly cried.

She nestled into his warmth for a few minutes but didn't want to be too quiet for too long. "Do you really want me to open your gift now instead of waiting for Christmas morning?"

"Yes. Without your parents watching, even though they know what it is."

She didn't know if his statement should have made her nervous.

Since he'd probably done his best wrapping it, Rochelle

carefully picked the paper off then flipped open the box.

Inside was a small diamond ring. Not an engagement ring but a different kind of special ring.

He slipped his arm around her waist. "It's a promise ring. My promise to you that I love you and will cherish you until the time is right to formalize things and ask if you will do me the honor of being my wife."

A tear leaked out of her eye. Gently Kade wiped it away with his thumb, which only made more tears happen. "I love you, too," she choked out. She had a feeling it wouldn't be long before he did formally propose, because in a way he just had. She already knew what her answer would be.

His hands trembled slightly as he plucked the tiny ring out of the box and slid it on her finger. "I trust those are good tears."

She nodded, swiped them off her cheeks, then dug through her backpack. "This gift is for you. I was going to give it to you at church after the service, but I think I ran out on you."

He wasn't as careful in unwrapping her gift. He tore off the paper and stuffed it in his pocket. "A snowglobe. Is that Snowflake Tower inside?" He shook it and watched as the glitter floated down. "This is fascinating. Where did you get it?"

"I made it. After all, I know how much you like snowflakes. I thought you'd put it on your desk at the office."

"There's the snowflake logo on the side of the building." He shook it again and watched, entranced, as one large heart-shaped piece of glitter floated down amidst the snow. She could see the exact moment he noticed it.

"That's to remind you every day how much I love you. I guess that's my promise to you."

He kissed her slowly, but when she leaned into him, he stepped back. "As much as I want to kiss you right now, we should call it a night. I don't want your parents to suddenly decide they're not so sleepy anymore. It's also going to be a very early morning. Your family is going to get a lot of visitors all day."

Rochelle grasped his hand. "They're your family now, too."

"Yeah. I guess they are. Thank you for the best gift of all."

At that moment, the clock on her parents' mantel struck midnight. Kade grasped her hand tightly as they listened together to the melody then the chimes.

When the last tone sounded and the echo in the quiet living room faded to silence, she gave his hand a squeeze.

"Merry Christmas."

GAIL SATTLER

Gail loves to write about different locations, but she really lives in Vancouver, BC (where you don't have to shovel rain) with her husband, three sons, two dogs, and a lazy lizard named Draco, who is quite cuddly for a reptile. When she's not writing, Gail keeps busy running Mom's Taxi and playing her bass guitar on her church's worship team (loud). She also plays jazz bass for a local band, and that's loud, too. You're invited to visit Gail's Web site at www.gailsattler.com.

A Letter to Our Readers

Dear Readers:

In order that we might better contribute to your reading enjoyment, we would appreciate your taking a few minutes to respond to the following questions. When completed, please return to the following: Fiction Editor, Barbour Publishing, Inc., P.O. Box 719, Uhrichsville, OH 44683.

1. Did you enjoy reading *A Connecticut Christmas*?
   ❑ Very much—I would like to see more books like this.
   ❑ Moderately—I would have enjoyed it more if _____

   _____

   _____

2. What influenced your decision to purchase this book?
   (Check those that apply.)
   ❑ Cover   ❑ Back cover copy   ❑ Title   ❑ Price
   ❑ Friends   ❑ Publicity   ❑ Other

3. Which story was your favorite?
   ❑ *Santa's Prayer*   ❑ *Stuck on You*
   ❑ *The Cookie Jar*   ❑ *Snowbound for Christmas*

4. Please check your age range:
   ❑ Under 18   ❑ 18–24   ❑ 25–34
   ❑ 35–45   ❑ 46–55   ❑ Over 55

5. How many hours per week do you read? _____

Name _____

Occupation _____

Address _____

City _____ State _____ Zip _____

E-mail _____